SCARS

A Novel

OBED OLIVARRÍA

metamorphosis
PUBLISHERS

Names: Olivarría, Obed, author.
Title: Scars / Obed Olivarría
Description: Metamorphosis Publishers
Subjects: LCSH: Serial-Killer–Fiction. | Torture–Fiction. | Revenge–Fiction. | Fatherhood–Fiction. | Rape–Fiction. | Murder–Fiction. | Home-Invasion–Fiction. | Forgiveness–Fiction. | Spiritual-Crisis–Fiction. | Identity–Fiction. | Classism–Fiction. | Racism–Fiction. | Personality-Disorders–Fiction. | Ethics–Fiction.
BISAC: FICTION / Psychological. | FICTION / Thrillers. | GSAFD: Mystery Fiction | Suspense Fiction

Print ISBN: 978-1-966179-98-6
eBook ISBN: 978-1-966179-99-3
Library of Congress Control Number: 2024923595

First Edition

Book and Cover design by Obed Olivarria
For information contact:
www.obedolivarria.com
.

Book interior and cover design by Obed Olivarría.

Printed in the United States

OTHER TITLES BY OBED OLIVARRÍA

PSYCHOLOGICAL SUSPENSE NOVELS

The Flight of the Butterfly

Broken

Dilated Pupils

NON-FICTION

Divine Masterpiece

Threefold Love

Seeking

Found

For Zowie.

Thank you for being amazing, my princess.

Content Warning:

Scars includes graphic content that some readers may find distressing or triggering, including graphic depictions of violence, rape, homicide, and its aftermath. Topics covered in the story also include moments of extreme violence, hate crimes, sexual assault, and instances of suicide ideation.

These scenes are not meant to shock, but to portray the raw depths of pain and the power of forgiveness and redemption. If you find the first few chapters difficult to get through, please know that healing lies ahead in this story. While unflinching in its portrayal of grief and rage, *Scars* is ultimately a story about the healing power of love, the struggle of holding onto faith in the darkest moments, the resilience of the human spirit, and the quiet heroism found in forgiveness.

Scars is graphic, gut-wrenching, and powerful. Yes, some will be offended or may need to walk away; but others will walk through that fire and come out changed. I understand if you put it down. After all, this isn't a book for everyone—it's a book for those who need it.

FOREWORD

Some stories are not easy to tell. *Scars* is one of them. As a writer, psychologist, and father, I don't typically set out to create something purely for shock or entertainment—though there's a time and place for that. In this particular case, I wrote *Scars* because I believe that fiction—at its best—can illuminate the darkest corners of human suffering and, in doing so, reveal a flicker of hope.

This story was born from the realization that so many people walk around carrying invisible wounds—trauma, loss, guilt, pain they don't know how to name, much less heal. I have met them. Some have sat across from me in my office. Others have opened up after a public talk or in quiet conversations. I've seen the aftermath of tragedy—not just in victims, but in the brokenness that ripples outward to families, spouses, and communities. Pain doesn't stay isolated. It spreads. And so does healing.

When I decided to write *Scars*, I knew I wouldn't sugarcoat the horrors at the center of this story. The crime at the heart of the novel—the brutal rape and murder of a young girl—is not something that should be made palatable or glossed over. It is disturbing. It should be. My decision to include graphic content was intentional, even agonizing at times. But I wanted readers to feel the full weight of grief, the raw confusion of rage, the suffocating silence of guilt, and the unbearable agony of "what if?"—because that's the reality so many live in every day.

Scars is not just about the violence itself, but about what comes after. It's about the struggle to go on. It's about two parents who lose their way in their grief. It's about the questions we all ask when faith fails to offer quick answers: *Where is God in this? How do I forgive the unforgivable? Am I still a good person if I want revenge?* It's about redemption—but only after traveling through the fire.

Some chapters in this novel are written from the point of view of the killer. That decision was not made lightly either. As someone who works in the mental health field, I have long been fascinated—and disturbed—by what drives certain individuals to hurt others. While I do not excuse evil, I believe that understanding it is part of what empowers us to confront it. In entering the mind of someone with deep psychological and personality disorders, I hope readers will come face to face with the disturbing humanity of those we label as monsters. Evil doesn't always come cloaked in horns; sometimes, it wears the face of a neighbor, a stranger, or someone with a buried wound of their own. And most times, they have their own story to tell—a story worth listening to.

As mentioned in the content warning, if you are sensitive to heavy topics, I understand this novel may not be for you.

But if you can walk through the first few chapters, I believe you'll see why this story needed to be told the way it was told. *Scars* is not about death—it's about what it takes to live after death. Not just survive, but truly live. So, if you can, while reading the difficult chapters, please be patient and carry on. It's okay to be uncomfortable. In fact, that is the point. I hope you get goosebumps as you read from the perspective of evil.

Though, most importantly, I hope this story opens your eyes, moves your heart, and reminds you that even the deepest wounds can begin to heal. That justice, while often flawed, still matters. And that forgiveness—however impossible it seems—is still the most courageous act of love.

One last thing before you dive in, I also want to acknowledge something important. The antagonist in *Scars* is a man from the Appalachian region, and he and his family speak in a way that some might recognize as stereotypical or "redneck." Please know this was never meant to be insensitive, prejudiced, or demeaning.

I based this character loosely on someone I met—an honest, vulnerable man who grew up in that same environment and shared parts of his life story with me. He turned out to be a resilient and kind human being, in spite of having an incredibly difficult upbringing. But one of his siblings didn't fare as well and made tragic choices that affected many around him. That story stayed with me. What

I wrote was not meant to generalize or insult a culture, but to explore how pain, trauma, and circumstance can shape the paths people take—for better or worse. I write with respect, not judgment. I hope you do the reading with the same respect.

Thank you for reading.

– Obed Olivarría

CHAPTER **ONE**

KARL MUNSON REMOVED SCARS FOR A LIVING. But Karl Munson was a scarred man himself. And he was not okay with that.

He surveyed his surroundings, as the clinking glasses and empty chatter sounded distant in his mind. He was connected to these people, although he wondered why he was even there. He was treading holy ground, and with it he had to force a polite smile into place and pretend that the people around him didn't disgust him. He was at a church fundraiser party in an art gallery in downtown Glendale with other wealthy members of his church.

The forty-seven-year-old wasn't a pessimistic man, nor did he think of himself as better than his peers. He just happened to know what some of his peers did in their free time and didn't condone any of it. It also irked him that they only attended his home church mostly because it was a must to them, not something that they sincerely wanted to do.

Karl was unaware of it, but his peers looked up to him. They found the plastic surgeon to be a genuine person, and often joked that his job as a plastic surgeon left certain things questionable. Still, the doctor laughed with them, unfazed by their comments. He didn't care what they thought of him, and often tuned things like that out. It was easier not to listen to them. But through it all, he was a good, selfless man with a good heart, and his community knew this well.

His wife tugged on his arm. He looked around to see her smiling face and couldn't help but return the smile. Deborah, two years younger than him, was beautiful. She had long brown hair that she liked to braid, and wide green eyes that never seemed to dim, not even now that she had reached her middle age. She pressed a manicured hand against his arm and told the other members that she wanted a word with her husband.

"Thanks for saving me back there, Deb. I couldn't listen to them drone on anymore. I don't even know why I bother with these parties anyway," he said to her.

"Oh, don't be such a downer, babe," Debbie replied, laughing. "We both know that you'd be too bored back at the house. You'd be itching to keep up with all the gossip."

"I think you're mistaking me for you!" Karl retorted with a grin. "Gossip is not for me."

"I'm only teasing, don't you worry. Anyway, I am not the one that wanted to get you out of there."

It wasn't Debbie that wanted the word, but their pastor. Mark Gomez was the Senior Pastor at the Ebenezer Christian Church in South Pasadena, CA, a very affluent and influential non-denominational church in the greater Los Angeles area. Pastor Gomez was also someone that Karl looked up to, and he turned to the spiritual mentor whenever things were tough.

Karl frequently invited the pastor and his wife, Mary, to dinner. This was always a big gamble for the Munson family, because Mary had a very specific list of things that she ate and didn't eat. It wasn't because she was picky, though; it was due to her allergies. The pastor often asked if it wouldn't be better if the Munson family joined the Gomez family, since it would be easier.

Throughout the years, the families had developed a great friendship. Debbie and Mary especially got along great. Debbie was always complimenting the pastor's wife on her sense of style and choice in books, though she did it to her husband. That was why Karl was so happy and thought himself to be lucky, with Debbie as his wife. She was a kind soul, and very adamant about justice. These two traits—kindness and seeking justice—was what drove her to be involved in social justice matters, often going as far as taking time away from her job as an orthodontist to help a struggling teen.

Debbie led Karl into a small work office, so they could all speak in a quieter setting. She lightly tapped on the door and pushed it open. The pastor greeted her with a thankful smile for rounding up Karl.

"Ah, Karl!" the pastor said, delighted, before extending a hand to the fair-haired doctor. "I trust you are well?"

"Indeed. And you?"

"Couldn't be better, but I must ask a favor of you…" The pastor averted his gaze, took a deep breath, and motioned for the couple to follow through a second door, down a long corridor, and outside.

Pastor Mark abhorred asking for money, even if it was for a good cause. That much Karl knew. Karl had once considered paying an amount of money into the church's account each month for the pastor to use as he wished in his church ministries, but Gomez had turned it down, feeling this to be unethical. Karl had asked why Pastor Mark was so against it, because Karl had more than enough money to live off. Why couldn't he help?

Instead, Karl and Debbie would stick to giving twenty percent of their earnings. They had also opened an account and continued to put the money away for a rainy day. They knew that either the church or this ministry that they were fundraising for this evening would eventually need it. Karl had told Mary about this account. Mary had been dumbstruck, unsure of how to react.

She was a social worker by profession, but she spent her days wholly running Angel Wings, a non-profit organization that supported teenagers in need in the Los Angeles Metropolitan Area. The fundraiser this evening was to benefit Angel Wings, and so far, they were doing great.

"The church is need of the... money... that you put away for us," Pastor Mark said, flinching.

Of course Mary had told her husband—they told each other everything—and then the pastor had accepted it. It was something Karl had relied on.

"Of course! How much money would you like me to withdraw?" Karl asked with a smile.

"Do you not wish to know what it is for, Karl?" Pastor Mark asked carefully.

"I trust you, and I know that you will put the money to good use," he reassured the pastor, before taking out his admittedly outdated checkbook and wrote a large check in the name of the church. "This will help greatly with our taxes anyway," Karl told the pastor with a grin, as if giving a solid excuse of why he contributed so much.

But the truth was that he loved the feeling of giving and, if he could, he'd always be signing checks to help others.

"Your contributions are always greatly appreciated," Pastor Mark stated, slowly reaching for the check.

He didn't want to appear too eager for the money.

"We're always in the mood to help," Debbie chimed in. "It's brisk out here. We should go back inside and mingle some more. We all know how much of a party animal Karl is."

The two men laughed and Karl kissed his wife's cheek. "You're just full of jokes this evening. Aren't you? What's got you in such a chipper mood?"

"What reason have I got to be upset?" she replied as the three of them returned to the party.

Later that evening, Karl stepped out of the party salon and took his phone out of his pocket. He dialed Naomi's number; he was worried about his daughter.

"Hello? Daddy? I can't really talk right now. Kind of busy." The phone line went dead and Karl frowned.

She was usually more talkative, but his little girl was growing up and she didn't always have time for her old man. She was at home with her friend, Sophia, and they were most likely either playing music loudly, which meant that he would hear complaints from the neighbors once again, or watching a movie. In which case the music was also loud, since the two girls liked to watch musicals and sing along with it.

Naomi would prefer to watch *Chicago!* And she would even attempt to do the dances. Sophia preferred *The Sound of Music,* and Karl thought that the teenager did a better job at the opening song than Julie Andrews did.

He logged into the surveillance app on his phone. His daughter and her friend were now swimming, and Karl had no doubt in his mind that music was blaring in the background. Through the video feed, he could see that the girls seemed to be having a good time. This app allowed Karl to monitor the house remotely. He'd never had many issues with security before, but it never hurt to be a little cautious.

There was already a text message from his neighbor to please turn the music down. He sighed and sent his daughter a message to do as the neighbors asked. She replied with a smile emoticon, which he hoped meant that she would oblige. At least the girls were safe.

He returned to the party, where his wife and Pastor Gomez were proudly discussing the plastic surgeon's contribution with another few people.

"I just checked in on the girls," Karl said to Tanner Waller, Sophia's father. "They're fine. Just taking a swim."

"And probably discussing some movie star's abs," Diana Waller said, unable to hide her smile.

"Naomi is more of a bicep girl," Debbie said playfully before the four parents rejoined the discussion.

⇁⋅⇃⋅⇂⋅◿⋅◿⋅◿⋅◿⋅⇁⇂⋅

"Your dad again, huh?" Sophia said as Naomi dropped her phone back on her towel. It was getting too cold and she was anxious to get back in the house. The girls jumped out of the pool and dried themselves off.

"Yeah. And yes, I know that this is the second time he's called. The man is a little overprotective. What can I do about that?" Naomi shrugged as she grabbed the remote and raced Sophia back into the house.

A little overprotective? That was an understatement.

"Do you know how much begging and pleading it took before he dropped the call every fifteen minutes rule?" Naomi smiled at that, remembering that in the end it was her mom that made him change it to make sure she picked up every time they called. *So far so good,* she thought as she lowered the volume of the speakers.

"Wait. What are you doing?" Sophia demanded.

"Apparently the neighbors called Dad about the noise. So, it is either we lower the volume, or he comes back home and ruin all the fun."

"Noise? What noise? Your neighbors have very bad taste in music." Sophia complained. She fell back to the couch and picked up a fashion magazine. "Do you think I would look nice with this hairdo?"

She showed Naomi a picture of a model with rainbow-patterned hair as she played with her own.

"Maybe, but I think your hair is better the way it is now. I wish my hair was as full as yours," Naomi replied. She put a hand to Sophia's fiery red hair and ran it through her fingers.

Her own hair was long and straight, but not as full as Sophia's.

"Trust me. You don't want my volume. If only you knew how long it takes to dry this hair in the morning, or keep it down when it gets hot, you wouldn't want it."

"Oh, yeah? Then why haven't you hacked it off?"

Sophia thought about the question for a few moments before she finally smiled. "Okay, maybe it is cool having hair this thick. But trust me, maintaining it is hard work. Now, Chloe's, though! That is a girl that has a lot of hair and knows how to maintain it nice," Sophia said, talking about a classmate of theirs.

"True. You know, I heard that she goes to the salon every week to make it look like that."

"Well, I wouldn't mind going to the salon every week, or every day, rather." Sophia picked up her bag of nail polish and began to go through the bottles, trying to figure out what color she was going to use for the week. "She doesn't even have to do her nails herself. That is the kind of life that I could easily get used to."

"Anybody can get used to—" Naomi paused midsentence and looked sharply towards the back of the house. "I think I heard a noise."

Sophia looked up from what she was doing. "What do you mean 'a noise'?"

"I don't know, but I think I heard something at the back."

"Probably your neighbor's stupid cat again. You'd think that thing is too old to do more than just eat and poop," Sophia joked.

But Naomi still looked unconvinced. She peered outside towards the back, where the pool was.

"Come on, Naomi, this is Oak Knoll. This is Pasadena! Nothing bad ever happens here. Stop imagining the worst and help me decide which color I should go for."

Naomi glanced one more time at the back, then shrugged. Sophia was right. Nothing bad ever happened in this part of town.

⁂

Back at the party, Karl kept his eyes on the exit.

"What's going on in that brilliant head of yours?" Debbie asked.

"I have this sickening feeling in the pit of my stomach."

"No more wine for you!" Debbie chuckled and snatched his glass away from him.

"I'm serious, Debbie. I feel like something's wrong. I don't get this feeling very often. I think I need to call Naomi again."

Debbie kissed his cheek and turned his face away from the door. "That's just the responsible father in you trying to protect our precious princess. She's growing up, dear, and we promised to cut down on the amount of times we call her. You must give her some space. If she needs us, she knows our numbers."

"You're right. Everything's going to be fine."

Mitch Petersen pulled himself up and settled on a thick tree branch. The thick bunches of leaves obscured him from his prey, which he was thankful for.

Teenage girls. Both around sixteen, or so. *They're both hotties; most likely popular with the boys at their school,* thought the peeping tom. He wasn't wrong about that. Athletic bodies. Fit. He shook his head—*no, no getting hard now.* Yes, they were pretty. Their bodies were young, and tight, and... *No, Mitch.*

He watched the two girls as they each cuddled a pillow and shared a large bowl of popcorn between them. The lights were off, and the only source of light was the dim glow of the television screen. His gaze flicked to the screen. Some sort of musical was on. He snorted. *Girls.* He would hate them if it weren't for their bodies.

And then there was Joy. Kind of stupid, but she was a good lay and did whatever he told her. The eighteen-year-old girl never questioned him. She was such a passive little bitch. Whenever he would say that he wanted to do her, the meek lassie would just open her legs like a submissive whore.

He looked at his prey again. The one girl was asleep, and the twenty-eight-year-old man couldn't help but fantasize about running his hands over her young, pert body. The one that wasn't asleep softly slapped her friend's arm to wake her. They said something and both nodded. They had agreed to something. The one girl started to tie her hair into a high ponytail as she made her way outside, clamping her hairband between her teeth to open the sliding door.

Her friend soon joined her with two full glasses of soda. That one, the one with the soda, he identified as Naomi. The other was Sophia, then. He'd heard their names as they talked, but had been having a hard time to figure just who was who. Naomi was the taller of the two, with a lean body and long brown hair that she had tied into two braids. Sophia was a redhead, shorter, but with more voluptuous curves. Mitch couldn't keep his eyes off her. Then again, he liked the slimmer and taller one better. She was prettier. Ah, who was he kidding? They were both hot! Either one would do. And, yes, these two would fight him. They would scratch and slap and kick and even bite. He couldn't wait.

He palmed himself; he was already hard. He wanted to take it out and give it a peek of the two pretty girls. Young, tight...

The girls started to undress, revealing their swimwear. Naomi wore a bikini, showing off her flat and smooth stomach, while the other girl wore a black one-piece suit that showed off her ass. *My goodness!* He breathed in deeply. Naomi switched on the nearby Jacuzzi, and delighted yelps came from her friend.

Mitch craned his neck—he wanted to hear that again. Would she be able to make those sounds when his hands were around her pretty little neck? She was wearing a fine, silver necklace too. That would be his soon. But those sounds... Oh, if she made those sounds he wouldn't be able to last long. Then again, he would be hard again soon. There were two girls to pleasure him, two beautiful little necks that needed a new necklace, made of his fingers pushing into their throats.

They jumped into the pool together. They laughed loudly when they came up for air, and each got a floating tube, where they lazily drifted in the water. This disappointed Mitch. He had enjoyed his view of their half-nude bodies.

"Did you see Chris's abs?" Sophia asked, "Dude, I wanna lick 'em."

"Eww!" said the more pious of the girls while laughing. "You're gross, dude..."

Mitch stopped listening. He couldn't give a damn about these girls and their thoughts on boys. This continued for a while, the girls alternating between the pool and the Jacuzzi, each time offering the stalking predator a good view of their wet, firm bodies that now stood up in the cool night air.

Soon the conversation turned to volleyball, to which Mitch only paid slight attention, before they headed back inside. He had been palming himself through his dark jeans and was disappointed that the two beautiful bodies, with their voices that he wanted to hear soon—screaming in pleasure or in pain, it didn't matter—left him alone. They decided to take showers and order pizza.

Mitch could get behind that. He wanted to see those bodies closer. He wanted to touch them, caress them, dig his hands into them. Yes, this would be good.

The long wait would soon pay off...

CHAPTER **TWO**

MITCH JUMPED OUT OF THE TREE, landing firmly on his feet. He glanced up at the house, a smirk forming on his thin lips. The two teenaged girls were inside the house, presumably taking showers. He vaguely wondered if they shared a shower and what they did in that shower. Were they truly innocent little girls, or were they a bit more playful than that?

He marched over the green lawn, frowning distastefully at the glasses, paper plates, and sweet wrappers that the girls had left outside. And the stupid little girls had left the glass sliding door unlocked. He smirked again, opening the door silently. He closed the door behind him. He was pretty sure that no one else had been at the house, but he did this just to be safe.

The house was lavishly decorated, not strange for a wealthy family, but quite foreign to Mitch. His own family wasn't materially wealthy. At least he didn't think so. But they were a large family. It was him, his idiot of a girlfriend Joy, his father, sister, brother... the list went on. They all lived together, as if they were one happy family.

While in this rich man's place, twice the size of his own home, lived three people. Three fucking people! What did they need all this crap for anyway? It was stupid to surround themselves with nice things, because they just died in the end.

The tall, muscled man tore his gaze away from the massive television and leather—or faux-leather, either way—couches to a large cabinet that was filled with photos of people he assumed were family members of the family that lived here. He recognized the parents of the one girl. She shared her mother's beauty and her father's intelligence shone through her eyes.

He moved past the large cabinet, promising himself the opportunity to peruse the house later. He pitched his ears for the sound of the shower, or showers, since he wasn't sure where the girls' bedroom was. Mitch turned his blue eyes up the spiraling stairs and grinned.

With strained ears, he slowly made his way upstairs, making sure that the girls didn't hear him. All he heard was the gushing of water. Soon, he found the room where one of the girls was showering. He went in, not exactly caring about who it was that he found.

It was the hall bathroom, and he assumed that the other girl was taking a shower in her en-suite bathroom. He nearly laughed aloud. How rich were these people? Kids got fancy things like en-suite bathrooms when they were the president's kid, or a prince, or something like that, but not when daddy had money.

Pfff... Rich people.

One of the girls came out of the bathroom, a towel wrapped around her body and another tied around her hair. She had left the shower running, she probably would get back into it. Or she thought she would, Mitch thought excitedly. He pulled out his engraved knife.

"Hey, Na—"

Mitch surged forward, his arms outstretched, and grabbed her around the torso. His large hand covered her mouth before she could scream.

"Hey, girlie," he crooned into her ear as he pulled her towel from her body. Her breasts sprang free, and he groaned gutturally.

Mmmhmmm. Those tits...

Her scream was muffled against his hand and she even tried to lick his hand off her face, but he just laughed at this.

"You think a little of your spit's gonna stop me?" he asked before drawing his engraved knife up to her neck.

She looked at it with large eyes, terror written all over her face. Mitch Petersen was in heaven. That terror gave him a high that rivaled even the best lay he could get. But instead of drawing the knife over her pretty throat and creating a scarlet smile with blood dripping onto her naked chest, he pressed the hilt of his knife into her throat.

"See, if I slit your throat, it isn't fun. I don't get to see the light leave your eyes." He dug his nose into her neck. She smelled sweet, like lavender and cream. Her shampoo. He twisted her head and forced her to look at him. "But if I strangle you... you get to feel this..."

He pressed his crotch into her naked rear. He could come all over her right here and right now. But, then again, the other one was prettier. He wanted *her*. Yes, he would have the taller one instead. That innocent baby face just made her even hotter.

Sophia resumed her resistance with new vigor, struggling and flailing as she tried to scream around the palm covering her mouth and the sharp knife pricked against her throat. With a hard push, Mitch thrust his knife into Sophia's throat, choking the air out of her. His other hand never left her mouth. He waited until she stopped moving, and until her young body slumped against his, before he let her fall. Her body hit the floor with a soft thump, and when her head hit the tiles there was a louder crack. He kicked her unresponsive body to make sure. Nothing but a lifeless sack of flesh and bones on the floor.

Mitch wandered to the room where he heard the other shower. The rich kid's bedroom. The brunette teenaged girl turned the tap off, and the water stopped, only a few drops hitting the small wet tiles. He heard the shower door open, and he stopped to survey the room. It was huge.

Of course, it's huge! He snorted.

The bed—a king size bed with soft pink linen with a light-blue flowery decoration on it. The girl was a bookworm, with a massive bookcase against one wall. Her taste in literature showed that she was religious and a bit of a fantasy dreamer as well. Mitch waited.

The girl entered her room, her body covered in a towel and another one thrown over her head, just like the other girl. She didn't look around, not that she could, she had loosely thrown the towel over her head. Brown hair peeked under the towel. She crossed over to her chest of drawers and let the towel fall to her feet.

That body. My goodness, that *body*. She was better than the redhead. Her stomach defined by ab muscles, her tits small, but pleasant, and she was nicely shaved and smooth down the rabbit hole. He knew he wouldn't last long.

"Sophie! You need to hurry up!" the teenager yelled loudly as she pulled on a pair of pink girly panties that matched her room. "The pizza is going to get here soon, and that movie isn't gonna watch itself!"

She pulled the towel from her head, and Mitch surged forward as she turned around. She saw his face and opened her mouth to scream, but he hit her over the head with his large hands. She hit the floor, her consciousness lost. Mitch pulled her to her pretty pink-and-blue bed and threw her taut body on it. It lightly bounced. He couldn't keep his eyes off her pinkish nipples.

He allowed himself one more minute to look at her body. Young, tight. Dark brown hair and long eyelashes. Gorgeous.

He tore her ridiculous panties off her body—there was a freaking cartoon character on it! He laughed again in disbelief. He proceeded to tie her hands to a bed pole with some scarves from her closet. She would probably wake up soon. He then pushed the torn panties between her pink lips.

He bent over and pushed his face up between her legs. She smelled so good. He started to lick her. *Mmmhmmm... so good. It would have been better if she was wet, though.*

She woke up and tried to scream, but her underwear blocked her screams. All that escaped was a muffled yelp.

"Girlie..." he said under his breath before relieving himself from his restricting jeans. He was ready.

Her eyes widened as she saw his thing, and she began to panic even more. She tried to kick, but he quickly put an end to that too by tying her left leg to another bed post.

"I'm going to fuck you so hard," he said conversationally, "and I don't care if you cry, or scream, or bleed. Because all I care about is a good time tonight."

She managed to push her panties out of her mouth with her tongue.

"Please!" she cried—no, sobbed—while tears ran down her pretty little face. "You don't have to do this."

"I know," he said, "but you see, I want to."

She screamed. "Help! Sophia! SOPHIA!"

He slapped her harshly across the face. "Your little friend is dead, so shut the hell up."

She sobbed even harder. "SOPHIA!"

He shoved his hand to her mouth, muffling her yells. "Shut. The fuck. Up."

She tried to get up, but her own scarves kept her from moving. Fresh tears welled up in her eyes. He loved it. She tried to kick him with her only loose limb, but his hand caught her leg quickly.

"Do not fight me."

There was no foreplay—good. He hated having to pretend to care about the girl's orgasm. He gripped her head in place and licked her neck. He couldn't wait! He could smell her fear, and she reeked of terror.

"I'm going to give you the best cock that you'll ever have. You should thank me for this."

She sobbed and begged him again to stop, but he just laughed. Her protest only excited him more, and her squirming body was a hot promise to the fire that he would find in her when he entered her.

He enjoyed the fight. Joy just opened her legs, but this little cunt... she was gorgeous, *and* she was a fighter. This excited him. He liked the sound of her cries. No, he loved it.

"Why are you doing this?" the girl asked in confusion.

"Because I can," he replied before punching her in the face.

He began to stroke his pulsating member softly with his hand close to her bruised face, while promising her a wonderful experience in a semisweet voice. He looked down at the monster in his hand and a crooked smile appeared on his lips. Mitch was proud of himself.

Her face shook, trying to face the other way. Disgusted. Terrified.

Mitch laughed and made his way on top of her. He grabbed her by the hips as her body quivered from the soft sobs she was still uttering.

She went completely rigid under his touch and started up her desperate plea once again. "Please... no... Stop." The tears were heavy.

Little did she know that her pleas only encouraged him to go on. Her sobs were like an aphrodisiac, and he needed more of them.

Mitch positioned himself on top of her and felt the shock that went through Naomi's body. She squirmed, struggling to move away, but it was useless. Though her pleas grew stronger, they were music to his ears.

Mitch struggled, but with a hard thrust, he plunged himself inside her with brutal force. Her face red and wet, sobbing quietly now. The pain was excruciating. Her body became wilted, as if wanting to die. She clenched her teeth.

He pulled out and saw that there was blood on his tip. He chuckled as she continued to cry silently. But he wasn't done. He began once more and thrusted harder. Now her screams were like sirens, loud and desperate. He pulled back and immediately thrust back again. It hurt so badly, her screams were evidence of that, and he thought she would pass out. She still wiggled, trying to escape his burning body, useless as it was.

His movements went faster, Naomi's screams of pain and her sobbing filling his every sense, making the experience the hottest he had ever had. A fulfilled fantasy. He groaned as he pounded harder and harder. He pressed his fingers deeper in the pale flesh of the young girl's hips, as he plunged deeper inside of her tight body with each thrust.

"Shit!" he screamed back at the teenager he pounded his hips to hers. "You are so tight!"

He felt he could not postpone his orgasm much longer. He knew she was bleeding, his flesh had stopped scraping her inner walls some time ago and he could feel the wetness that was surely not vaginal secretion, sopping with every thrust he gave her.

"Ah!" he continued. "You are such a hot little bitch!"

Mitch's hips thrust into her repeatedly. Her screaming had stopped again, but her sobbing continued. All she could still say was a quiet "Please," a word she uttered every time he plunged inside her, making it sound in his mind like she begged for him to continue. A little moan accompanied the little word due to the force of his thrusts and it drove him over the edge.

Naomi was barely conscious. Mitch grinned, reaching his hands forward and closing them around her thin throat.

"Now you die," he said as he pressed the air out of her body, and refused to let any more in.

She gasped—or tried to— and he felt her body strain beneath him.

Then her sobs stopped, her body grew limp, and as Naomi Munson released her last breath, Mitch ejaculated inside of her. He pulled out, released her neck, and drew back. Remains of the semen burst out and fell over the young lifeless body.

He looked down to see the damage he had caused. The evil monster felt pride. Her bed was covered in red where her legs met, the red now staining the pretty pink. Her vagina was swollen and red from the action that he had done.

He couldn't resist it, he wanted to know what it tasted like. He flicked his tongue over the swollen flesh, tasting blood and something else too. Bitter.

You're welcome, bitch. Mitch grinned at the dead girl before tucking himself back into his jeans and zipping himself up.

He left her there, ravaged, her bed full of blood, tears now drying on her pretty face and around her now empty eyes staring at oblivion. Exiting the room, he stepped over the redheaded girl's body as he made his way downstairs. He had promised himself that he would take a look around the rich people's house, and he was damn well going to do that. He wandered into another room, bigger than the teenaged girl's. *It must be the parents' room*, he figured.

The room was also lavishly decorated, even more so than the downstairs areas. The bed was huge, and deep purple curtains were draped around the bed posts. Above the bed hung a massive portrait of the two parents with smiles on their faces. The girl looked a lot like her mother, who also had dark brown hair and large brown eyes. Pretty women would be his death.

He walked away from the bed to one of the closets. One whole side of the room was filled with doors made from light wood. One of the free-standing closets stood open, revealing a massive flat screen TV and a Blu-ray player with several cases stacked on top of it. Mitch guessed that the other closets contained more than just clothes.

He opened the one closest to him, finding a bunch of neatly folded ties and socks. The tall man shook his head in disgust and moved on. He wasn't interested in freaking socks! Where did these people keep the good stuff? He didn't see any safes standing around the room, so it had to be either in the closet or behind the portrait above the bed.

He glanced at his watch; he had been there for around twenty-seven minutes. He could still hang around for a bit. The parents were at some stupid party. Most likely one of those parties that rich people go to, just to show just how ridiculously rich they were and to throw their money around as if it was confetti.

Rummaging through the closets, he finally found some jewelry. It looked like a gold necklace, and a large leopard hung from it. A pendant. *Leopards? What the hell?* He vaguely thought that his girlfriend would like it and stuffed it into his pocket. Then his eyes landed on a watch. There were diamonds around its face, and the band was most likely leather. He liked this one; he would take it for himself. He stuffed it into his pocket too, though more carefully than he did the pendant.

He decided to leave the bedroom. The truth was that he really didn't need stuff to make him happy, though that leather watch would look good around his wrist, and he would be happier if he could look better, even the tiniest bit.

He went downstairs again, his hand lovingly trailing along the banister as he descended. He went back to the dining room, where the large cabinet with a multitude of photos stood, and he surveyed the lot. Photos of a happy family, and presumably extended family too. Brunette women, like Naomi and her mother, were all over the cabinet. They were all good looking. He picked up a recent photo of the teenaged girl, where she was alone in the frame, wearing a sheer white dress. Her hair came down on her shoulders and she had a happy smile on her face. The building behind her was one he recognized—a church. Of course, these people would be churchgoers, because they were such a perfect family. Probably the type of people that swore and cussed worse than he did, who drank a bottle of whiskey an evening, but then tried to sanctify their souls by showing up at church with halos around their heads the following Sunday morning.

He tucked the photo into his jacket pocket, the edge just showing slightly. He took a few smaller frames too, all with the pretty teenager in them, and one with a toddler Naomi where she had a gap-toothed smile and pigtails. Man, this girl was hot.

The doorbell rang, and Mitch's heart nearly stopped. He heard it hammering in his chest, and as he felt it, he made a run for it. He slipped out the door to the patio and made his way back to the tree that he had initially used to get inside.

SCARS

CHAPTER **THREE**

"WE'LL BE HOME SOON, DEAR." Debbie said, leaning on her husband's shoulder.

They sat in the back of the Uber town car that they ordered to get them home safely. Karl's stomach was still swirling with nerves. A pit formed in the back of his throat. He expected to find Naomi and Sophia passed out on the couch, with music blaring and pizza boxes all over the floor. He knew that was the least of his worries, because his gut was never wrong.

Not forty-five minutes had passed after the atrocities, when Doctor Karl Munson and his wife, Deborah, returned home. Karl knew that something was wrong the minute that he heard silence, because whenever his daughter and her friend were together, there was never silence. It was either loud music, a very loud TV, or very loud laughing. But never silence. Naomi liked waiting up for them, because they always made sure to take one of the souvenirs for her.

"I am going to check if the girls are asleep upstairs, babe. Would you please put the kettle on?" He asked his wife, pressing a kiss to her cheek.

"Okay, honey. Some tea?"

"Yes, please. Coffee will just keep me awake," he said making his way to the stairs.

As he passed the cabinet, he noticed that something was off. He didn't know what, but that only made his suspicions grow, and the ache in his stomach burned. He heard that the shower was running, and thought it was a bit late for a shower.

When he reached the top of the stairs, his heart stopped. Sophia was lying on the ground, naked. Her eyes open, her mouth agape, with terror written on her face and dried tears on her cheek. Dead. A lake of blood below her head. A wound in her neck.

For a moment, Karl had no words. He was frozen in time, still as a statue. This couldn't be real. He had to be imagining it. Did he have too much to drink? Did someone spike the punch? His mouth moved, and he struggled to find his voice.

"Deb..." Karl said, and his voice faltered. He nearly fell to the floor, unable to believe his eyes. "DEBBIE!" He finally yelled with strength, voice filled with panic.

Debbie came running, and when she wanted to go up the stairs, he stopped her from above.

"No, Deb. Stay there and call the police."

"Karl, what is...?"

"Call 911 now!" he screamed.

He had never yelled at her, which made his wife start and dash into the kitchen to find a phone. Karl heard his heart rather than felt it.

Wait. How was he sure that she was dead?

With hope, the doctor surged forward and put a hand around her neck, keeping his eyes off her nude form. He was a doctor, for crying aloud! Why didn't he do this first before assuming the worst?

But he had been accurate in assuming the worst-case scenario. Her body wasn't even warm. How could this have happened? He had checked on them an hour ago, and they had been *fine*.

Naomi!

He leapt to his feet and ran to his daughter's room. A cry of shock and anguish left his throat when he saw his daughter sprawled on the bed. Her hands were tied up, so was one leg, and between her legs, a crimson mess.

"NAOMI!" he cried out, hoping against all hope that she would open her mouth and talk to him.

He fell to his knees, his entire body shaking. Tears formed in his eyes, and he looked up to the ceiling.

"Naomi..." he whispered as he stood up and dragged his body towards her. He felt heavy as his heart pounded in his ears. He placed his hands on the side of the bed and pulled himself up to face his daughter.

He didn't need to feel for a pulse, because it was obvious that she was dead. His surgeon's brain told him this, but his heart refused to accept it. Tears poured down his face and he blubbered incoherently. With a shaky hand, he stroked her hair carefully. It hadn't fully sunk in what he was facing. His body was in shock, unable to comprehend the reality of the situation. He stared at her, and then his stomach rumbled violently. He stumbled as he tried to stand and forced himself towards her bathroom.

He barely made it to the toilet, where his entire dinner went spiraling into the porcelain bowl. There was so much blood... and the terror the girls must have felt... He spluttered again, his stomach now empty.

Karl wiped off his face with a towel and felt the cold floor underneath him. He traced the patterns on the tiles, and the room started spinning. He felt like he'd get sick again, but there was nothing left to expel. His body convulsed, and he started dry heaving. He was on all four, crying uncontrollably.

"Naomi!" he cried once again, hoping this was just a dream and he would wake up to see her beautiful, smiling face. "My baby!"

"Karl? They're on their way. Can I come up?" Debbie called from the stairs.

Karl staggered outside still struggling with his dizzy spell, keeping his eyes away from his daughter and her friend.

Before he could stop her, Deborah had made her way up the stairs and she saw the redheaded teen's body. "Sophia? Sophia!" she screamed and collapsed on the last step.

She looked up at Karl, holding onto the stair railing, and her mouth dropped open.

"Stop, Debbie," he said.

But she didn't listen.

She ran towards Naomi's room, and upon seeing the massacre, she fell to the floor by the bed, her legs no longer able to keep her standing. An anguished cry escaped her lips, and Karl pulled her away from the scene.

"Don't touch me!" Debbie shrieked. "My baby needs me!"

"There's nothing we can do for her now," he replied, pulling her into his chest.

As he said it out loud, he finally realized what had happened. He didn't want to keep looking at it, and he didn't want her to look at it either. She struggled against him, screaming at the top of her lungs that she didn't want to leave her baby.

"They're... dead... Deborah, they were... strangled," he managed to say, and then his throat closed, He couldn't say anything else.

He knew it was more than that. It was obvious.

The sound that came from his wife was heart wrenching, and he just kept her in his arms.

"We need to go downstairs and wait for the cops," Karl said in a broken voice. "Please, Debbie, we can't stay here. There's nothing else for us to do."

"I won't go!" Debbie screamed. "I'm not leaving her, not again. You were right."

"Debbie..."

"Karl, we should have come home sooner. We should have known what was happening!"

Karl looked at Debbie and held her, so she stayed facing him. "No, don't start that. This is no one's fault except for who did this to our girls. This is not your fault, Debbie. You got that?"

She nodded and buried her face in his chest. He almost didn't believe his own words. On some level, he thought Debbie was right. Could it really be their fault? Could they have prevented this from happening?

"*You* said they were fine!" she managed to whisper. "You checked and said that they were okay."

Karl didn't know what to say. He softly pulled her downstairs, as she went limp in his arms for a the last few steps. She crumbled on a couch, sobs coming from her.

"Why? Why, God? My *baby*!" She couldn't stop crying and screaming, confused.

She buried her face in a decorating pillow. Her body shook, and Karl kneeled to sit beside her. He was still, solid. His eyes were dead, and on the inside, he was a mess of pain and confusion.

The police arrived soon. The sudden noise startled both Karl and Debbie. They were still on the couch, not looking at each other, and completely silent. It took Karl a moment to bring himself back to reality and stand up to answer the door. It was just one man in a lone squad car at first; but when he saw the bodies, he called for more support.

"There will be more of us in here soon," affirmed the officer. "Please, come with me to the kitchen so that I can get your statements."

"What? You think we're responsible for this?" Karl growled, and clenched his fists.

Debbie was silent, lying on her stomach, facing the door.

"Not at all." The officer said calmly. "It's just standard procedure so that we can get the full story of what you saw. Every little detail can help us catch who did this to you."

"Did this to *us*?" Karl asked and stepped forward, very close to the officer's face. "This isn't about us, this is about *those* girls up there! They are the victims here. You better start showing a little more respect, young man..."

"Enough!" Debbie shouted; she was now standing, dried tears on her face. "Let's go to the living room and talk. I'll make you a cup of tea. Or would you prefer coffee?"

"I'm fine, ma'am." The officer said. "Thank you. Let's just get *you* comfortable."

Debbie walked to the living room, and collapsed on the couch. It was like she had no control over her body's movements.

"The Wallers!" Debbie squealed and ran to her cell phone on the coffee table. "We have to call them! Tell them what happened. Oh, I don't even know where to start."

Karl grabbed the phone from her. "I'll do it, darling. Go sit. Rest."

He dialed their number and asked the Wallers to come over. It was easier to explain everything in person. Then, he joined Debbie on the couch.

Soon their large house was overrun with men and women, most in blue and black, but some on suits, with red and blue lights flickering outside their windows. The Wallers had been called too, by both police officer and their friends, and they were on their way.

Karl settled on the couch with Debbie. Detectives stood in front of them with sympathetic stares. He explained the story to two detectives, Robert Park and Kimberley Ramirez, who had given each of the Munson's a warm cup of coffee and a blanket. Deborah couldn't say a word now, and she was silently crying on the couch.

"My wife and I were at a party, with the Wallers in downtown Glendale, not too far from here. We always left the two girls alone. There are security cameras and they have always been safe. This is a safe neighborhood and they are... were... good girls. They were smart. I checked on them an hour before my wife and I left the party, and they were fine. They were outside, chatting and swimming. And when I came home, I knew something was wrong. The girls always had loud noise around them, but now... there was nothing. And..." He gestured a hand to the upstairs floor, and the detective interrupted.

"I'm sorry for your loss, Dr. Munson." Detective Park sat on the couch's armrest, and put a hand on Karl's shoulder. "But I must ask you for any, and all, security footage. This is crucial to our investigation."

"Of course." Karl stood up, but was pulled back down when Debbie grabbed his arm.

"Please, do not leave me by myself." She whimpered.

He leaned down and kissed the top of her head. "I am not going far. Just stay here, and I'll be back soon. Okay?"

She nodded and took a sip of her coffee. Karl led them to his study on the first floor, and he showed them the night's footage. He let Detective Ramirez sit in his chair and entered his password to view the videos.

He started where he had called his daughter, and waited until they went inside. His breath caught when he saw a man entering their home – dirty blond, large, muscled, clad in jeans and a trench coat, and the doctor thought that he was a real hillbilly. He left later, when a pizza boy showed up at the door. He must have been terrified to hear the doorbell ringing, and he fled much faster than he had entered. After a while, the pizza boy, looking very annoyed, left the house.

Karl was wide eyed and felt the blood drain from his face. "No, this can't..." He whispered, mostly to himself. "I just spoke to her. I should have known..."

"Sir." Detective Park called his attention. "Maybe it's best if you wait outside."

"No!" He screamed. "This is *my* house. I'll be where I want to be. You will not keep me in the dark on this."

"Very well, sir." Detective Park replied, and bent over to review the videos with his partner.

They ran through it multiple times and studied it carefully. Karl leaned against the window ledge and watched with them. He crossed his arms and looked straight at the perpetrator with each run through.

"Park, you don't think that's...?" Ramirez said to her partner, who had gone white in the face.

"Yes, I do." Park said before she even finished her question, and then he opened his mouth to say something else, his face turned to Karl but his eyes still on the screen. Some voices downstairs interrupted him.

"Deborah, what's going on? What's with all the police?" It was Sophia's mother, Diana Waller. "Where is Sophie?"

Karl ejected the burned DVD of the night's footage from his desktop and handed it to the detectives, who thanked him before they made their way downstairs, where the Wallers were waiting.

"Karl!" Tanner Waller said, relief evident on his face. "What's going on? Why did you call us? And what's with all the police?"

"I'm very sorry to tell you this, Mr. Waller." Said Detective Ramirez after she introduced herself. "Your daughter has been murdered tonight."

"WHAT?" Both parents protested, as Diana started to cry.

"No! This can't be! Karl, you checked on them..." Tanner said, unbelieving.

"I'm sorry for your loss, sir." Said Detective Park, indicating to some of the sergeants to make more coffee.

"How could this have happened?" Tanner asked, his tone accusatory.

"It isn't their fault." Said Park quickly. "The man who did it is a fugitive from the law."

"You mean... you know who that.... monster is?" Karl couldn't find another word to describe the scene upstairs, or the perpetrator.

"Yes. His name is Mitch Petersen. He is a suspect in several murders and rape cases. The man is a nut case... borderline personality disorder, antisocial, narcissistic, delusional... You name it, he's got it. But unfortunately, we haven't been able to track him down." Ramirez informed them all.

Diana gasped at this, tears streaming down her cheeks.

"What do you mean that you haven't been able to track him down?" Karl shouted at Detective Park, spit flying as he let loose his anger at the next available target.

Park understood his grief, and after seeing what had been done to the victims, he knew that being the scapegoat was a small price to pay. He became a police officer to stop crimes like this from ever happening, not to catch the perpetrator after the crime had been committed.

"Why is someone like that in our city, in *our* neighborhood, and we are just hearing about it, after he murdered...?" Karl broke down then, unable to finish the question, his shoulders slumping, as the picture of Naomi lying in bed, violated in a way that no human being should have ever been flashed across his mind. "He killed my baby! He... he..."

"He may have killed them..." Tanner said. "But those girls were *your* responsibility." He poked his finger into Karl's chest. "You're the reason they're dead. You didn't take enough precautions. I trusted you, and now my daughter is dead! And it's all *your* fault!"

Tanner lunged forward, trying to attack Karl, but the Detectives held him back.

"Tanner, you cannot blame our friends!" Diana exclaimed, her voice high-pitched and shaky. "Don't turn on them. We're all in pain. Each of us is a victim."

She ran into the living room and hugged Debbie. The Detectives brought Tanner to another room, leaving Karl alone.

He stared at his feet, and tears rolled down his cheeks. "Is this my fault?"

Falling to the floor, Karl began sobbing into his hand, his cries only overshadowed by the loud crying his wife.

A sergeant offered the Wallers cups of coffee, and they took it absentmindedly. It was clear that they were still trying to process the information. And, even though Park and Ramirez knew they were a little bit lucky that the two of them had not descended into hysteria like the Munson's had, he knew that the waterworks were going to come soon, and he sure did not wish to be there when it did.

The rest of the night was a blur. The two teenage girls were taken away, their bodies zipped up in two black body bags. They would be undergoing tests for signs of rape, to determine a cause of death, and neighbors were questioned. It would have waited until morning, but their neighbors were so nosy that they all stood huddled outside. Morbid curiosity, Karl liked to call it. Their home was designated to be a crime scene, and the couple decided to spend the night in a hotel. The Wallers did offer them a room for the night, but they declined the offer.

Karl didn't sleep that night, even with a sleeping pill and half a bottle of whiskey in his system. He didn't even drink. But this night was different. All he could see was his daughter and her friend's faces; their last emotion had been terror.

Karl and Debbie laid in bed, leaning against the headboard. "Do you think we should go stay with the Wallers?" Debbie asked. "It might be better if we stay with friends."

Karl barely heard what she said. He was lost in his own thoughts. His only reply was a grunt.

He turned off the lamp and rolled onto his side. "Just sleep, Debbie."

How could anyone do this? How could anyone live with themselves if they did this? Mitch Petersen was no man, Karl Munson decided. He was a monster.

There were monsters among the citizens of the greater Los Angeles metropolitan area. They tended to blend in, however, as chameleons. They were hard to discern from normal citizens because they faked normal behavior. But they were dangerous, nonetheless. And these were the scariest killers of them all because you least expected it from them.

According to Detectives Park and Ramirez, Mitch was wanted for questioning in a series of murders and rapes throughout Southern California. And this video obtained from the Munson's would surely put him behind bars for life, if not worse.

Mitch Petersen... a serial killer and rapist? Indeed. A monster? No doubt about it.

A serial murderer, by definition, was someone that committed the unlawful killing of two or more victims by the same offender in separate events. Real life serial rapists and killers were rare, but they sure were real. Not all were evil geniuses as the media liked to portray, however. While some, apparently, were contributing members of society who appeared normal, others were peculiar loners.

Mitch Petersen was the latter. There was no contributing to society for him. It was a dog-eat-dog world, where the fittest would survive. And he was at the top of the chain. The man was a basket case. The list of mental health issues that this man had was ever-growing. He was an emblematic sadistic predator who came from an abusive background, who targeted vulnerable victims, because it made him feel powerful. He was audacious, ruthless, confident, at times even charismatic, and determined to win at all costs. But he was a remorseless bully, and always had been as such. The rules didn't apply to him because he was free from any moral or ethical insight.

Some people killed for financial enrichment, while others as a form of revenge. For some others, however, the motive was sexual power. Mitch, on the other hand, killed for pleasure. There was certainly some enrichment and the obvious sexual release; but he mostly did it because it just felt good. Because he could. Because life to him was a game, and he always won in this game. He was a winner in life. And he always got away with it. Doing this excited him.

Mitch had spent a good part of his upbringing behind bars. He had been taken in before for numerous misdemeanors and even a few felonies across the United States, but he had never been arrested or even suspected for murder or rape before. If that had been the case, he wouldn't have seen another day of light in the outside. But it didn't matter, because he was unafraid of punishment.

Full of hostility and shame, driven by paranoid delusions, and motivated by sadistic ideologies, paired with a substance abuse and a history of traumatic family violence, Mitch had gradually lost any sense of empathy, ultimately becoming a cold-blooded and methodical hunter. And young girls were the prey. He lived for this hunt and this hunt was his life.

The latest two in his quest had been delicious. His patience had paid off; it had been a good day for him. The monster and his little monster were at ease, and there was no stopping them any time soon.

The game had to go on, for the hunter was hungry.

SCARS

CHAPTER **FOUR**

GRACE MILLER SLOWLY OPENED HER EYES, and for the first few minutes she just lay in her bed. It was easier to pretend this way. Easier to pretend she still had to wake up very early to make sure that Brittany was ready for school. She used to hate having to go to her room to wake her up, then again to make sure that she truly was awake, and finally to drag her butt to the bathroom where a splash of cold water would do the job properly. Now, she would give anything she had, and then some more, just so she could get to do that with Brittany one more time.

But Brittany was dead—had been dead for three years now—and Grace was waking up alone in the house that she used to share with her husband and daughter. As usual, the silence was one of the worst things about being alone. The way every movement echoed against the walls, the floors. Even worse was the cold. No matter how warm the weather got, or where she was, she still felt cold. A cold that was deep-rooted in her bones, one she had started to feel the day the police had stood outside the door to tell her they had finally found her daughter's body of her.

At first, Tony had been a little relief in keeping the cold at bay. His arms had been around her when he'd told her that the cops must have made a mistake. Then the way he'd held her when they had gone to the morgue and confirmed that the body with the broken face and crushed neck was, indeed, their daughter. That was the day when his arms had stopped being the safe haven they used to be. Later they had found out the battered face and crushed throat was the smallest of the injuries their daughter had suffered. And she had suffered a lot, so much that the cops had called Tony aside to confer with him on whether it was wise to talk about the extent of her injuries in front of his wife.

Three days after she'd learned of her daughter's death and how she had died, Grace had suffered her first breakdown. In the next two years, she would have to spend three more long stays in the hospital, once courtesy of a full fist of over-the-counter pills and a bottle of red wine.

That was the last time, and it was when Tony had finally told her that he was tired of her crap and that he wanted a divorce. He'd moved out that same day. Three months later, Grace Hall became Grace Miller once again. As for Grace, she couldn't understand how easy it had been for him to get over their daughter's death. How fast he had been to go back to his work, to think of having friends over. How quick he had been to suggest that they clear out their daughter's room. And then there was that day when he had brought up the suggestion that they tried having kids again. It was one of the times when Grace wondered if she had married a monster.

Even though several people told her that four months was enough time for some people for that kind of grieving, and that Tony was right in trying to move on from what was clearly a nightmare, she didn't believe them. She refused to accept the fact that it was easier for some people to move on. After all, three years later, she was *still* grieving. She couldn't really blame him, though; he hadn't been the one who had screamed in their daughter's face that she could get out of the house if she could not abide by her rules. And, even though Tony said he didn't blame her at all, she couldn't help but think that, deep inside, he did. She could never forgive herself.

Grace got up from bed and put on her bathrobe before walking into the kitchen to turn the coffee maker on. After that, she grabbed the vacuum and got to her first task of the day, making sure that the house was spotlessly clean, even though she had done this exact same thing yesterday, and the day before.

Even though there was no single speck of dust to be found in the entire house, she still cleaned it from top to bottom. It had started one day when she had remembered how she usually chastised Brittany for tracking mud into the house, or complained about her not doing laundry or helping with the house chores. She had gone into a frenzy that day, cleaning the whole house from the attic to the basement. As if that would bring her little girl back, as if she was telling Brittany that she would never be mad at her again.

She had fallen asleep exhausted that night. But the next day, she did the same thing, this time leaving the attic and basement out of her route. Tony had tried to stop her once, and she had nearly bitten his head off. Well, now, he was no longer around to stop her. Now she would scrub, and she would clean, and she would dust for as long as it took.

She finished with all the rooms upstairs, except one. Then, she cleaned the entire ground floor, after which she sat at the kitchen table with all the mail that had been delivered that day and her old laptop. First, she read the paper, taking note of all crime stories and trying to draw parallels with Brittany's murder. Then, she went online to all the forums and chat sites that she had registered with, trying to find out if anyone had seen or heard anything about a killer who went after runaway kids. When she was done, she closed the notebook she that had been writing in, then went back upstairs and into the untouched room from earlier.

This time when she cleaned the room, she only tackled the dust, making sure that Brittany's table was still as cluttered as she had left it. The clothes in her closet were clean, but still the exact same way that she had left them, Grace made sure of this. Some people might call it an obsession; she didn't. It was just something that she did, because until Brittany's killer was found, Grace couldn't shake the feeling that Brittany was not yet at rest.

It was the third day after Naomi's and Sophie's murder, and just like the two days before, Karl was at the police station to ask if there were any updates on the manhunt for the monster, Mitch Petersen. However, unlike the two previous days, this day he had asked Debbie to stay back at home. It was partly because he knew she needed the rest; but mostly because he was sick and tired of hearing her cry. Which was all she did.

She cried.

She cried when people came to pay their condolences. She cried some more when some of the girls' classmates dropped by with a large bouquet of flowers and a card. She cried when they tried to talk to the detectives about the case.

Then, cried some more when she heard that there were no new leads that had come up yet. She even cried when they turned in to sleep at night, not that Karl had been able to sleep a wink. But come early morning, and she was *still* crying.

Karl, on the other hand, was determined that if nothing, at the very least, the killer would be brought to justice. It would in no way compensate him and Debbie for their loss, but knowing that Naomi's killer walked free while her body lay lifeless in a morgue somewhere made Karl feel even more useless as a father. He was supposed to protect his daughter; he was supposed to watch her grow up and get old. He was supposed to give prospective boyfriends the scary father talk, and hold her hand when she suffered her first heartbreak. He was supposed to watch her get married and spoil her children, his grandchildren. Then one day, he was supposed to die knowing that he had a daughter to bury him in the proper way. He was not supposed to bury *her*. That was never how it was meant to be. It was not the norm.

Karl heard a door open and Detectives Park and Ramirez walked in. He noticed the look of resignation on their face, and knew deep inside that he should probably leave them to do their job. But he couldn't leave them; he couldn't sit back at home, nodding his head at the empty platitudes of his church members. If he heard anyone say anything such as "God knows best" or "She is in a better place" one more time, he might be tempted to strangle someone. No, she wasn't!

She was dead. Period. And bringing God into this situation only made matters worse for him.

Standing up from his chair, he went to meet the detectives.

"Dr. Munson..." Detective Park said as soon as Karl came within earshot. "We already told you that we would let you know as soon as we get any breakthrough in the case. You should be at home with your wife."

Karl looked at him like he was crazy. "And do *what* at home? Make cookies? I need to be here! I need to know what I can do to help. This monster cannot be allowed to do this to someone else."

"We are trying our possible best, Dr. Munson," Detective Ramirez said. "It's just that—"

"Your possible best? What is that even supposed to mean? Your possible best should have been to catch that monster... that... sick son of a bitch before he did this. Or at least to have alerted people in the city to the fact that a deranged sexual pervert and serial killer was living amongst us. Maybe if you had, we would have done your job of locking him up for good and my daughter would still be alive!"

For a moment, all eyes in the station were on them, before everyone resumed whatever it was that they were respectively doing. Detective Park stared down at his shoes as if he was trying to decide something, and then, finally, lifted his head.

"Okay. How about this? I will share what we have so far with you, as well as how we are working towards apprehending this Mitch Petersen. If you think you have an idea on how to help, let us know, and we will decide if it is an idea worth exploring. Is that okay with you?"

Karl quickly nodded his head, happy to finally have something to do. "That's better than sitting at home wondering if this is really your priority."

"Okay, then, Dr. Munson, I can assure you that finding Mitch Petersen is our number one priority," Detective Park affirmed. "Ramirez, take him to Conference Room B. I'll go grab the files and meet you down there."

Karl followed Detective Ramirez down a long hallway to an empty conference room. At first, he stood awkwardly behind her as she went to put on the light and set up the projector. Then, when she was done, she indicated to him that he could have a seat anywhere. Karl chose the chair closest to him and sat down.

"Would you like some coffee, Dr. Munson?" She asked him after about five minutes of awkward silence.

"No, thank you. I'm fine," Karl quickly replied; too quickly, he thought to himself.

But the arrival of Detective Park saved him from any other embarrassing episodes. Detective Park dropped the carton that he was carrying on the table.

"Like I said before, we are doing everything that we can to catch and arrest Mitch Peterson as quickly as possible. We've put out an APB with his picture, and also offered a reward to anyone who has any information that could lead to his arrest—"

"Double the reward for that! I'll pay anything." Karl interrupted him and slammed his fist against the table in front of him. "Make sure they know that if anyone can help us catch this guy, I will pay them handsomely for it."

The two detectives looked at each other, before Detective Ramirez continued. "The thing is in this type of situation, especially when money is involved, the tips we usually get are typically false. Sometimes people are eager to say they saw something when they didn't. But after carefully going through all the calls and messages we receive, we know little about the culprit's movements."

"People say they saw him walk around, but no one can tell in exactly what direction he came from," Detective Park added. "We already know he gained access to your house from the tree at the back, but it is still hard to figure out if the crime was planned or if it was a random act of violence, since he didn't try to hide from the camera or make any plans for keeping his identity private."

"What does that tell us?" Karl asked, looking at the two of them.

"Well, honestly..." Detective Ramirez looked at him, deciding honesty was the best approach in this case. "...it tells us nothing. Mitch was on parole, but his PO said that he broke parole about three months back and subsequent visits to the address he'd left at the parole office yielded no results. At first, he wasn't a suspect for these types of crimes. Otherwise he would've never been out. Normally this automatically meant that a warrant was issued out for his arrest, but there was no sighting of him until..."

"Until he killed my daughter." Karl said, staring down at the floor.

"Yes, until that."

"So then, what's going to happen now?" Karl asked.

"Now, you leave us to do our job," Park said. "We already have his description. His picture is everywhere. It won't be long before someone sees him or sees something that will eventually lead to his arrest. I know it's hard; but it's best for everyone involved if you leave us to do our job."

Karl thought about this for a moment. "Okay. When can we get Naomi back? Debbie and I want the funeral as soon as possible."

"The coroner is still carrying out his autopsy and we want to make sure that we get as much DNA evidence as possible."

"DNA evidence? What do we need that for? We already have him on tape. Isn't that enough?"

"Yes, we do. But it's still best not to take any chances."

"Don't waste my time, Detective. Quit playing this game. I want my daughter back, now." Karl stood up and puffed out his chest to look stronger.

"This isn't a game!" Detective Park cried out. "We're not trying to torment you or make your life more difficult than it already is. We are doing our jobs, and this is the way it must be. You're feeling a little lost right now—"

"Don't tell me what you think I'm feeling! You have no idea what this is like." Karl wiped a tear from his cheek.

On the way back to the hotel, Karl drove through his neighborhood. The house was still being treated as a crime scene. He parked across the street from his house and thought about what Detective Park had said last. Karl wasn't scared that Mitch Peterson might not be found guilty, because Karl knew that, if it came to it, there would be no trial at all for Mitch.

All he was waiting for now was to find the man who had murdered his daughter. He sat in his car for a few minutes before revving the engine and speeding off. He didn't know if he should go back to the hotel or find another place to go. It didn't matter. Everywhere he went, all he could think about was Naomi.

There was no escaping it.

Grace barely got out of the way as a man stalked out of the police station, someone else with a problem the police could not solve. She walked in and went straight to the desk of Detective Ortega, the person in charge of Brittany's case, and saw that he wasn't there. Looking up, she greeted the next person she saw.

"Hello, Detective Park."

"Hi, Grace," he answered, looking up from the file in his hand and smiling when he saw that it was her. "How are you today?"

It was no surprise that he knew her. In fact, everyone at the station knew her by now because of how often she came by. The day she'd seen Brittany's body, she had returned home crying, unwilling to accept the fact that her baby was no more. Then, for three months, she hadn't wanted to have anything to do with the investigation. Officers came by and Tony had to beg her to answer their questions.

After that, she'd had her first breakdown. While she was in the hospital she'd woken up one day with this burning desire to bring Brittany's killer to justice. So, she had started, first with the detectives assigned to her case. Hounding them every day for answers, bringing them clues of other similar crimes, and having to tell her story so many times.

That was the hardest part of all, having to relive her story so many times to the cops as they tried to find clues as to how they could track Brittany's movement after she had left the house. Even now, she still vividly remembered what had happened that day. How she had chased her daughter into the arms of the man who had taken her life.

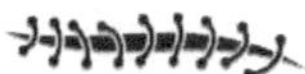

Grace walked into the house. It was quieter than she expected it to be. Tony was playing poker at his friend's house and wouldn't be home until later that night, but Brittany was supposed to be home from cheerleading practice by now. She went into the kitchen and discovered the sink still filled with dirty dishes from breakfast that morning, and the chicken she had instructed Brittany to bring out of the freezer to defrost for dinner still in the fridge.

Angry, she took out the chicken and, after placing it on the sink, she tackled the dirty dishes. When she was done, she decided to change her clothes. As she walked up the stairs, she realized she was not as alone as she'd thought she was. A noise came from Brittany's room. At first, she thought her daughter was on the phone and was about to call out to her, but when she finally heard what was happening, she couldn't believe her ears.

Enraged, she grabbed the doorknob to her daughter's room and fount it locked.

"Brittany!" she immediately yelled. "I know you are in there and I sure as hell can hear what is happening inside there. Come out right now."

There was a sound of a scuffle, and Grace thought she heard what sounded like a window being opened. But before she could run downstairs and around the back to see who it was, Brittany opened the door and immediately leaned against it.

"What is it, Mom?" she asked, trying to look cool.

But Grace pushed past her and went straight to the window, where she caught the running figure of a boy in their backyard.

"Who is that?" she demanded from her daughter.

"Who is what?"

"Don't play dumb with me, Brittany! I am not in the mood. Don't tell me you had that Wilson guy in here."

Brittany threw her face in the air as she walked back to her bed and grabbed her phone from the nightstand, ignoring her mother.

"Answer me when I'm talking to you," Grace commanded, moving close to the bed.

"Yeah, mom. Wilson was here. So, what? This is *my* room, remember? I can do whatever I want in here."

"No, you can't!" Grace said, getting in Brittany's face when she tried to ignore her. "As long as you are still living under this roof, you don't just get to do whatever you want. And especially not something stupid or something that is threatening to ruin your life."

Brittany rolled her eyes, then mumbled. "I'm sick of this house and its stupid rules. I can't wait to be eighteen, so I can leave."

Grace laughed at her comment. "You say that, all talk about leaving and whatnot, as if it was so easy. Well, try it and see how easy it really is."

"You always do that, Mom." Brittany stood up, and Grace was surprised to see that she was close to tears. "You think that I can't take care of myself, like there is anything special in what you guys do. I am old enough now to decide what to do with my life. And if I want to have sex, I'm going to fuck whoever I want, whenever I want."

Grace was shocked at her daughter's unexpected tone.

"Well, isn't that what you want to talk about? You were wondering if I was having sex in here with Wilson, right? Well, I wasn't. At least, not yet, Mom. But trust me, I am starting to think about it now."

"Exactly what do you think you know about this? What if you get pregnant? What would you do then? How would you deal with that? It would ruin your life, Brittany! Have you thought about that?"

"This is not the 80's, mom." Brittany smiled at her mother mockingly.

"Maybe not, and maybe I can't stop you from doing what you want to do. But as long as you live under this roof, you obey *my* rules. No questions asked. No ifs or buts. Hopefully, one day you will be smart enough to see that this was all for your good."

"Then I'll get out from under your roof."

"And do what?" Grace demanded, trying to tamp down her anger, but finding it hard to do so. "You can't even put a couple of dishes in the dishwasher or defrost a piece of chicken, and you're talking about moving out on your own. First learn to wipe your own ass and then talk to me about growing up."

"What the hell, Mom? I am so sick of all this. I'm sick and tired of you treating me like a little child. I'm done with you trying to control my life." Brittany cried as she ran out of the room and down the stairs.

A few seconds later, Grace heard the porch door open and her daughter walking out of the house. She sighed and walked down the stairs, refusing to feel guilty that she may have been too harsh on her daughter. Six hours later, Tony came back and learned from Grace that she had gotten in a fight with Brittany and she hadn't returned home. They spent that night calling all her friends and trying to find anyone who had seen her. Early the next morning, they were at the police station to report her missing.

Two days later, they viewed their daughter's corpse in a morgue.

⊰⊱⊰⊱⊰⊱⊰⊱

"I am fine, Robert," Grace replied him, all formalities aside, fixing a small smile on her face. "Have you seen Detective Ortega around, by any chance? I've got something for him."

"Um, Ortega? Yeah, actually. I thought I saw him at his desk just now." Detective Park tried to look behind Grace, aware that it wasn't rare for Ortega to take to his heels once he saw her coming in. "What is it that you want to give him?"

"Oh, just some notes I took from the papers today and from some online forums that I checked out this morning," Grace said, raising the paper up.

"Well, why don't you hand them over to me and I'll give them to him as soon as I see him?"

Grace hesitated when Detective Park stretched out his hand to take the information from her.

"Are you sure you're going to give this to him? It's very important! I saw on one of my online chat groups that some cops in Ohio caught a serial killer who used to prey on runaway girls at the bus station. I think this could help.

Maybe if you guys call down there and ask if he was anywhere around here around the time that Brittany was killed…" Grace choked up a little at the word "killed" before continuing, "I just really need to know that you guys are still working on this case."

"Of course, Grace! We're on your daughter's case on a daily basis."

Detective Park knew that a case still being under investigation didn't necessarily mean the detective assigned to it was actively pursuing it. Normally, the first three months of a case were when any active investigations were carried out. After that, it heavily depended on how high-profile the case was, the caliber of the victim involved, and how much interest the media. By the end of the first year, the best most detectives would do was wait to see if they got any noteworthy tips on the case, and even then, that was casually followed at best.

The amount of crimes committed in a day in the greater Los Angeles area alone was so staggering, it was almost impossible to follow them all. The main reason why Brittany Miller's case was still declared open and active was mostly due to Grace's active badgering and incessant visits to the station. For all intents and purposes, Brittany's case was closed and declared as unsolved. Until something significant happened to open it again, it would remain that way.

Still, Detective Park understood Grace's pain, knew her history, and knew the hope that Brittany's killer would one day be caught was probably the only thing that still kept her up. So, he collected the papers from her, placed them on his desk, and wrote a note to himself to hand it over to Ortega.

"Thank you, Detective. By the way, how is your sexy Latina partner doing?" Grace asked him with a wink.

"Oh, Ramirez? She is fine. Probably around here somewhere. Most likely getting coffee." He replied, ignoring her wink and double meaning.

"You cops and your coffee. Just like donuts." She smiled, touching him lightly on the arm. "You know, I made the mistake of drinking station coffee once. It's something I never want to try again."

"Well, you know us. We've got lead lining our stomachs," the middle-aged Korean man joked back at her.

She waved at him as she left the office, stopping briefly to talk with Officer Leslie, who was just returning from maternity leave.

"Was that Grace Miller?" Detective Park heard someone say behind him and turned around to see it was Ortega.

"Come on, you fool! Don't play dumb like you didn't run out of here the minute you saw her walk through the door."

"I did and I'm not sorry. That woman is really something, isn't she? I mean after all this time, she still holds out hope that we can find the killer."

"Well, you can't really blame her, can you? I mean to lose your only child like that." Detective Park said, and they went quiet for a few minutes in agreement. "So, no new leads on the case?"

"No, nothing at all. But then, the trail went cold almost immediately after the crime. It doesn't help that we couldn't build a timeline from her leaving the house and getting to Echo Park. We don't know of anyone she knew in that part of town, and none of her friends heard from her that night. Not even the boy she was allegedly dating. Honestly, the case was all messed up from day one."

"That sucks, man." Detective Park shook his head in pity as Ortega took his seat.

"Sometimes, I think of just telling her the truth. That we may never find the killer. But then, I remember how fragile she is. I don't think I can do that to her."

The two of them got lost in their thoughts for a few moments before Detective Park waved bye and walked back to his desk. The papers he'd collected from Grace were still where he left them, forgotten.

CHAPTER **FIVE**

EBORAH MUNSON STARED AT THE PEOPLE sitting around her in the hotel room. Most of them had been there the day before as well, and the rest were also there to pay their condolences. Debbie wished that they could all go to hell. Then she immediately regretted that thought. She was a Christian and she wasn't supposed to have such thoughts. Besides, it wasn't their fault that Naomi was dead.

"I heard the school is planning to have a memorial service for the girls," Gina said as she unwrapped a plate of cookies.

Debbie immediately tuned out from yet another discussion on how people planned to remember her daughter. She looked around the hotel room and decided she hated the place. She wanted to go back home, back to the house where she had raised and nurtured her daughter. The bed sheets had been confiscated as evidence, but Debbie still hated knowing that Naomi's room still contained hints of that monster. She needed to scrub and vacuum every inch of that room, to clean and preserve the memory of Naomi.

"Do you think that you'll be available to attend?" Gina was asking Debbie. "We already talked to Diana, and she said that she and Tanner can make time on Wednesday."

At first, Debbie looked at her, not quite grasping the question. Then she realized that she didn't care what they were talking about, and their presence was in no way helping to deal with her grief. Standing up, without saying a word, she walked into the bedroom, leaving her friends all alone and talking to themselves.

Karl had taken an entire suite in the hotel, and Debbie knew it was mostly because he wasn't yet ready to deal with the scene in the house. But she... she needed to see what had happened. She needed to know exactly how much her baby had suffered. Because not knowing hurt so bad. Like it had hurt yesterday, at least until... She heard the voices of the women murmuring in the other room, but was not at all in the mood to be polite to anyone anymore. They didn't know what she was going through, so they could judge her all they wanted. It wasn't like they were any help anyway.

She took one more look at the mini-fridge in one corner of the room. She knew the alcohol inside was the only thing that had helped silence the voices for at least a short while. It wasn't long before she opened the fridge and grabbed several of the small bottles kept inside it. With shaky hands, she unclasped the first one. By the time that she poured the fifth one down her throat, her hands were no longer shaking at all. For a little while, her imagination didn't run as wild, her senses dulled by the alcohol. This way, it was easier to think good things. Like how cute Naomi had looked on her first day to school. Or how proud she and Karl had been when her team won the Regional CIF Volleyball Championship.

Debbie leaned against the wall with the empty bottles at her feet. She looked up at the ceiling and a whimper escaped her lips.

"Why did this happen? Why? I hear about this kind of thing all the time on the news, but I never thought it would happen to us. It's not supposed to happen to people like us. We're good people! Is that why you took my daughter? Did we need some bad in our lives to balance out the good?"

She grabbed an empty bottle and put it to her lips. She held it upside down, trying to pour out every last, bitter drop.

She could tell from the silence that her friends had finally taken the hint and left. But her ears still pricked up when she heard footsteps on the other room. For a brief moment, she was seized with terror and glanced around frantically for something that she could use as a weapon.

Karl poked his head into the room and she breathed a very audible sigh of relief.

"Any news?" she asked from where she sat on the floor.

"No, but they said we can move back into the house tomorrow. Although I still think we should stay here for a while longer. I already called a cleaning company to go in and clean the place before we move back in."

"No!" Debbie screamed, half-rising from the floor.

Karl looked at her, shocked at her reaction.

"I want to do it myself!" she insisted vehemently. "I need to be the one to clean her room myself."

"Come on, Debbie. Not again." Karl looked at her like she was crazy. "Why the hell would you want to put yourself through all that?" Then more stubbornly, he added. "It's not like we can do anything to bring her back."

"That may be true, but I'm not going to forget her just like that. You may have pushed her out of your mind, but I'm her mother. She'll be with me forever."

Karl's insides attacked him. He wanted to run to the bathroom and throw up. He couldn't let his true emotions show. He had to be strong for the both of them. The best way to honor Naomi was to keep living. She would have wanted them to be happy.

"I didn't say anything about forgetting her. It's been two weeks already, and I know there is no accepted time frame for when and how to mourn. But I really think we should start moving on with our lives, babe."

"I don't want to move on with my life!" Debbie snapped. "I don't even have a life anymore."

She was wailing now. Destroyed. She threw the tiny bottles at Karl, but they barely reached him. In that moment, Karl felt nothing. His entire body shut down. He just wanted this part of his life to be over.

Karl looked at her as she bawled into her hands and sighed. He was tired of spending the day cooped up with her. He knew she had started to drink, and at first didn't mind her finding something to ease the pain. But by now, she couldn't sleep without it. He smelled alcohol on her breath when she came to bed and every other time he came near her. He could already see the small bottles in her hand and on the floor next to her and knew she'd been drinking again. He pretended not to notice, but the signs were clear.

Sometimes he wished he could find his own escape hatch too, something to dull the red haze of pain that seemed to now live constantly with him. But Karl knew his only escape hatch would come when he finally got his hands on Mitch Peterson, the monster. Until then, he would happily live with the pain, unlike his wife.

Naomi and Sophie were buried three days later. As Karl watched the pallbearers lower the coffin into the ground, it hit him hard that he would never see his precious daughter again. It was fact. Everything he had done in his life up to that point became useless. As he dropped a rose into the grave, he promised himself that, no matter how long it took, Mitch Peterson was going to pay.

After the service, while people came to pay their final respects to the girls, Karl spied Detective Park and Detective Ramirez standing at the back of the crowd. He led Deborah to the limo that would take them back to the funeral parlor, then excused himself and returned to where he had seen the detectives. They were about to leave.

"Detectives!" he called out and they turned back, waiting for him to catch up to them.

"Dr. Munson," Detective Ramirez said. "Just came by to pay our respects. We really are sorry about what happened to Naomi."

"Yeah, yeah…" Karl brushed aside their condolence greeting. "So, any headway made in catching this Mitch guy?"

Detective Park looked at his partner, before looking back at Karl. "I don't think we should be discussing this here today. Maybe you should focus on honoring your daughter's memory and not allow that monster to taint it."

"Don't you get it?" Karl asked, looking at both of them in turn. "He already did that when he entered what I created to be a safe haven for her and violated her in the most of evil of ways."

"He can only do that if you let him, Dr. Munson."

"What, so you're a therapist now, Park? Just tell me if you have anything on him. Have we gotten any tips, last sightings, anything of the sort?"

Detective Ramirez was about to answer when Deborah joined them.

"Karl, what is it?" she asked, looking at the three of them.

"Nothing, Debbie. Don't worry about it. Please, just go back to the car and wait for me there. I'll be done here soon," Karl said in a soft voice, trying to protect her.

But she dug her heels in. "No, thanks. I don't need any patronizing. If there are any news or updates, I want to hear them too. She was my daughter too. Don't you forget that."

Karl nodded in agreement. He understood his wife's desire to know just as much as himself and he felt bad for his response.

"We really are sorry for your loss. Our most sincere condolences," Detective Ramirez said again.

Deborah nodded in acknowledgement. "Thank you, Kimberly. Now, why haven't you caught the monster responsible for this? I mean, we even have pictures *and* a video of him, for goodness sake!"

"These things sometimes take time, Dr. Munson," Detective Park answered. "We've gotten several tips and we can assure you that we've followed down every single one of them without making any headway."

"Still, we were able to get a few tips that proved a bit useful in trying to get a read on where he might be," Ramirez added. "A couple mentioned they saw someone matching his description head west toward downtown on the night in question. They were able to give a close enough description of what Mitch Peterson wore that night, so we know that he headed there. All other tips that proved to be legitimate let us know that he stayed somewhere downtown during the period he was here."

Deborah was about to say something when Karl raised up a hand. "What do you mean during the time that he was here?"

"We can't say for sure, but we don't think he's around these parts anymore," Detective Park answered.

"And what does that mean then?"

"It just means it's a little harder to find him. He could be anywhere by now. But you better believe we're doing our very best to catch him. We'll get him," Detective Park added immediately. "His face is with every cop in the country and he's bound to turn up somewhere. Criminals always make mistakes."

The two detectives made their excuses and left, promising to call immediately as soon as anything else came up. Karl escorted Deborah back to the car and got in with her. As they drove to the funeral parlor, Deborah looked at Karl, who seemed to be lost in his thoughts.

"Do you think the detective was right? Do you really believe they'll get him soon?"

"I don't know what to think anymore, Debbie. I'm starting to get scared that the monster who took our Naomi away is going to get away with what he did."

"No, he can't! Don't even say that." Deborah shook her head, refusing to even consider the possibility. "I don't think God will let a monster like that keep on roaming around, bringing grief to other people."

Karl didn't say anything. He simply held her hand and decided to take the detective's advice to grieve in peace.

It would be a very long time before they held hands like that again.

SCARS

CHAPTER **SIX**

KARL AND DEBORAH sat across from Pastor Gomez. Neither of them looked at the other, and the pastor looked slightly annoyed.

"You're giving up?" the pastor asked, perplexed.

He didn't approve of their decision but, as far as Karl was concerned, the pastor didn't have a say in his life.

It had been more than a year. A whole year and a half had passed since the murder of his daughter and her best friend by that animal. Karl refused to acknowledge that such a monster had a name. What made things worse was the fact that the monster hadn't been caught yet. Who knew how many other girls he had raped in this time? How many girls he had killed? And who was to say that his victims were exclusively female?

In their entire relationship, the Munson's had taken on a number of hardships, but this one they couldn't work through together. The pastor had attempted to convince them to try and stay together, but after about a year, they were ready to give up. Well, not fully give up, but take some time apart. They weren't calling it quits entirely, but they were temporarily splitting.

Things were hard. They barely talked anymore besides "What do you want to eat?" And neither of them wanted to spend the rest of their lives with what the other wanted to eat until they died.

Karl had fallen in love with his wife for several reasons, one of them being the fact that he could discuss almost anything with her. They used to have deep theological conversations. They would converse about social justice issues. Now he just avoided her in hopes of not having to talk to her at all.

However, he wasn't the sole guilty party in this whole thing. She avoided him just as much. Karl, who was normally a very religious man, had stopped attending church. He hadn't done so consciously, rather finding himself volunteering his doctor services on Sunday mornings more often. That was just how it started. Deborah hadn't gone to church, but it was because she hated going alone. And that was how their church attendance had started to decline.

With their decline in visits to their church, their faith in God also took a nosedive. Well, how could their faith not lessen? Their sixteen-year-old daughter—who had been and a good kid—had been *raped* and *murdered* in their own home.

If that wasn't enough, her friend had been strangled too. How could anyone keep believing in God when that kind of evil happened? To make things worse, the monster that had caused the whole tragedy was still on the loose, wrecking lives everywhere he went.

Karl shivered at the thought of what his daughter's final moments. He imagined the terror the girl must have felt as that monstrosity stole her innocence and promptly murdered her. The Munson's had been told she had been alive for most the rape. Sophia had not been raped.

Mitch Petersen, it seemed, had fled the scene on the arrival of a pizza delivery boy. Said boy had waited at the front door for ten minutes, ringing the doorbell twice a minute, before he left their house with a scowl on his face. He had heard nothing. Nor had any of the neighbors. The neighbors, who usually complained at the music being too loud, had heard nothing this time. It was unbelievable!

"Look, Mark…" Deborah said. "We're not giving up. We're giving each other space."

"And that almost always leads to divorce!" the pastor snapped, but soon regretted his loss of temper. "I know what happened is a tragedy, but you two need each other now more than ever. You need to support and love each other. That's the vow you two made when you got married in this same church twenty years ago."

"We're not planning to divorce," Deborah reassured. Tiredly she continued, "We just... need time."

"I still love my wife, very much," Karl said, glancing at Deborah, "but we're living past one another and it is getting ridiculous."

"We're hoping the whole 'absence makes the heart grow fonder' thing works for us," Deborah said, a hint of a smile ghosting around her lips.

"Unfortunately, it doesn't work that way—" the pastor began, and Karl grew irritate at his spiritual leader and friend.

"Your way isn't the only way that works," he snapped, "and we already decided to do this."

"But you also abandoned the church," the pastor tried again, but to no avail. This time it was Mrs. Munson who intervened.

"So, what if we are?" she said, looking at the pastor with cold eyes. "I thought church was about our personal relationship with Jesus, and not about the people in the building?"

The pastor said nothing. It was pointless to continue. Karl knew that they had won, at least this time. For the last six months, elders of the church had arrived at the Munson home at random times to try and convince the couple to come back to church, but both Munson's had thrown themselves into their work. The Gomez couple had less luck than the elders. Now the pastor, in a final attempt, had even made the Wallers speak to them. Nothing worked. All it did was succeed in making the couple annoyed and irate.

"If you'll excuse us, Mark," Karl said, getting up, "we have to get to work."

"Please, you must reconsider," the pastor pleaded. "Let's talk through this again."

"I've had enough talk. I'm ready for some action, which no one in this town seems to understand. Nothing gets done. Everyone runs around like chickens with their heads cut off. You can't change our decision. This is the best path for us." Karl stormed out and slammed the door behind him.

Debbie cleared her throat and stood up. "He's right. This is final," she said while fixing her skirt.

"Come now, Debbie! You were always the more reasonable one. Karl is so stubborn. Is this really what you want?"

Debbie sat down again and pondered his question. "I don't know what I want, except my daughter back. I'm numb. My prayers are never answered and I'm completely alone."

"You have God and the members of the church."

Debbie shook her head and wiped her tears with a tissue. "They don't understand. They never will."

"What about the Wallers? Maybe they can give you more insight? They understand the pain you're going through more than any of us. You're right about that much."

"I can barely look at them without blaming myself for Sophia's death. I'm sure they blame us too. We don't have much of a home here anymore. We've lost everything." Debbie stood up once again and walked to the door, then looked back at the pastor and smiled. "We have many good memories with this church, but nothing lasts forever."

"Put your faith in God!" the pastor shouted as she left the room. "He has the answers you need."

They had used their lunch hours to inform the pastor of their decision. They had gone into it knowing that he wouldn't be happy about it. But, then again, the pastor had no say in their marriage. Yes, he had tried to counsel them, but he wasn't a psychologist. And the Munson's had started to see marriage counselor six months after their daughter's death, on top of their usual weekly visits to other therapists to try and come to terms with what had happened. But neither of their hearts were in it, because how on God's green Earth could one come to terms with the brutal murder of their own young daughter?

Deborah followed Karl, running in her heels to catch up, both ignoring the pastor's protests. Outside of the building, they turned to one another. Karl couldn't look at his wife because he saw Naomi in his wife's expressions. It just hurt too much.

"Are you sure about this, Debbie?" he asked, secretly hoping she hadn't changed her mind about their arrangement.

It wouldn't matter whether he lived in the house with her anymore or not, since they slept in separate bedrooms anyway. He just couldn't take the dull silences anymore. It wasn't as if they didn't have anything to say to each other; it is just that, when they did talk, they either didn't listen or didn't care anymore. And when they did talk... Oh, when they did talk, it wasn't so much talking as a screaming contest. They blamed each other for the stupidest things—about a lone sock that didn't have a mate, about the toilet seat, about their spending habits... It wasn't as though they couldn't afford to spend money. The fights weren't really about the spending, but more about the attempts to fill the void left by their beloved Naomi.

Nothing helped. She'd tried shopping therapy for a while, but no amount of clothes or jewelry dulled the pain. She had gone from drinking wine here and there with a meal, to inhaling full bottles in a single sitting. He hadn't been much of a drinker either, but had recently found a new love affair with whiskey. Except drinking didn't help either; it only dulled the pain temporarily and then simply made matters worse.

Deborah used to love to hear about Dr. Munson's patients and some of the ridiculous requests that he would get on the job as a plastic surgeon. Nowadays, however, she just didn't care to ask. Though maybe she had asked those questions in favor of their daughter. No, it couldn't be, she had always been interested in his strange clients, even before they had Naomi.

And before, she would entertain him with stories of her colleague and friend, Justine, who was an odd soul. She refused to wear what could be considered normal clothes, choosing to wear long, eccentric dresses and jackets, no matter what the weather was. Justine also would come up with some strange stories that always amused the plastic surgeon. But now those tall tales were simply a thing of the past.

"I'm sure," was all Deborah said before she placed a quick kiss on his cheek, got into her car, and sped away back to work.

He sighed, looking back at the church building, finding the pastor outside. Karl gave him a wave before getting into his own car, trying to ignore the pastor's obviously sad, yet judgmental look.

Karl looked at his watch. They wouldn't mind if he was a few minutes late. He was good at his job, so he knew he was worth the wait. He looked at the church, then started his car.

"If God is so forgiving, then he'll forgive me if I never come here again."

At his office, he found his business partner, Dr. Carlos Montes, and insisted on a meeting in the latter's office. The two men had a fruitful business together, both becoming rich in their practice through the years. But it was no use denying that Karl's work had suffered the past few months.

"Look, Carlos," Karl stated, sitting across from his partner. "I'm going to be blunt. I really need some time off."

"Finally!" his partner said, to which Karl looked up in surprise. "I was expecting this a few months ago, but you're a stubborn old bastard."

"Excuse me?" Dr. Munson said, confused. "You were expecting this?"

"Yes, I was. You deserved some time off after what happened, but you threw yourself into your work. Now, I think it's time for you to take leave. You don't have to say how long, just let me know whenever you plan on returning," Montes said seriously. "You know that I've got it covered, bro."

Karl smiled at his partner, thankful. It was the first time in a long while that his face had been graced with a smile, and the sensation was alien.

"Go. Now." Dr. Montes waved him away. "And relax. Find yourself, Karl. Do what you need to do. Then, and only then, come back to us."

Karl was thankful for his partner and friend. The fact that he didn't put up a fuss was great. Karl shook his Montes's hand and left for his house.

He honestly hated the house now. A large building, which was probably one of the reasons why Petersen had decided to target them in the first place, that was empty. It held no warmth, no laughter, and no children. Oh, what would he have given to hear the latest annoying pop song coming from his daughter's bedroom. That room stood closed. Neither of the Munson's had been in there since the incident. They had had it cleaned, and still kept it up weekly, but didn't dare to go inside it. At least, Karl didn't. He didn't think he would be able to take it.

He went up the stairs to his own bedroom and packed. He took a few items of clothing—nothing formal; he didn't plan to attend a black-tie event while he took his leave—and stuffed them unceremoniously into his suitcase. He then packed his books and his guitar and loaded them into his gray Range Rover.

He let the cleaning lady know he wouldn't be home for several days and she didn't need to worry about his room. Now she only had to worry about the main bedroom in which Deborah slept, and Naomi's room, which basically required dusting and some light sweeping.

He took the keys to his summer house off the hook and left his wife a note.

Deb, I am going the mountains for some time. Call if you need anything. —K.

Even if they were on the rocks, he still didn't wish for her to worry. He dearly loved Deborah, but he couldn't love anyone if he was so unsure of who he was.

He didn't like who he had become. His decline in attendance to his church was one thing, but he'd also stopped giving. He didn't know why, because he had always loved the feeling of giving. Oh, the church still got their money, but he used to like anonymously donating money to people who needed it, like a poor family who couldn't afford to send their children to school, or a teenager's college tuition when they were bright, but couldn't afford to go to college. He never told anyone, but he did like to see the faces of the people he helped.

He should give again. Maybe he would feel better. He didn't know who he was anymore, and he was tired of the dark cloud that always seemed to hang over his head like a foreboding storm. He desperately wished to avoid *that* storm, because he didn't know who he would be afterwards.

Karl Munson got into his car, pushed the gear stick, and raced off to his summer house by the lake. He tried turning on the radio, but every pop song playing on every station reminded him of Naomi. When he turned it off, the silence was deafening. He was trapped with his own thoughts, tortured by them. Nothing he did could help him escape the memories of his little girl. He hoped a fresh scenery would dull the pain.

As Karl drove down to the lake, he tried to tamp down the guilt he felt at the fact that it seemed like he was abandoning Debbie. He told himself it wasn't that he was abandoning her; he was simply going to the lake house to try to find the old him. He needed to find the Karl who couldn't do without her, the Karl who used to be so madly in love with her that he couldn't stand being away from her.

Now, however, she merely served as a reminder of a time he feverishly wished he had back. The fact that he knew it was impossible was a pain he was still struggling to learn how to deal with. And since Debbie had been the only one who had to suffer it with him, she'd proven to be the handiest of targets. It was hard to heal and move on when the person you were supposed to heal with was the most potent reminder of what you were trying to get over to begin with.

There were days when he woke up, looked at Debbie, and realized he was staring at the closest resemblance to what Naomi would have looked like if she had grown up. It made him want to fall to his knees in tears, but since he couldn't, anger was his only other outlet for his pain. Since the monster who was the cause of this was still on the run, his loving wife was, unfortunately, the only person he could get angry at.

He remembered when Debbie and he used to go to the house on the lake for the occasional weekend. They had taken Naomi with them once, but later decided the summer house would be his and Debbie's escape every once in a while. Except on long summer breaks, when the whole family had spent a few weeks at the lake.

He remembered the last trip the three of them had taken to the summer house. He had come in, only to see Debbie and Naomi watching *The Bachelorette* on TV and talking about who they felt was going to be eliminated next.

"Hi, babe!" Debbie greeted him when she heard him come back from work.

"Hey, Dad," Naomi said from where she lay her head on her mother's lap.

"Hello, my gorgeous ladies. What are you guys up to?" he asked, hanging his car keys on the hook by the entrance to the living room.

"Watching *The Bachelorette*," Naomi answered him excitedly as she made space for him to join them on the couch.

"No, no, no. We have to watch something other than that if you want me to join you."

"No, we don't," Debbie answered.

"Yes, we do! I've been at work all day and I think that for once I should get to watch what I want to see. It's not fair that I always lose," Karl said, trying to look serious.

Debbie and Naomi stared at him for a few seconds before they both burst out laughing. Karl sighed theatrically, but also had a smile on his face.

"Well, that's why you also have a TV in your room. You can go and watch men shoot guns and blow up stuff there if you want," Debbie said when she and Naomi finally stopped laughing.

Karl looked at his wife with a smile. "You know, one of these days, I am going to win the battle of the remote control."

"Oh, Dad, it's not even a competition. You love me too much to ever actually do that to me," Naomi said, batting her eyelashes. "Or do you want us to put it to a vote again?"

Karl rolled his eyes at that. "One of these days, I'm telling you, we're going to get a boy, and the playing field is going to become even."

"In your dreams, that is. Get ten boys and we're still going to have the upper hand," Debbie said as she finally leaned in to kiss her husband.

He smiled at her, and for a moment they shared a tender look between them, a visual reflection of the feeling in their heart.

There was a time when talking about having another kid would have brought a painful look to her eyes. But after they had Naomi and considering what they'd needed to go through to get her, Karl and Debbie had decided they would never ever see having an only child as something other than what it really was. A blessing. An opportunity to shower just one person with all the love they had to give. And they adored Naomi.

"Hey, why don't we head out up the mountains to the summer house this weekend?" Karl suggested, as he looked at the two most important people in his life. "Let's escape this heat for a couple of days."

Debbie seemed to consider it for a few minutes, but Naomi was quick to protest.

"*All* of us, or just you two? Because there's no way I'm wasting a whole weekend away from all my friends."

"You have friends over there too." Karl said, seeing that Debbi was already warming to the idea.

"No, I don't. *You* have friends that I end up having no choice but to talk to, since I have no actual friends," Naomi said, groaning in objection. "Come on, Mom. Back me up here."

Debbie smiled at this, before she said, "Actually, honey, I think I'm going to agree with your father on this one. It's been a while since we went away just us. All of us."

"Finally, someone is agreeing with me! I don't believe it." Karl gave a victorious whoop. "Besides, it's summer. I'm sure there will be other families there too. Maybe you can find a friend or two your age."

"Yeah, who knows? Steve's school may be on break too," Debbie said with a waggle of her brows as she winked at Naomi.

Naomi blushed deeply at that, immediately staring intently at the ceiling. "I don't know who you're talking about."

"Oh, yeah! I remember him," Karl said, joining in the fun. "Isn't he that cowboy kid you had a crush on the last time we were there."

"No, he is not. And no, I didn't have a crush on anyone," Naomi denied vehemently as she sat up and folded her hands.

"Okay, you didn't. But still, it would be nice to go and spend time away. Wake up and go fishing, sit down around the fireplace and make smores, just the three of us, and talk until late into the night."

"Well, it may have been fun if Dad hadn't decided it would be better if we didn't have a TV in the house," Naomi said, looking at her dad.

"What's the point of having a summer house if we're going to go down there and do the same thing that we do here, though? Watch TV? Are you serious? You have the lake! The boat. The hikes. The forest."

"Yeah, but TV is fun. You gotta admit it. Besides, if you really want me to have a good vacation, then instead let me head down to Cancun and the Mayan Riviera with my friends," Naomi said, looking really hopeful.

Karl had to hold himself back from bursting into laughter. It was clear she thought she could convince him to finally allow the trip abroad she had been angling to get for a while now.

"Yeah, that is definitely NOT going to happen," Debbie said beside her and smiled as Naomi groaned.

"I never have fun at the summer house. At least, not anymore, anyway. I wonder what you guys do there without TV or internet service all the time."

Karl and Debbie sent each other with a knowing look, mischievous smiles on their faces.

"Use our imagination," Karl said while winking at Debbie, who blushed and laughed softly.

"Eww!" Naomi screamed, sitting up straight as it dawned on her what all the winks and smiles meant. "That's gross. Thanks for the mental image. Now, for sure, I don't want to go to the summer house. Can I stay with Sophia while you guys go?"

In the end, of course, they had all headed for the summer house, where Karl and Naomi spent the day out on the lake fishing. It didn't even matter that they hadn't caught a thing. In the evening, the whole family went out to eat at one of the restaurants in the nearby town of Big Bear, since it had more food options than the town of Lake Arrowhead.

Naomi had a great time, after all.

It was the last vacation the three of them had taken together, the last time Karl had really gotten to spend time with his daughter, and he was hoping that maybe some of those good memories would help his soul with the healing it needed. He loved his wife and, while he could never ever imagine a life where she wasn't with him, he knew he needed to find a way to get over the demons he was fighting so that he wouldn't lose her too.

He thought about the murder a lot, as well as the fact that Mitch Peterson was still at large. He wondered what the police could have done differently to catch him, or exactly how he had managed to elude capture all this time. Sometimes he wondered if Mitch hadn't done a face change or something to make it harder for the police to identify him. It was a farfetched theory, but as a plastic surgeon, Karl had seen firsthand the way a little nip and tuck here and there could lead to a whole different look. Sometimes, he found himself looking at total strangers and wondering if they could be the monster who had killed his baby.

Yes, Karl knew he was slowly losing it. Hopefully, this alone time at the lake house could be the start of his healing.

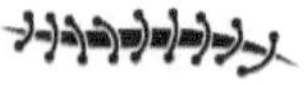

The autumn leaves were falling, little birds were chirping, and the sound of a little girl laughing echoed round the garden. Tony and Grace had just moved to their new house in a quieter neighborhood and a safe haven for their little girl to grow up in. Brittany was all excited, running up and down without a care in the world.

Grace stood at the porch, fulfilled. She now had everything that a woman like her could wish for—a good home, a happy child, and a supportive husband. She had a good life.

While she stood elated, her little daughter ran up to meet her. She carried something in her chubby palm.

"What is it, honey?"

Brittany showed her mom a pretty butterfly she had caught, and she was excited. Brittany wanted to keep the butterfly as a pet.

"Brittany, you can't keep a butterfly as a pet. They are meant to be free!" Grace said with concern.

"But Mom, I want to keep it. I love its wings. They are so colorful and pretty. They are the prettiest things that I have ever seen," Brittany cried back.

Grace smiled affectionately as she gently drew her daughter close to her. "We can't always have what we want, honey. Besides, the prettiest thing here is you."

Brittany, however, didn't want to listen. She wasn't ready to let go of her treasure.

Grace had to try again. "Did you know that butterflies are messengers? They carry the wishes of little children."

"I didn't know that," the child replied as she held the butterfly in her hand. "How do I make the butterfly send my message?"

"Just whisper to it and let it fly away, and your wish will come true."

Brittany did as her mother told her. She whispered to the butterfly and released it. The butterfly hurriedly left Brittany's chubby hand, flapping its beautiful wings as it flew to the sky, enjoying its freedom once more.

At that moment, Tony came out of the house somewhat sweaty. He'd been working inside, as some parts of the house still needed repairs and he had decided to fix them himself. Brittany rushed to meet him.

"Daddy, daddy! I made a wish. Mom said that butterflies carry wishes. So, I made a wish," Brittany squealed.

Tony carried her as he moved closer to Grace and smiled at her, pressing a kiss to her lips.

"Well, darling, you know that's all nonsense, because if I remember correctly, I think it's the moth that carries the wishes!" Tony stated, laughing.

"All nonsense?" Brittany quickly came down from her father's arm. "I need to catch a moth then!" she yelled as she ran into the garden, leaving her parents behind.

But now, Brittany would never catch butterflies or moths. She would never run again. She would never laugh again. Grace would never feel the warmth of her embrace ever again. All because of a monster.

"Are you okay, Grace?" her therapist asked.

Grace came back from her reverie and she stared back at the concerned face that was staring at her.

"I'm not okay. To be honest, I don't think I'll ever be okay again. I was someone who had it all, a good home, a good life, a good family. I was fulfilled. I was happy. But now all of that is gone. So, you explain to me, with all your fancy degrees, how can I be okay? Please enlighten me," Grace eyes flashed with anger.

"Let it out, Grace. Vent it out," he prompted her.

"I'm sorry, Doc. I shouldn't be shouting at you. You're not the cause of my pain," Grace apologized.

"No, no. This is a role play. You're meant to be angry with me," the therapist further encouraged her.

"Oh, but I assure you, you wouldn't want me to see me angry," she replied.

"Alright. If you aren't ready to talk about that, let's talk about your ex-husband."

"What about him?"

"Do you feel he blames you for your daughter's death? Do you think that's the reason why he left?"

"Tony was a good husband. I don't think he blames me. He supported me through it all, even though he was also going through the same roller coaster I was."

"Then why did he leave, especially when you were—are... in this state of mind, when you need him the most?"

There was an awkward moment of silence. Neither of them said anything for a minute. An eternal minute.

Feeling uncomfortable, she finally broke the silence. "Doc, it's ok for you to call it by its name. You don't need to be careful. After all, that is the main reason why I'm even here in the first place. Right? I *am* suicidal."

"You *were* suicidal, Grace. And I'm glad you're no longer in that state of mind."

Grace gave him a fake smile, requesting to use the bathroom. Once there, she stared at the mirror, her face was blank as a white canvas. No sign of emotion. Pale. Nothing there. Her orange sweatshirt was the only rose in her thorns, her hair neatly packed. She straightened her blouse, then went inside a stall.

The once emotionless face filled with pain; as if a sunny day had just unexpectedly grown stormy. Grace poured out her soul, her face becoming a waterfall of tears.

What the doctor had said was true, no matter how she tried to deny it or to forget the day Tony had deserted her. She had just come back from the police station, and that day she had been hopeful, for she had made a discovery she'd thought would help the police find her daughter's killer. When she got home, the look on Tony's face dashed the slight hope she'd had. He had already packed his bags and was waiting for her return, to let her know that he, the only pillar she'd thought she would be able to rely on, was leaving.

Divorce had never been conceived in her mind. Her parents had gotten divorced and their separation had scarred her. Since an early age, she had made a vow to never split with her spouse. But there had stood the man she'd sworn to stay with through thick and thin, holding divorce papers in his hand. Her signature the only thing still keeping them married. A twenty-year-old marriage was about to end, just like that.

She'd pleaded. She'd begged. She'd cried. She'd tried to reason with him. Grace had done everything in her power to make Tony stay. She'd promised. She'd threatened. But no; it had been pointless. Nothing had worked. Nothing could change his mind. Their marriage was over. The final blow had come when Tony had uttered those words, the words that had shaken her to the core and devastated her.

"I can't stand you, Grace. I just can't anymore. Every time I see you, all I see is the woman who drove my daughter to her death."

With that, Tony had left. He'd dropped the papers on her lap as he walked out of their house—the same house they had lived in for over a decade, the same house that was filled with all the love they had shared with Brittany.

Tony had walked out and never looked back. Not even once. Not even a little hesitation in his stride.

That was the first time she had ever felt loneliness. Brittany's death had caused her so much pain, but Tony's departure had left her naked to the pain. Suicidal.

Grace's emotions had been all over the place. While still in shock, she'd popped a pill out of a container and swallowed it. She'd popped another one, and another one, until the container was empty. But the pain had remained intact. She'd fallen flat on the floor and stared at the ceilings. Her life had flashed before her eyes. Darkness had enveloped her, welcoming her to its abyss. Her eyes had slowly started to close as she succumbed to the nothingness...

"Are you okay?"

Grace jolted back to reality, becoming aware of her surroundings. She was still in the bathroom stall. She fixed herself and came out.

An older janitor stood there, staring at her with concern. "Ma'am, are you okay?" she asked again when she got no response.

"Yes, I'm okay. Thank you," Grace answered and walked right past her, going towards the mirror.

Ignoring the other concerned lady in the reflection, she gazed at herself in the mirror, noting that her appearance was the complete opposite of how she had looked earlier. Her eyes were now puffy, the little makeup she had worn was now all messed up, and her hair was ruffled up. She patched up her face to the best of her ability to appear better, but the pain was still evident. Her agony was visible, no matter how hard she tried to mask it.

Turning towards the janitor, who was pretending not to stare at her, she finally said, "Thank you."

Grace headed out of the bathroom, back to whatever was left of her time in her therapy session. She walked up the hallway until reaching the door, but she stopped to take a deep breath before entering.

"Are you okay, Grace? I was just about to send someone to check on you," the calm man inquired.

Grace sat down, feeling as if the office was shrinking, trying to choke her. The books in the shelves were screaming at her with their silence. She was losing her mind. Again. Absentmindedly, she reacted when the man touched her.

"Calm down, Grace. You are safe," he assured her.

"That's what people keep telling me, to calm down and that everything will be alright. They say the worst is over and that it's time for me to move on. But the truth is that I don't want to move on. I don't want to calm down! How can I calm down when my daughter's killer is still out there? And why should I calm down when my daughter is lying six feet under?"

"It's okay to be angry, Grace."

"Hell yes, it is! Angry is exactly how I feel. And I know well I'm a bad mother, so please don't tell me or try to convince me otherwise. I was supposed to protect her, guide her, and shield her from the terrors of this world. Instead, I sent her away. I killed my daughter, Doc! I basically dug my daughter's grave and buried her. I know it's all my fault."

Grace burst into tears. But it was understood in the room that the only way she could heal was for her to release all the resentment she had pent up inside her. The crying was cathartic.

"You know, Doc... I've thought of different ways to kill the asshole, countless methods to make him suffer."

"Are you talking about Tony now, or the monster?"

"The monster, Doc! I'm serious. I'd tie him to a tree like a piñata, naked. Then I'd take a club covered with spikes and break every single bone in his body. But that's just the beginning. After that, I'd bathe him with boiling water to cleanse him of his sin and to make him feel the agony he'd caused to my daughter. Lastly, I'd take a hot rod and pierce it through his asshole until it came out of his mouth. That's exactly what I plan to do when I catch him."

Doc was concerned with what Grace was becoming. Any sign of improvement was now usually quickly tainted by threats like this.

Back at the house in Pasadena, Debbie was losing control. She'd cried when she'd found Karl's note, though she hadn't fully understood why. They'd agreed to a separation, and Karl couldn't get much farther away than the lake house. She'd called Karl's phone several times, hoping to hear his voice just once more.

Debbie got his voicemail each time she called. With each call, she would hang up, take a swig from the wine bottle she held like a baby, and throw the phone at the wall in her bedroom. When she went to retrieve it, she'd stumble and laugh about bumping into her dressers. Her vision was blurring, and the room spun rapidly.

At the last call of the night, she decided to leave a message. "Karl, honey? I hope you can listen to this. You must not have service right now. I miss you. The old you. The old us. I miss Naomi. Not a day goes by that I don't think about the family we used to be. I hope you're okay. I hope the time by yourself helps you heal. I think I'll be okay too. I have many friends here, though I've been ignoring a lot of them. Maybe I'll start going back to church. I don't know. Anyway, I love you, and I hope one day we can find our way back to each other. You deserve happiness, Karl. Even if that happiness doesn't include me. Stay safe..."

She wanted to say more, but the robotic recording cut her off. She threw the phone at the wall and pulled her blanket over her body. She hugged the empty wine bottle like a security blanket and closed her eyes.

"God, if you're listening," she mumbled, slurring her words. "Please keep my husband safe. I know you and I haven't been on speaking terms lately, but I hope you're still watching over us."

CHAPTER **SEVEN**

KARL PARKED HIS CAR by the lakeshore and entered his one-story house, the last one on the road, adjacent to the lake. He dropped his keys and wallet on the table. He dropped his stuff off in his room and collapsed on the bed. He rubbed his eyes and strained his ears. There was nothing. No sound. Just him and the wilderness outside. That was what he needed to move on with his life. As he lay there, the emptiness crawled through his body. The pain stung his heart, and a massive weight pushed on his chest. He had to keep moving. He had to keep himself occupied.

The lake house was peaceful and much cozier than the house in Pasadena. It only had two bedrooms, two bathrooms, a kitchen, living room, and dining room. The living room had sliding glass doors that opened to a wooden deck, which connected to a small dock on top of rocks where they could jump into the lake. The last three rooms were one large, open-space area, with a fireplace at one end for those icy winter nights and when they simply wanted to spend time alone.

He made a mental note to buy some firewood. He could use the sound of a crackling fire to soothe his messed-up nerves. And hot chocolate, the Mexican one in a yellow box with the picture of a grandma on its cover. This was Naomi's favorite drink, and it would help too.

He locked the house behind him and made his way to the local store in the town of Lake Arrowhead to buy some groceries: firewood, hot chocolate, milk, bread, cereal, fire starters, a lighter, frozen TV dinners, coffee, a case of bottled waters, and a bottle of whiskey for later too. And ice, which he almost forgot about.

"Hey, Karl!" said a voice behind him as he left the store.

Karl was now on his way to the pharmacy to hear if they could give him something over the counter to help him sleep, in case the whiskey didn't work. He turned to find his neighbor, Fred Williams, there.

"Hi, Fred." He shook the aged man's hand firmly. "How are you?"

"I'm doing well. I didn't know you would be joining us," the dark-skinned man said.

Fred Williams and his wife, Destiny, were the Munson's' neighbors for almost a decade now. They were both in their late sixties, or maybe even early seventies, and enjoyed their retired life in their big house on the edge of the lake, adjacent to the Munson lake house, while also doing the Munson family a favor by looking after the summer home. They were an African-American couple, very kind, and very white-haired too. They used to dote on Naomi whenever she was around.

"Yes. I'm sorry, I should have called. I'm going to be up here for a while," Karl said, falling into step with his friend.

"And Debbie?"

"She's still in Pasadena," Karl said softly, looking at his shoes. "We're taking some time apart after Naomi..."

He couldn't finish his sentence and hoped the aged man would understand. He did, because he nodded, not expecting Karl to continue with his sentence.

"It makes sense. Hey, do you want to have dinner with us tonight? Destiny is making steak, and you know she always makes enough for an army," Fred said as they stopped next to Fred's car.

"You know what, Fred?" Karl said, unable to keep a smile from his face, "I'd love to!"

As Karl watched Fred drive off, he thought about what it meant that he was finally willing to put himself in a social situation. Of course, the fact that it was Fred and Destiny helped too. He and Deborah used to have so much fun with the older couple, and he knew that with them, it would be safe; they would understand his grief. Fred had lost some of his close friends in the war, and his pain was still clear whenever he spoke about it. Karl wanted to ask him if it ever stopped hurting. Or at least enough that it was bearable.

He briefly wished that Deborah was here with him. He knew he wasn't the only one hurting, and he also knew well that what had happened pained Deborah even more than it did him. Not to put a quantity on their love, but Deborah and Naomi had always had a special bond. They had done everything together, and he knew that she needed him more at this point than anytime else.

A feeling of guilt enveloped him as he realized he was abandoning his wife in her hour of need. But he couldn't help but think of Naomi every time he looked at her, and those were memories that he wasn't ready to talk about.

He remembered thinking about going to college and talking about how they would miss her when she finally left the house. Back then, they had laughed and joked at the dinner table, saying Naomi shouldn't be surprised if they always paid her surprise visits at college. But what could they do when she had gone to a place where they couldn't go after her?

As he drove home, he looked around the town and realized that, even though Naomi had spent just a short time here, the place was peppered with memories of her. There was the shop where he'd liked to take her for ice-cream. Then there was also the restaurant where they'd held her twelfth birthday. The ghetto arcade place where she'd liked to hang out with the friends she'd made during summer was there too. But as Karl looked around, he realized he wasn't as sad as he normally would have been when he thought of his daughter and her memories.

Maybe it was because this place wasn't tainted with the ugly picture of her death. Maybe it was because this place was far from any association of those bloody bed sheets. Here, he could think about Naomi and smile a little at all the good times they'd had. And as he did, he couldn't help but realize that Deborah was a big part of all those memories too. He hated himself for letting it get to this point, the point where they were actually considering divorce.

Karl struggled with his thoughts. He wanted to give him and Debbie time apart to process their emotions. Yet, he didn't want to lose her, and that was what was happening. They were pushing each other away and leading themselves down a destructive path. He wondered if divorce was what he really wanted. In that moment, he didn't know why he'd gone to the lake house. He wasn't sure why this happy place should only be enjoyed by him. The image of Debbie danced in his brain, and guilt shot through him. He needed to heal. They both did. Was time apart really the right path?

Suddenly, he felt determined. It was time he started to heal, time he and Deborah started to heal as a family, starting from his dinner with Fred and Destiny. Then, maybe, he would call Deborah after dinner and the two of them could start figuring out how they would get back to what they used to be. Or at least the closest version to it that they could be after the death of their daughter.

Karl walked over to his neighbor's house. He wanted to bring them a gift, but he realized there wasn't much to offer yet. They hadn't restocked the kitchen in over a year. Knocking on the door, he felt anxious. It wasn't right being there without his wife and daughter. He was greeted with happy smiles and warm hugs from Frank and Destiny. He hoped he could get through dinner pretending that everything was all right.

"How is the business been going?" Destiny asked him later that night, while she poured herself some sweet red wine that Fred had bought for the dinner.

"Oh, just great," Karl said, but he didn't elaborate. He was telling an outright lie, but that was his sin to bear.

"And how's Deb?"

"She's… fine. Still working right now, so she won't be joining me for this trip," he said coolly, taking a bite of a well-cooked steak, just the way he liked it.

Fred had been right about Destiny making enough food to feed an army, because there were easily six pieces of steaks after they had each taken one. Still, the steak was delicious, so he had no qualms about it. He vaguely wondered if he would be able to persuade the elderly couple to send one home with him for a later meal.

"And how have things really been?" Destiny asked next, peering at the doctor over her spectacles.

Something about that look made him feel like a naughty child at school. He sighed and played open cards with them. He didn't want to talk about himself, but they were his friends. They deserved the truth.

"Not great. Deborah and I... Well, we've fallen apart. We can't really talk to each other anymore without it turning into a screaming contest. And no one ever wins, because it's an ongoing battle. We usually just stomp off to our rooms and let steam out, but it only continues the next day." He couldn't believe he had confessed all of that. "Our friends and the pastor aren't happy with our decision to spend some time apart either. The whole church hasn't been happy with us for not attending, but I'm too tired to keep up appearances."

He had no idea where that last bit had come from.

"Oh, honey..." the white-haired woman said, reaching out and squeezing his hand. "I can't promise it'll become easier, but know that the Lord has a plan for you."

"And why did His plan have to include killing my baby girl?" he asked, obviously irritated, setting down his knife and fork. His eyes burned and he blinked rapidly to keep tears from escaping his eyes. "Is God a sadist, Destiny?"

"Leave it, Destiny," Fred said gruffly, waving a large hand to quiet her down. "Let the man be."

"I'm sorry," she said and squeezed his hand again. "Please know we're here if you want to talk, Karl."

The plastic surgeon nodded appreciatively at her, his eyes no longer burning. But he felt his gut twist, as it often did when he thought of his daughter. He felt sick and couldn't eat anymore. He asked if he could take his food home to eat the next day. Destiny agreed and sent him home with a Tupperware container full of steak and baked potatoes, probably scared he'd starve himself to death.

Destiny and Karl said goodbye to each other and Fred walked him to the door. They both stepped outside and Fred left the door slightly open.

"Listen, Karl," he said and placed a hand on his shoulder. "I know you're going through a lot, and have been since... well, you know. But I need you to know you're not alone. We may not completely understand what you feel, but you can count on us to be your friends. I don't know what your relationship with God is like right now, but I know he's still watching over you. I can feel a holy presence."

Karl smiled and hugged his old friend. "Thank you. That means a lot to me. Please apologize to Destiny for my behavior earlier and thank her for the food."

"There's no need for that, my friend. She understands. All is well."

Karl waved goodbye as he walked away. He knew Fred's heart was in the right place, but on some level, a hint of anger rose through him. Fred was wrong. He was alone, and he would feel that way until Naomi came home. Karl seethed with anger, but let it all go when he returned to the house.

"What's the use?" he huffed. "It won't change anything."

At the lake house, he locked the door, put the food in the fridge, and retired to his bedroom. He fell onto his bed and stared at the ceiling in the darkness.

Why, God? Why Naomi? Why did You let this happen to us? Look at Deb. Look at my marriage. It's in shambles. I thought that You wouldn't send anything across our paths that we cannot handle. Well, I can't handle this! I am alone. And why am I even alive if nothing else matters anymore? Do You want me to end it? Is that it? I could just end it all, You know? But... I am too scared to do it. Carbon Monoxide poisoning? Hanging?

With those morbid thoughts, Karl fell asleep, his heart heavy and his mind even heftier. His face was wet with tears, tears he never dared to cry in front of his wife because he was supposed to be the strong one between them. He wasn't. He couldn't keep the charade up any longer, and it made him sick to think that he would have to go home and put on the charade again.

But not now. Now he was alone, and he could let it all out.

When morning came, Karl felt better. His face felt tight, so he quickly hopped into the shower. He decided to take the boat out on the lake that day, but first he had to get rid of the energy that he had. Energy that he had no idea where it came from, but he still needed to get rid of it.

A jog. Jogging would get rid of the energy and clear his mind. He could also enjoy the beauty of nature around Lake Arrowhead. Maybe he would even take a crack at the gym equipment in the lake house's garage. That was what the doctor did. He ran to get rid of the unexplainable burst of energy, and to get rid of the frustration and stress in his body. And when he came home, he went straight to the garage and did a bit of everything. Weights, steps, push-ups, pull-ups, and sit-ups. As many as he could, which weren't many. And then some more. His legs and stomach burned in protest, but he kept going. The burn distracted him from his dark mindset.

When he was done, he was so sweaty that he had to take another shower. Afterwards, he set out for the marina to take out his boat. This was something he hadn't done in a long while, and something he'd craved to do at the same time.

"Karl?" a voice said once he entered the marina.

Karl whirled around and smiled at Stanley Jones, marina worker and friend. "Stan," he said, sincerely delighted, and shook his friend's hand.

"I've kept an eye on your boat for you," the tall, gangly man said. "The workers clean her once a week, and we kept her out of the rain too."

"Thanks, Stan!" Karl said. "You're still the man! Hey, would you like to join me for dinner tonight?"

He had no idea why he asked, but he was pleased that he had.

"Sure, if it's okay with Mrs. Munson?" Stan asked, lifting an eyebrow.

"Deb's not here, it's just me," Karl said and grinned, though the grin felt forced.

Stan's resolve faltered for a minute before he returned the grin. "Sure, I'll bring the drinks."

After that, Karl made his way to his boat. He drove her out to the water and relished in the view mother nature had provided.

He stopped the boat in a place where he could see water in every direction. The land was distant enough, so Karl didn't feel constricted. He lay on a chair and put his sunglasses on. The water crashed against the sides of the boat and the sun's heat was cooled by a blast of wind. Karl closed his eyes and didn't think about anything. Whenever an image of his family came into view, he would shake his head and start over again.

Karl sat up and felt restless. He didn't know whether to read, drink, fish, or do something new entirely. He leaned against the railing and looked out at the water.

What would happen if I kept going? What would happen if I sailed this thing to the ends of the Earth and never looked back? Would I be any happier? Would Debbie? Would I be able to forget my life?

Karl looked at the sky and scowled.

"You're quiet lately. Don't You think I deserve a sign? What do You think I should do? Any suggestions?" He waited a minute, then huffed. "Yeah, I didn't think so."

He sighed and headed back to the marina.

The answers I'm looking for aren't out there. Do they even exist?

CHAPTER **EIGHT**

FRED WILLIAMS LIKED TO THINK that he lived a relatively quiet life. He lived in the mountains with his wife and barely any neighbors, for crying aloud. Of course, there was the Munson family who lived next door, but they only visited the house in the summer. That was why, when Fred saw the Munson patriarch outside the bottle store, he was surprised. He knew the Munson's didn't drink; they were devout, and frankly perhaps a little too conservative, Christians. But he liked to think that he hid it well, and even invited Karl for dinner.

Fred liked Karl, but since the death of his daughter he had changed a great deal. He was now a lot more drawn into himself. Fred enjoyed the stories that the plastic surgeon had told him of his work, but nowadays, those stories were limited. He could honestly say he had sorely missed Karl's company the previous summer.

The two of them would go out onto the lake with fishing rods, even if Karl hated fishing, and they would just hang around, as the young ones would say. But now, the doctor was obsessively working out, it seemed. He did try to come around to their house every now and then, bringing gifts and asking Fred to go out with him on his boat. Fred had accepted, and it had been fun, but not as it should have been the first time. The second time, it went better. The third time, it went great.

But at least Karl seemed to be doing better. As good as he could. Still, the mountains were relatively quiet, even if there was an extra person on it. Karl generally didn't bother them, and that was one of the reason that the Williams couple had moved out here.

The mountains were quiet, the loudest noise was that of their own TV playing football games or their radio playing Motown tunes, or perhaps a motorboat or jet ski going across the lake. The people were nice, especially to the elderly couple. Stan at the marina gave them free boat rides every fortnight, and Judy at the store gave them extra discounts when she could. They already got military discount, but she hooked them up on top of that.

So, when a group of hillbillies entered his home uninvited, he was understandably upset. He and his wife had been enjoying a siesta when the noise started.

"Tiny, look at this TV, man!" said a voice. "Can we get it?"

"Shut it, Paddy. The neighbor is home!" said another voice, presumably this Tiny person.

"We've been scoping this place out for a while now. Usually the man is out for groceries, and the wife is at the farmer's market. We can loot this house!"

"Shut it, both of you," said a gruffer voice, and both men fell silent. "Laura, check upstairs."

This all happened while the old man was asleep, so he didn't really hear any of this. What he did hear was a shrill female voice alerting her companions that the house wasn't empty.

Fred was yanked from his bed by strong hands. Even though he was ex-military, he was an old man and he only had so much fight left in him. He called out to his wife, but his only response was a muffled scream. He was surrounded by a group of people who chuckled and made no attempt to answer Fred's questions.

"Why are you here? What's going on?"

They'd pulled a pillowcase over Fred's head, in the hopes of increasing his terror. Fred wasn't afraid, not for his life, but for his wife's. They were both swarming with confusion and fear. Fred stumbled as they dragged him down the stairs and kicking and scratched at them, but to no avail. They enjoyed his persistence and ultimate failure to overpower them.

They pulled the pillowcase off and his head, and the next thing that the aged man knew, he was sitting back-to-back in the living room on a chair, tied to his wife. Tiny, who was, ironically enough, the largest of the felonious group, had found a bunch of zip-ties on the kitchen counter and had tied them up. Fred's heartbeat loudly, and he was terrified of what was going to happen next.

"Please, let her go," he croaked at Tiny, who just laughed.

"Nah, old man. I like her." Tiny put a large hand on Destiny's head and stroked her hair lovingly. Destiny shivered and wrenched her head back from his touch, knocking Fred's head. He didn't say a word, terror gripping his heart.

"We get to have some fun, eh?" said the girl, who couldn't be older than 21. She was small and petite, but her teeth looked awful. Her two front upper teeth were stubs, and the stubs were blackened. She would have been pretty if she had kept her mouth shut.

"Control yourself," yet another voice said.

Fred tried to look around, but was unable to. The man was out of sight. His voice was strange, as if he had been smoking for three decades and there were holes in his lungs.

"Get the stuff first, you idiots. Tiny, Paddy, go!"

The muscled man, who looked very stupid, and the other man, Paddy, disappeared out of the living room.

"Please, take whatever you want; just leave us alone. We won't say anything," Fred tried to bargain, but the girl just laughed—a high-pitched, cruel laugh that sent shivers down the old man's spine.

"Baby girl…" the out-of-sight voice said. "Find something to shut him up with."

The girl disappeared, and Fred didn't say anything. He had no idea who these people were, or why they had chosen the Williams residence. The elderly couple weren't rich. They were pensioners, for crying out loud. The military years had given them a good life, but the most expensive thing they owned was the 4k Ultra-HD TV that the men seemed so fond of. He loved watching football on his "baby". But why them?

The girl reappeared with two pairs of socks and she stuffed them into their mouths. Neither of the elderly couple protested, hoping that this would be over soon if they just cooperated.

"Daddy!" said the girl, Laura, facing the voice that Fred couldn't see. "Look what I found." She held up a pair of shears. "Can I use it?"

"Yes, but on the nigger bitch," said the voice—the father—and the girl let out a laugh of pleasure.

Fred's eyes widened. What did they think they were doing? He had no idea what the girl wanted to do with shears, but it couldn't be good. Then he heard his wife's muffled scream and knew that she had been cut. He screamed, trying to see what was going on, his head twisting painfully, but he saw nothing. Just heard the muffled screams, and then sobs, of his wife.

"Pa..." The call came from the other room; it was Tiny. "You think this is worth something?"

"Just bag it. We'll toss it out if it isn't," the voice said again. "Paddy!"

The other man, the one with the mullet, poked his head into the room. "Yes?"

"Come here and tell this man what my daughter is doing to his wife."

The man came forward, peering curiously over Fred's shoulder to see what his girl was doing. When he saw it, he laughed. Loudly. Annoyingly. His teeth were no better than Laura's.

"Oh, she is just cutting off your wife's pinky toe!" Paddy said delightedly, unable to keep his delight to himself. "There is so much blood. Baby, how long 'til it's off?"

"Two more snips, at most," the girl said happily. And then there was the sickening crunch that told Fred his wife had lost a toe. He screamed, but the sound was muffled.

"Now him, honey," said the disembodied voice.

Laura walked around them, while Paddy bent down and took the man's shoe off.

"Thanks, baby." The girl kissed Paddy—a prolonged kiss that Fred closed his eyes to. "Go get 'im."

He slapped her bottom, and she sat on the floor, cross-legged, before taking Fred's foot in her hand. She peeled off his sock and he kicked. She laughed again and held his foot tightly. The dirty blonde girl lifted a pair of bloodied shears, smiled horribly at him, before digging the shears into his foot. He screamed—or tried to. She had shoved it into the middle of his foot and turned it. The girl had surprising strength for such a petite creature.

She pulled the shears out and turned it towards his toes.

"This little piggy… went off," she said in a singsong voice, and then she started to saw into his toe.

He screamed again, and again the sound was muffled by the sock that had been shoved into mouth. She snipped, snipped, snipped… and then there was a loud crunch, and his toe was completely off.

Blood pooled around his exposed foot, and he felt hot tears ran down his face. The girl recited the poem *This Little Piggy* with every snip, or saw, or whatever it was.

"Now… a few fingers," said the girl.

Fred was trained to endure this type of torture, but his body hadn't been exposed to it for a long time. He squirmed in his chair, trying to hold his wife's hand. He desperately wanted to tell her to stay strong, that everything would be all right. He tried to block out the pain and go to his happy place. He imagined his wife and him going for a walk. The birds tweeted brightly, the leaves rustled in the trees. He would find himself in complete peace until suddenly, his wife would scream and break him out of his daydream. Fred felt faint. He could tell he'd lost too much blood. He only hoped that they'd been more merciful to Destiny. He couldn't hear her anymore. She wasn't moving. A tear rolled down his cheek. Was she dead? Soon after, Fred, just like his wife, lost consciousness.

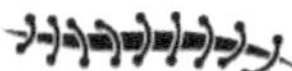

Karl Munson fumbled with the keys to his house. It was just like him to try and carry every single grocery-filled plastic bag in one trip, while he knew perfectly well this would cause him to struggle when opening the door. He always knew, but he never listened to the nagging voice in his head.

Wait... What was *that*?

He glanced over to the Williams's residence. He heard something that sounded oddly like laughter. Except it didn't sound like Fred's wheezy voice, and it surely wasn't Destiny either. It did sound like a woman, however. Karl shrugged it off; maybe they had company.

Finally, succumbing to the annoying voice in his head, he put some bags down, opened the door with his leg and carried the bags inside. He quickly put the food away.

He wasn't sure what to do next. He felt lost. Sitting at the kitchen table, he read a newspaper a week old. He remembered the time when every piece of news was about the death of his daughter. It killed him that her story faded as quickly as a fad. It had once been all anyone could talk about, and then suddenly it wasn't.

He was enjoying his time at the lake house as best as he could, but there was no avoiding the fact that he dearly missed his wife. And, of course, Naomi. His daughter. His baby girl, who was named after the mother-in-law of Ruth from the Bible. Karl and Deb had always liked that story. Ruth and Naomi, after their respective husbands died, found a new home with Boas, after her mother-in-law, Naomi, had told her to pick up wheat as the farmers left it. Naomi. A selfless creature. A woman who was willing to give up her own dreams and life in order for her mother in law to be safe. *Naomi.* It was a worthy name.

Oh, how he missed his baby girl.

But there it was again. Karl heard raucous laughter coming from the house next door. He glanced out the window, but saw nothing. The curtains were closed at the windows he could see, but that laughter was severely unnerving. It seemed as if it was... cruel. It was the same laugh he'd often heard from the teenage boys after church when they were being particularly nasty to either each other or about someone.

It was a sadistic laugh he had learned to fear. And one that his neighbors would never utter, or would allow anyone in their home to utter, unless they had no choice. They were kind people. Some of the few truly kind people left in the world.

So, this laughter was highly suspect, and he decided to find out what the reason behind the laughter was. The doctor donned a pair of sneakers, ones that didn't squeak, and made his way to his neighbors' home.

Luckily it was dark, because if it was someone who had invaded their house, he wouldn't be seen. He made his way over as quietly as possible, using the path by the rocks under the deck that he usually did when he went jogging in the mornings. But it was no use; their deck doors were blinded shut. He went around instead, toward the front of the house, wishing for better luck. This would be better anyway, because it was dense with trees that he could hide behind. This path led past the Williams's residence and around the lake, where he usually waved at them and they invited him for a morning cup of coffee. It led to the main road by the mountainside.

Karl put his head between two branches and could see through a window on the other side of their big house, facing their other neighbors, who were almost never there during the year. He knew this was a window that the Williams never bothered to close or hang curtains in front of.

He drew in a sharp breath when he saw them. His neighbors, Destiny and Fred, were tied up back-to-back.

There was blood on the floor, a deep red that told Karl they were still bleeding, and the laughter came from two voices. One was a young, dirty blonde woman who sat at Fred's feet with a pair of garden shears, and she was... she was *snipping off Fred's thumb*. No, it was more like she was hacking at it, since garden shears weren't usually sharp enough to cut through human flesh and bone. And with every hack, she laughed cruelly and recited the rhyme *This Little Piggy*, even if she was busy with fingers.

Fred was unconscious.

There was a male voice too, and he apparently found what the blonde girl was doing to be hilarious. He cheered her on, and walked past the doorway, facing the outside.

Karl ducked his head, but it was too late. The massive man hanging outside had seen him and was excitedly yelling at his comrades. The plastic surgeon let out a rather unmanly shriek and ran as fast his legs could carry him. He felt around in his pockets...

Why hadn't he taken his phone?

It was lying on the dining room table.

The doctor put the pedal to the metal, as he often liked to say, and decided to run back to his summer home to get his phone and call the authorities. His daughter and her friend had died because of an unwanted visitor in his house. He'd be damned if the same happened to his elderly neighbors. God only knew what Fred and Destiny had already been through. Whatever it was, he knew it was far from good, if he had to judge by the blood on the floor and that sadistic woman's laughter.

He ran this route daily, so he knew it quite well. He knew there was a poison oak tree on the left, he knew there was a large rock in the middle that he had to run around, and also a large tree root in between both homes, just before he reached his house. But it was dark, and he couldn't see much by the dim light of the moon, just shadows cast by the trees.

"STOP!" a voice yelled behind him, and Karl ran even faster.

His heart was thundering in his ears. No, wait, that was footsteps behind him.

"Stop! I'll kill you!"

Yes, because warning someone of their impending death is the right motivation to give someone when you are trying to get them stop running away from you. Karl laughed nastily, and swerved around the large rock that he knew about. His chaser wasn't as lucky and hit the large rock full-on.

Karl let out a breath of relief. Only to have that feeling stolen from him.

"You *idjit*!" a male voice called, and Karl heard the man swerve around the rock.

There were two chasing him! One was down. And now... if only he could get the other man to trip over the tree root...

Karl fell, a sickening crack was evident in the dark night. As luck would have it, he had fallen over the tree root that he had tried to make his chaser fall victim to. Karl tried to force himself to his feet and continue the run, but the moment he put weight on his left foot, it gave in under him. He had twisted his ankle. A sharp pain shot up through his leg, and a loud thud echoed through the woods as he fell again, and the thundering footsteps that had been following came to a stop next to him.

"Why did ya gotta run, boy?" the man asked.

Before Karl could even think to answer, he was kicked in the face by a worn-out working boot. He felt his body been thrown over the other man's shoulder, like a pig carcass at a butchery. The doctor struggled against his captor, kicking with the foot that wasn't sore and slamming his fists into the man's back. This man wasn't that big, but he sure was strong. Karl's foot connected to the man's neck or chest somehow, and the man was breathing heavily. But he wouldn't stop.

"Tiny!" his captor called when he neared the Williams's residence, and a large man came outside.

The colossal male was holding some sort of frozen meat to his forehead.

"What?" Tiny – who wasn't as tiny as his name, or nickname, implied – demanded.

He was brutish, his voice was rough, and he glared at Karl. Karl refused to stop struggling, because he didn't want to be the victim of a horrific toe-cutting home invasion.

"Help me! You idjit!"

Tiny threw the frozen meat aside and took Karl from his captor, who, Karl was delighted to see, was sporting a large purple bruise on his collar bone.

Karl was carried into the house and saw Fred looking at him with wide eyes, while Destiny, it seemed, was unconscious. Fred shook his head vehemently—*no. NO! NO!* Karl could hear the muffled denial, and started to scream threats at Tiny, the blonde girl and the other guy who'd caught him.

"Gag him," a voice said from the darkness, and Karl's head whirled around to see what the source was.

He saw an old man, with a tough face and looked like an older, but smaller, version of Tiny. He looked almost frail, and Karl would pity him if it weren't for the fact that he seemed to be the brains behind the whole thing.

The blonde girl pushed a piece of cloth into his mouth, while Tiny forced him into a chair, holding him down with immense strength, while his original captor, who he identified as Paddy after the old man ordered him to, tied his hands together with cable ties. They were tied uncomfortably tight, as though gagging him and tying him up wasn't bad enough, they also wanted to cut off the circulation of blood to his hands. Maybe that wasn't such a bad thing, since they seemed to enjoy blood sports.

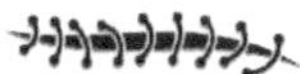

Grace had just finished cleaning the whole house. It was so clean, that even dirt itself wouldn't want to stain it. The more she cleaned, the more she hoped Brittany would just magically walk in and mess up the whole house. As she cleaned, she stared at the front door, hoping, wishing. But there was nothing. Nobody came through the door. Certainly not her Brittany. Brittany wasn't coming back.

Grace sat down on a lounge chair in the living room, stacks of newspaper, magazines, and all sorts of journals were neatly piled on the coffee table. After cleaning the house, the next thing on Grace's agenda was to start her perusal. She had become a sleuth. She would go through every story, looking for any small detail that resembled her daughter's case. She felt that the more she combed through the reports and articles, the more her soul connected with her daughter. Seeking out and finding the killer would be the only thing to give her the closure she desperately needed. She was determined to find this monster.

After going through the newspaper and drinking lots of coffee, she had jotted down any case she thought would help Brittany's case. And then she would call Ortega. He was the man the justice system had put in charge to catch her daughter's killer. But to her, it felt as if the detective was no longer interested in the case. Which is why she would help solve it. The more she tried to help, however, the more she felt abandoned.

She picked up her phone and dialed Detective Ortega's number. But, once again, the call went to voicemail, as did every other call. Any healthy person would have figured out by now that the person one the other end was trying to avoid them. Unfortunately, Grace didn't have the luxury to think like that. She opened a burner phone she had just acquired and made the same call. To her surprise, it didn't go to voice mail.

"Ortega speaking," the voice cordially answered on the other end.

"Good day, Detective. This is Grace Miller…" Grace felt an unease as she introduced herself.

"Good day, Mrs. Miller. It has been a while. How can I help you?"

"I've found some more clues about the case, and I really think they will significantly help you in finding the culprit this time."

There was a pause on the line. A short silence. "I can assure you, ma'am, there is no clue that you would want to bring us that we don't know about. We're working on so many leads. Please, do not worry about this. Trust me on this; we're doing our best. And soon, your daughter's killer will be captured."

"But how can we be sure? How about I come to the station tomorrow so we can compare notes? What time will you be available?"

"Ma'am, let me be frank. You don't need to come down to the station. All you need to do is to mourn your daughter and take your needed time to heal."

But the time for mourning was over. Now it was the time for action. She was ready for action. She would do her part. She is tired of crying and asking questions without getting any convincing response. She understood now that the only person who could really answer her questions was the killer. And she was going to go to any lengths to make sure all her questions were answered.

"Were you by any chance able to go through the notes that I gave Detective Park for you?" Grace inquired.

"Not yet, Mrs. Miller. Unfortunately, I have been ridiculously busy. But I can assure you that as soon as I am free, I will go through it," the detective promised.

"How can you say you're busy, Detective Ortega? This case should be a top priority. A mad man is on the loose and hurting other young girls like Brittany, and you're telling me you're busy? What kind of detective are you?!"

"Look, I get that you're grieving and all. I respect that. But I'm sure you wouldn't take it lightly if people started questioning you on how to do your job. So, for us not to say things that we will later regret, I'm just going to end this call now, Mrs. Miller. Have a nice day."

Detective Ortega hung up, leaving Grace alone with her demons. She stared at the phone expecting something to happen, anything. But nothing ensued. She dropped the phone. The detective's words had punctured her soul.

Grace continued with her routine, reading her newspaper, and taking down lengthy notes anytime she saw something relevant. Her coffee cup was now empty. She stood up and headed to the kitchen to refill it. She came back to the living room with her coffee and continued with her obsession.

She would find the monster, no matter what. With or without help. No one was going to take away the only closure that she could have. She would find the killer, and she would look at him and make him know that he was going to pay for everything he had done.

Everything.

SCARS

CHAPTER **NINE**

KARL KEPT AN EYE ON HIS CAPTORS. Paddy, who had run after him, Tiny, who seemed to be the muscle of the group, the girl, who he later learned was Lauren, a Meth addict, if the black nubs of her teeth were any indication, and the brains of the operation, the old man. The old man kept smoking nonstop. One cigarette wouldn't be completely finished before he had stuffed another cancer stick into his mouth.

"Are you calm now?" the girl with the disgusting teeth asked.

Karl nodded slowly. The girl was way too close for comfort, and he would prefer it if she would stand a few feet away from him. She stank. Ugh! For all he cared, she could go jump off a cliff, but his luck wasn't that good.

Lauren pulled the spit-drenched cloth from his mouth. "Don't scream, don't talk, unless Daddy says you can. Got it?"

He nodded again, slowly.

"Who are you?" the old man asked, his question ending in a cough.

Karl's mind reeled. His thoughts were jumbled. He was a mess. All he could remember was his name, which he relayed to his captors.

"And what were you doing outside?" the old man—"Daddy"—asked.

"I was jogging. I'm... a neighbor." He inclined his head to Fred and Destiny.

He made sure not to say from which side he came.

"Did he have a phone on him?" the old man asked, looking to Paddy.

Paddy shook his head.

"I saw him, Pop, and he ran. I ran after him. And then Tiny, Pop... Tiny ran into a rock! One day we gotta start calling him Rocky instead o' Tiny 'cause of all the rocks in his head! Hahaha. Anyway, he fell, but he had nuttin' on him."

"You're sure?" Cancer stick man said, and Paddy nodded eagerly.

"Baby girl..." The old man said, this time to the blonde. "Gag him again. The police ain't coming."

"You sure, Daddy?" But even while she asked, she forced the cloth back into his mouth. "Daddy, can I get new shears? These are taking forever!"

"Tiny, go get your sister some new shears," the old man ordered the massive one, who, Karl could now see, had no neck, just muscle.

All that this giant was wearing was jeans, boots, and a vest that would be flattering if his muscles didn't look like they had been built with the help of a multitude of steroids. Tiny exited the house and went looking for shears.

Lauren, on the other hand, went over to the fridge and pulled out the half bottle of wine that was left from when Karl had visited Fred and Destiny for dinner. She popped the cork and drank it all down, while Paddy helped himself to whiskey.

The next thing he knew, the kitchen was on its head! The toaster, who Paddy—clearly drunk from having drunk an entire bottle of whiskey—had stuffed full of bread because he demanded toast and Lauren refused to make it for him, had caught fire and was now half-melted on the floor, where Tiny had dumped a bucket of water on it.

The old man was laughing hysterically at this and pulled everything out of the refrigerator that he could lie his hands on, until he found a dozen eggs and started throwing them at Fred and Destiny. Yes, the old man, who probably had lung cancer from the way he kept smoking, was pelting an elderly black couple with eggs.

How juvenile.

Karl couldn't believe the scene.

The old man was obviously struggling to breathe, because he kept coughing loudly and his laugh was hoarse.

The nastiest part was when the blonde girl and Paddy had started kissing sloppily in front of them all. At the same time, Paddy kept sticking his hands down the girl's shorts. Karl was suddenly glad that he hadn't eaten dinner, or lunch, or he would have thrown it up. And he would have been forced to swallow it down again due to his gag. Those teeth... He shivered, nauseated.

"Move it," the old man barked, and the kissing couple moved to the kitchen, continuing their awful kissing.

Karl could have sworn he saw a string of yellow spit between them as they took a second to breathe. The old man, whose face was littered with wrinkles and dark liver spots, smiled fondly at the girl. When he opened his mouth to speak, his yellow teeth were visible, showing he had smoking those damn cancer sticks for most his life.

The old man turned to the captives. "My pride an' joy."

None of them dared to reply or even so much as nod their heads, because if they gave the wrong answer, they might end up with a cigarette in the eye.

"Listen, boy. Lemme tell you 'bout me. You see... I'm from West Virginia," the old man said, sitting beside the counter island in the living room, taking a long draw from his cigarette. "Used to be a miner there, in the coal mines. Spent half the day underground with a pickaxe and hacked at the damned coal. An' why? Why did I waste my life in that motherfucking forsaken place? My lungs were sick, an' the more I stayed, the sicker I got. The doctors said my lungs were black 'cause o' all the coal. I nearly fucking torched the place 'cause it made me so sick." As if to prove to point, he coughed loudly, and it sounded as though he was digging up slime somewhere in his nasal cavity.

Karl stared at the old man. Why the hell the man was telling them this? Was he entertaining them? Or just himself?

"Me wife died when Lauren was jus' a kid," the old man continued. "Died in a car crash. Some idiot didn' look where he was goin' and hit her when she was on her way home. She died there, on the road, bled out. An' I started to work the night shift, 'cause no one else was gonna raise 'em. Tiny's got the brains of a parakeet, and Lauren was jus' a babe. Couldn' leave 'em, could I?"

The one ironically called Tiny didn't look fussed at being called stupid, he just glowered at the captives with a scowl that would put a boar to shame. Then again, Karl thought, the large and ironically named man probably took it as a compliment. The old man then ordered his idiot of a son to move the elderly couple away from each other so they could all look at him. Fred's chair was pulled away harshly and now he was between Karl and Destiny.

"Raised 'em all on my own. An' now I'm done with the mine, and took to a life o' crime, 'cause I showed 'em to stand up for 'emselves, because we lived in a bad place. My kin followed me here, to this damn mountain full o' rich fucks, an' now we're here." He looked at the kitchen he was in and pulled his face into an ugly scowl. "Rich people make me sick."

Karl was suddenly happy that they hadn't ever invaded his home in Pasadena, because they would have had a field day. And they would probably have killed him and Deb, shouting obscenities and claiming that they were too rich for their own good.

The plastic surgeon wished he could tell the old man that rich people often worked for their money and it didn't just fall into their laps. He himself had to study nearly a decade to be what he was and to be where he was.

"I wanna do it now!" Laura yelled, and all attention he had for his victims turned to the kitchen, and he made his way, groaning loudly as he did so.

"No, ya can't!" said Paddy, slapping his girlfriend's hands away from the table, or so it sounded. "Ya gotta wait, ya cunt!"

Karl looked at his neighbors. Destiny wasn't wearing any shoes, and her one foot was badly mangled and missing at least two toes, and he could see the faint outline of Fred's sidekick in his pants pocket. Fred was an old military man, and he never went anywhere without his sidekick, which wasn't his phone but a Swiss army knife. Destiny, like Karl, had taken the distraction as a good sign and extended her good foot to her husband's leg. She wiggled her toes and forced it out of his pocket, or tried to.

He couldn't believe it. He had thought that she would not be the type of woman to take action, but rather to take what she was getting and just wish it over. How wrong he was, he thought with delight.

The silver handle of the knife glinted from Fred's pocket. Karl kept an eye on the arguing couple—whose shouts were now threatening to reach freakishly high octaves—but they didn't notice Destiny. His gaze flitted to the Williamses. The knife clattered to the floor, and Karl's heart jumped into his throat.

The blonde looked up and saw Karl looking at her. She narrowed her eyes and made her way from the kitchen. Her boyfriend in tow.

Heart thumping, Karl brought his one foot down loudly, and Destiny jumped and did so too. She closed her eyes for effect, and Karl decided that glaring at the drug-addicted girl was the best he could do to avoid suspicion.

The girl saw Destiny with her eyes closed, cackled loudly, and shook the old woman harshly.

"Wake up, ya old bitch!" She slapped Destiny's head to the side. "Come on, come on! Do ya want me to get the shears again?"

Destiny's eyes opened widely, fear evident. The girl just laughed and went back to the kitchen, still cackling wildly. Karl's eyes were on the knife that he could see clearly behind Fred's chair, but none of the thieves saw it, already too busy arguing about Laura's wish to have a hit.

The argument simply continued. Paddy just observed them, his eyes raking over their tied hands. The old man in the kitchen coughed loudly again, and the couple returned.

"They're still tied up, Pop," the boy toy said, "and ya can't do it here, ya cunt. Do ya want the coppers to find the DNA all over the place?"

Karl let out a muffled laugh. They had already left more than enough DNA for the police to identify them. He also had a suspicion they were all wanted for some crime or another, and their DNA would only convict them further. The girl's obvious drug addiction, the large oaf's tattoos... it was obvious.

Karl glanced around. Tiny was still gone. Presumably looking for the shears his sister wanted. They were alone again, and Karl heaved a sigh of relief, glad the knife hadn't been seen.

Fred glanced to Karl, his eyebrows lifted. *Is it safe?* Karl peeked into the kitchen again and nodded minutely, unwilling to draw attention to himself. The blonde girl kept looking at him on the order of her father and giving him feedback.

"Yeah, Daddy, they're still there," she said calmly to her father every minute or so, before turning to her boyfriend and yelling at him.

The language she used made Karl's ears ring and his heart ache. The girl seemed to know every awful synonym for the words vagina and penis.

Fred used the foot that was still in his shoe, and tried to draw the knife towards him. It was their only tool to escape, and while Karl had no idea how they would use it with their hands still tied, it meant that they at least had something to use.

It meant *hope* that they otherwise didn't have. It meant *hope* that they would lose if the meth-head, old man, idiot, or drunken idiot found it and took it. Then again, if the captors found it, it meant that Karl and his neighbors would meet their end both violently and sooner than these monsters had intended for it to happen.

Fred drew the knife towards him too vigorously and it went flying beneath his chair, ending up between Destiny and Karl. Karl groaned, certain the noise would attract the perpetrators.

Fred was panicking, and trying hard not to make too much of a fuss. Destiny stretched out her undamaged foot and just barely reached the Swiss Army Knife with the tips of her toes. She managed to kick it towards Karl, who stopped it with a sneaker-clad foot and covered it just in a nick of time before their captors re-entered the living room.

Grace walked into the Vons around the corner from her house to shop for groceries. She had visited this place to buy things for Brittany, from her favorite snacks and drinks, and all the other junks that she had warned her not to eat. But now, here she was buying them. She remembered when Brittany had followed her to the store, how she had run to get her favorite cereal, and how she would beg when she told her they would not get it. But now, Brittany wasn't around and Grace was getting everything that would have pleased her.

She passed through the liquor section, feeling a certain pull. Curiosity. Grace had never really been much of a drinker. In fact, she hated it after seeing all the evil that it caused in her life as a child. She had always dreaded the moment when her father started banging on the door at night, cussing and shouting. He'd only cussed when he was drunk. Her father was a good man, but when liquor was added to the equation, it was as if he became someone else. Something else.

She had watched how her mother had suffered during those times. She would get beaten like a dog at night, and the next morning she would be treated like a princess, showered with all kinds of gifts. Her home was a mixture of heaven and hell; but liquor was the key that opened hell's gate.

Ever since then, she had promised never to open it. But now, doing exactly that was beginning to sound enticing. She was already living in hell, after all, so why not live it drunk? Perhaps she wouldn't feel its severe burning...

However, she knew that if she surrendered to this numbing vice, she would lose track of her daughter's case. She wouldn't be as efficient in her search for the monster. She needed to be at hundred percent capacity if she wanted to catch the killer. So, she walked away, not giving in to temptation.

She walked to the counter, paid for all the goods, and walked back to the parking lot. The air was a chilly; too bad she didn't wear her sweater. She headed to her blue sedan. As she reached for the keys, she passed a car and halted. It wasn't the car that interested her; it was a bumper sticker attached to it that called her attention.

God loves you.

That message infuriated her to the core. The statement made her nuclear. She was about to go off like an active volcano.

God loves me?

It infuriated her to believe there was truly a God that really loved. She wanted to see the owner of this car. She was burning with questions, and this person needed to reveal to her the extent of this God's love. If it was even true.

She didn't have to wait long, however. A man in a suit walked up to the car. He was in his late forties, with an aura of peace, someone who could believe that kind of statement.

"Can you take that sticker off your car, please? It's annoying," Grace snapped at the man.

The stranger was perplexed, looking over to see where the upset woman was directing her gaze. He saw the bumper sticker. "I don't see anything annoying about this declaration."

"So you believe God truly loves us and that there is just a magical being that sits on a magical throne and watches over us, loving us unconditionally?" Grace asked with a bitter laugh.

Mystified, the man engaged her, "Okay, fine. You don't have to believe in such things. But it is *my* car, and I believe it."

Enraged, Graced rebutted, "Tell me something, then. Why does God let bad things happen to good people? Why does He allow so much suffering if He truly loves us? Why is there so much pain?"

Grace was in tears now. The stranger felt Grace's pain and was deeply moved with compassion. Without saying a word, he drew her close and opened his arms as if to hug her.

"I understand your frustration and your doubts. I've experienced pain as well," he said.

It was an odd sensation, a person she didn't know was now hugging her, comforting her, but she didn't resist. In fact, she welcomed it. She needed someone to rely on, a close friend perhaps, but here was a complete stranger doing what no friend of hers ever had. They had all disappeared from her life a month after the incident with Brittany. They had called to check up on her once in a while, but soon, she had forgotten what the ringing of her phone sounded like. Nobody called. Nobody cared. They had all left her alone with her misery.

"My name is Mark," the man said.

"Grace." Her anger had died out and now she couldn't utter another word.

He invited her to a coffee so they could chat. They walked to a diner in the same business center in Eagle Rock.

"Tell me, why you are so angry with God?" Mark asked.

"I'm not angry at Him," she replied while sipping her hot coffee. "All I am saying is, I don't think God exists."

"Okay, let me rephrase my question, then. Why are *you* angry?"

Grace shed a tear, but remained quiet.

"Okay, I'll go first. When you cried in my arms, I felt your pain, I felt your sorrow. It was as if I was face to face with your suffering. I have a close friend," he continued. "He's a very good man. A Godly man, you could say. Someone you wouldn't wish evil upon, but something horrible happened to him. Something despicable. His teenaged daughter was raped and killed in their home when he was out on a date with his wife."

Grace became instantly interested in what the man was saying. "Wait! When and where did this happen?"

"Um, not long ago. Next door, in Pasadena. Why do you ask?"

"Have they caught the killer?" she probed further.

"No, not yet. The police are still investigating—"

"Can I meet them, the parents of the victim?"

Pastor Mark stared at the peculiar woman, not knowing where this was going or what this was all about. He put his cup down and changed his tone. "To be honest, I don't know the answer to that. They're really in a low place right now, if you know what I mean. But if you tell me why you have this sudden interest, maybe I could make a meeting happen."

Grace, however, wasn't going to let her cat out of the bag just yet. She wasn't ready for another intervention. She just wasn't ready. So, she stood up in hurry, having barely sipped her coffee. "Forget it. I have to go now. Thank you, Mark. It was nice to meet you."

Grace left Mark in the booth, confused as to what that had been all about. But she didn't turn back. She was out of the diner in a flash. Mark left a $20 bill on the table and rushed after her.

"You forgot your purse, Grace!" Mark called out, catching his breath. "I'd like to see you again," he added once he reached her and handed her his business card.

She accepted her purses and his card, looked at it, and noticed his title. Without saying a word, she entered her car. She zoomed off, leaving Mark in the parking lot.

She got on the 134 freeway and looked at the card that Mark had given her. He was the Senior Pastor at the Ebenezer Christian Church in Pasadena. She dropped the card in her purse and, while driving, she went over what Pastor Mark had told her. Why didn't the detective tell her that her case wasn't the only one? Was this monster a serial rapist-killer?

She needed to see the pastor's friend. It might just be the clue that she had been looking for!

Detective Ortega was getting ready to leave. Stressed out and tired, he wanted to wind down at the bar, take a few shots, hopefully get lucky, and take a hot girl home to warm his bed. Just as he was about to leave, Detective Robert Park entered, too excited.

"You need to see this!" Park exclaimed. "The clue that I have been looking for has been under our nose this whole time."

"I am glad for you, homie, but right now, there is somewhere that I need to be at. Tomorrow, however, I am all ears."

"Easy, tiger! This concerns your case too. Remember the notes Mrs. Miller handed to me to give you?"

"Yes, which you haven't given to me, by the way."

"Well, I accidentally saw some of it. And with it I was able to piece the puzzle together."

"What are you talking about, Park?"

"Here, take a look for yourself." Park showed Ortega the note. "We both thought we were working on two separate murders. But, what if there is only one perpetrator? What if they're the same person?"

Ortega looked at him, a quizzical look on his face. He dropped his stuff back in his desk and got back to work, suddenly energized. The hot girl from the bar could wait.

This was the best part of the job. Any new lead was a stimulant to keep them going. These moments that made it all worth it.

Ortega smiled at his colleague as he took off his jacket and said, "Okay. Let's take a look."

CHAPTER **TEN**

DEBORAH MUNSON WAS NOT A HAPPY PERSON. She hadn't known true happiness in over a year, and it was a very frustrating state of being to be in. Everyone kept asking her how she was.

How did they think she was? Her whole life had revolved around her family. Her job had been secondary to her husband and child. It was even secondary to church. But now? Now... now she had no happiness. Yes, there were fleeting instances of joy, but it was just that—a fleeting instance. And it was not happiness; it was temporary. Soon, she always sank back into the darkness that consisted only of loneliness and sorrow.

And hatred.

She absolutely abhorred it. Sure, she smiled to her patients at her practice, and she falsified the smile in the presence of her parents. They had always been clueless when it came to her emotions, but it hurt even more that they didn't see her suffering now. And if they did, they just ignored it. She needed her mother. Deborah felt like a little girl again, and she needed her mother's hug and comfort. The woman wouldn't have to say anything, she would just have to hug her and hold on to her.

But her mother was a stoic person; very cold and distant. There was no doubt that the elder woman loved her daughter, but she just wasn't a very affectionate mother. That was why Deborah had made sure to be affectionate towards Naomi. It was also probably why Deborah now craved that affection.

One evening, Debbie was forced to go to her parents' house for dinner. They used to have the occasional family dinner when Naomi was alive, but when she'd died, the dinners stopped completely. Her mother didn't want to be there either, but her father was trying to rekindle the relationship with Debbie.

Debbie sat at the table, holding her knife and fork. She barely touched her food. She was hungry, but she wouldn't feel any better if she ate. Nothing would make her feel better. Not even time with family.

"So, Debbie…" her mother said. "How are things?"

"Really?" Debbie scoffed and dropped her silverware. They clattered against the plate, making everyone jump. Debbie hadn't realized how silent the room had been until then. "I haven't seen you in over a year and that's all you have to say to me?"

"What else do you want me to say? 'Are you over your dead daughter yet?'"

"Clarice!" Debbie's father snapped. "You promised me you that wouldn't bring that up. I'm trying to have a peaceful family dinner here."

"You won't get any peace with her around," Debbie said and nodded her head towards her mother. "Do you even know how to have a sentimental conversation? Have you ever showed any compassion? What about when Naomi died? You do remember her name, don't you? You didn't call us or anything. How do you think that made me feel? Your only granddaughter, Mom! Seriously?"

"We were giving you space," Clarice responded and shrugged. "We thought you would call us if you needed anything. That's what families do, right?"

Debbie stood, fists clenched and heart racing. "I wouldn't know. I never had much of one." Debbie stomped out of the room to grab her coat.

Her father ran after her. "I'm sorry, Daddy, but I can't do this," she snarled.

"It's all right, dear. I'm sure she'll come around one day. I guess this just isn't the right time. I'm so sorry."

"You have nothing to apologize for," she huffed. "Only Mom does. I'll call you if I need anything," she said before storming out of the house.

She walked to her car, forcing her tears to stay where they were. She didn't want to give her mother the satisfaction for pushing her buttons.

Debbie sat in her car for a long time to compose herself. When she left, she vowed to never return. She didn't know how well she could keep that promise, because her father was always very persuasive. Her father was the only one who cared for her. She didn't have a mother. Not a biological one, anyway.

She had only one person to whom she could turn for that type of motherly affection—Destiny Williams, their elderly neighbor at their summer home. But she had no idea what her husband had told the Williams couple, and she didn't want to bother them either. Her husband needed space; he needed the elderly couple too. Perhaps he needed them more, since she was sure he blamed himself for the two teenage girls' deaths. She didn't. She knew the Wallers didn't either.

Only around her husband did she let down her guard and allow the smile to slip. In front of him, she didn't have to pretend. She was miserable, and so was he. They lived in a hated, yet needed, silence. She didn't blame him. That much was sure. She did not and could never blame him. If anyone was to blame, it was that animal, Mitch Petersen...

His image was branded into her memory and she would most likely murder him in the most violent way she could if she ever got hold of him. What he had done was despicable and nauseating. It was just awful.

Even if she and Karl barely spoke, and while this was making their marriage and life together harder, it was easy to be around him. He was her best friend, and he made her feel better, no matter what. He always had. And now he was gone, she couldn't find a reason to stay alive.

Her husband was gone. Her daughter was gone. Her house was a mess of memories that hurt her so much she couldn't stand it to go home. She threw herself into her work, choosing to sleep in her uncomfortable office chair rather than her Tempurpedic Cal-King bed at home.

She was considering selling the house, but she would need her husband to do that, since it was under both their names. She was intent on discussing it with him when she saw him again. For now, she was happy living in silence, dedicating every waking thought she had to her work and falling asleep with a bottle of Jameson next to her. She knew alcohol would not solve her problem, but it numbed her feelings for a bit.

But now it wasn't enough. She had been forced to go home after exterminators showed up at the office for the bi-yearly fumigation, and she couldn't stay there. She was now in the large empty house. And she was alone. She didn't even bother to put the light on, nor did she notice the answering machine's light flickering. She didn't think anyone cared enough to call and check on her. She got text messages from her husband every now and again from their summer home.

He'd sent pictures of Fred and Destiny, and that had made a small smile appear across her lips. It was a shining ray of hope in an otherwise dark world. She never answered. What could she say? There were no words to express how she felt. She didn't even know how she felt.

Deborah walked up to the bedroom she used to share with Karl and sat on the bed. She didn't feel like taking a shower, or a bath, or even watching television. All that she wanted to do was sleep, even though she wasn't tired.

Sleep was the one thing that would take her attention off her dull existence. Television only made her miss her family. Naomi liked to watch series with cute boys and magic in it, and with high school girls being thrown into strange circumstances. She also liked watching the music channels. Karl, on the other hand, liked thrillers and foreign romance films. She'd always laughed at the strange combination of his tastes, but now she missed it.

Could she end her life? Nobody would care. Karl would care, maybe, but perhaps just for a minute, and then he would move on. He always would. He had always been the stronger one between the two of them. He was the kinder one, the patient one, and the one who held them all together. She didn't have her pillar of strength anymore, and she was so utterly alone.

There were plenty of other orthodontists in the world, and she wasn't special in her field. She didn't even have a child to live for anymore. Why did she even bother to go on?

Next to her pillow, on the nightstand, stood an array of pills.

There were pain killers, for the days when she had headaches and needed to concentrate. There were stronger pain killers, for when her arthritis acted up and she needed to wear her knee brace. Multivitamins that she drank to keep her from getting sick. A case of folic acid pills, to keep her hair and nails strong. Some anti-depressants that the doctor had prescribed for both Karl and Deborah after Naomi's death. And then there were the sleeping tablets that the doctor had also prescribed.

The sandman had refused to visit the pair of them, yet it was the only way they could escape their harsh reality. A reality where someone had broken into their home, raped their daughter, and killed her. A reality that spoke of heartbreak and cruelty.

Not for the first time, Deborah wondered why their daughter had been taken from them. Naomi had been a good kid; she had gotten good grades in school, she had been active in church, she hadn't slept around, drunk, or smoked. She didn't... hadn't lied much, she never stole, she had been such a humble little girl. Why her? Why their darling daughter? If anything, the most problems that she had ever caused them was probably turning the music or the television on too loud.

Why Naomi? Why their princess?

It would be the best way to die. Deborah thought, picking up the white tub and glancing at it.

Take pills and go to sleep. It was easy. She wouldn't have to think about it anymore.

She wouldn't have to live with the grief of a daughter taken from her and a husband fleeing from her. She wouldn't have to live with constant headaches that said she slept too little and concentrated too much on her work. She wouldn't have to live with a permanent crick in her neck that meant another night had passed on the uncomfortable couch in her office. It meant she wouldn't have to answer questions from her co-workers as to why she was in the same clothes for three days in a row...

A jolt of anger boiled though her. She desperately wanted to stop feeling anything. She swiped the bottles off her nightstand in a fit of rage. Tears streamed down her face as she paced around her room. Why was she hesitating? What was the point? She didn't want to keep moving forward. She didn't have the strength to make her life better.

She stared at the medicine and opened each bottle. She dumped everything out on the floor. She sat beside the pile of pills, hugging her knees into her chest, rocking back and forth. The thought of Karl crossed her mind. What if he was never coming home? What if he didn't want to come home? He would live up at the lake house for the rest of his days and leave Debbie in the big empty house.

"Why didn't you take me with you?" she shouted. "Why did you abandon me when we needed each other the most? Couldn't you see I needed help? All I am is a burden to you. To everyone. Naomi is the only one anyone cared about in the Munson family. Now that she's gone, we mean nothing. Our lives mean nothing. The two of us could die today and there'd be no news story or big fuss. We'd disappear into the night and never be heard from again. And what if I die? Would I go to Heaven? Would I see Naomi up there? That's the only place she would be. What if Heaven is too big? What if I can't find her even there?"

Her body shook, and the tears never stopped.

"I know You're watching me. You must enjoy torturing Your creations. You must love seeing me in this pathetic state. I'm pathetic and weak. There's only one way to cure that."

She tossed two anti-depressants down her throat—she didn't want to change her mind later. The anti-depressants put her in a mind-set that she just didn't care, no matter the consequences. She didn't like taking them, because she wasn't sick. She wasn't chronically depressed; it was just because of what had happened. It made sense, didn't it?

She had met the real deal—people who had no control over their depression. They were the people that just randomly withdrew into themselves when the smallest thing had happened. She wasn't like that.

Was she?

She reached for the other pills, the ones that helped them sleep. She popped two in her mouth and lay down, keeping the pill bottle in her hand. Then again, thirty minutes later, she popped two more into her mouth. Then four. Then... nothing.

Suddenly, Debbie felt like she was trapped in a dream. Her body moved slowly, and no words were able to escape her lips. She saw Naomi, her eyes sparkling, and her laughter floated through the air. Then, a dark figure came up behind her. Debbie tried to warn Naomi, and reach out to her, but it was no use. Debbie was drifting away from her, and had to watch as the figure stabbed her in the chest.

Debbie's heart raced. She tried to run, but only moved backwards. She was surrounded by darkness, evil laughter, and a faint light that she would never reach. She turned around, looking for a place to go, but she couldn't see anything.

Suddenly, the dark figure jumped towards her and stabbed her too. Debbie gasped, and then there was complete darkness.

CHAPTER **ELEVEN**

"THANK GOD!" The woman's voice sounded terrified, but relieved to Deborah's ears.

"Will she be okay?" a male much calmer voice asked.

"Physically, yes. Mentally, I don't know." It was another woman, but she sounded businesslike, as though what they were discussing a budget that was due the next day. "Why would she do this?"

"We know why... Her daughter..." The hysterical voice said again. It was definitely female, and it was lined with worry.

"And our daughter," the man interjected.

"Yes. But still, Naomi was brutally raped before her death," the woman said again.

"Can you two wait out in the hallway? You're disturbing the patient," the businesslike woman said.

Deborah opened her eyes—or tried to—when she heard the voices subside outside. She smelled the sterile smell of a hospital and felt an icy hand around her wrist, taking her pulse.

"Mrs. Munson?" said the firm female voice, shining a bright light into her left eye after forcing the eyelids apart.

Deborah grunted in response. She felt groggy.

"Mrs. Munson, can you hear me?"

"Yes," Deborah hissed, unable to remember what had happened, though a heavy panic burdened her heart.

"Welcome to the land of the living," the female voice said again, and Deborah opened her eyes fully. "We're very glad you're still with us, ma'am."

"What's going on?" she asked. All that she could remember was getting home and going to her room.

"You tried to commit suicide, ma'am," Said the nurse, who was dressed in a stark white uniform. A Latina nurse. The badge on her chest said "Mary." She adjusted the drip that was attached to the orthodontist's arm. "But Mr. and Mrs. Waller found you just in time, luckily. Otherwise, it would have been a disaster."

The Wallers had found her?

"Shall I call them?" Mary asked.

Deborah nodded, swallowing.

The nurse left and soon returned with the Wallers. Both of them looked concerned when they came in, and relief washed over their faces when they saw that Deborah was alive.

Diana Waller looked at Deborah, which annoyed her. She felt like she was broken with the look her friend gave her.

"I'm fine," Deborah snapped at her friends.

"Obviously, you are not." Said Tanner Waller.

When his wife hit his arm, he didn't look sorry. He continued, "Look, I know it's hard. Where's Karl? He needs to come too."

"He's... out of town," she mumbled. "What happened? How did you find me?"

"Well, we had plans for dinner tonight, Deb," Diana said. "When you didn't show up, Tanner and I went to your house to check on you. You left the door unlocked, and we found you—"

"Okay, I'm caught up," Deborah said. "Thanks, guys. Next time, maybe you shouldn't trespass on other people's property. That's what got us all into this mess in the first place. I don't need you, okay? I just need to get back home. Stop trying to save me and pretend like you don't blame me for what happened."

"We don't," Diana said softly.

Tanner hugged his wife and stared at Debbie with cold eyes. "If it wasn't for us, you could have died. Why do you keep pushing us away like this? Don't think I haven't noticed the way you treat us when you're at our house or pretending to care what we're up to. You need help, Deb. You need your friends."

"You don't know me," Debbie scoffed. "Don't assume anything, because you're wrong."

"I'm not so sure about that," Tanner fired back.

Debbie pursed her lips and waited for them to leave. She stared up at the TV in the corner of the room and pretended she was the one on a television show. Her life was just an act, a stage play. She would follow through with the performance until she heard the crowd's applause. Then she'd walk off stage and hug and kiss Naomi.

Deborah knew that she hadn't tried to commit suicide, only tried to escape the pain of her harsh reality. She really wished they would stop looking at her like she was going to jump for the nearest knife and get to work on her veins.

"I didn't try to kill myself," she said again, just for emphasis, as she cast her eyes round the room.

The man and woman in this room used to be a very important part of her life, and next to Karl and Naomi, they formed the next closest relationship that she had. There was a time when they would have sworn to know exactly how each of them was feeling. She remembered when Diana had lost her grandmother, and how she had been there to help her grief.

To this day, Diana still joked about how she couldn't have gotten through that horrible experience without Deborah.

"I was just trying to get some sleep," Deborah said once more, angry that they looked like they weren't taking her word to be true.

"Really?" Diana asked, arms folded around her midsection. "When did a combination of anti-depressants and that many sleeping pills become your go-to sleeping aid?" Deborah was about to tell Diana how none of it was her business, when Diana suddenly burst into tears. "You have no idea how hard it was for me to walk into that room and see you like that, Deb!" She sobbed into her hands, as Tanner quickly came forward and wrapped his arms around his wife. "We had to stand there while they worked on you. I was out there, waiting for any news from the doctors and hoping to God that I don't lose another member of my family again." She looked down at Deborah, who now had the decency to look just a little bit guilty. "And the worst part was knowing that I was responsible for it."

"What?!" Deborah exclaimed, half-rising from the bed. "None of this is your fault." She reached out for Diana's hand and held it in hers.

"But it is. I mean, I remember when my nana passed away and you spent all those times with me. You have to know how much it meant to me to have you with me at that time," Diana said as she covered their hands on the bed with her other hand.

For a moment, Deborah stared at their hands, looking for a way to reassure her friend that none of this was her fault. "Well, that was because you allowed me to do so, Diana. It was easier because you were willing to accept help. I don't think I have made it any easier for anyone to actually help *me*."

"That shouldn't have been enough to stop me, though. I should have insisted. You're my closest friend! I should never have allowed you to push me away in the first place."

At the side, Tanner looked at his wife and her former best friend talking and knew they needed to do this. It had been a painful but amazing journey for him and his wife on healing from the pain of losing their youngest daughter, and the only one left at home. Their oldest daughter was out of the nest, gone for college and now married, living on the East Coast. And while having the support and assistance of the members of the church had been of much help, he knew that Diana had still missed having her best friend in this period.

There was a time when he had been mad at Karl and Diana for abandoning them the way they had, especially when they were the ones who best understood the situation, since they had suffered the same thing. But the moment he'd entered that room and saw the prone figure of Deborah on the bed as well as the pills on the bed beside her, he couldn't deny an overwhelming feeling of guilt as he realized that he had been a bit selfish himself.

A rush of pain and guilt washed over Debbie. All she had wanted to do was dull the pain. She had wanted a break, a fresh start, a new life without heartache. She never thought she would have this much of an effect on Diana and Tanner. Diana showed her pain through her tears pure and simple. At first, Debbie thought Tanner was blaming her for everything by the look on his face when she saw them. It finally struck her that is wasn't anger, but fear. He'd feared that he'd have to experience yet another death. Another painful funeral where no one knew exactly what to feel. Tanner and Diana had been by her side the whole time and she hadn't even realized it.

"We both lost our daughters that day," Deborah said, and even after all that time, there was no mistaking the crushing grief in her voice. "I guess we both needed to grief in our own way. Me... I can't even say if I actually wanted to kill myself or just find an escape from this feeling that seems to follow me everywhere I go."

Diana sat beside her friend on the bed and hugged her hard for the first time in a long time.

"Would you believe me if I said I've thought about it too? You know, finding a permanent way out. There was even a time when I wanted to sort of blame you for the whole ordeal," Diana said, and when she saw that there was no reaction from Deborah, she knew that her friend had also had such thoughts. "But it took friends, and a lot of prayers, for me to get to a point where I knew it was nobody's fault apart from the monster that actually killed her. I mean, I had to go through the point where I blamed myself and Tanner for Sophia's death."

She looked up at her husband with the kind of smile that Deborah used to give Karl in a time so long ago, it was even hard to recall.

"I just don't think I'm quite ready to get there..."

"Like I said, it took friends and a lot of prayers for me to get through all of that. And while I don't understand it and I'm certainly not ready to accept the 'everything happens for a reason' bullshit, I can say I'm at peace with all of this. All I know is that someday we will ask our Creator why this happened. And I also believe that we'll see my girl again. Naomi too."

Tears rolled down Deborah's face as she looked at her friend. "She would be so proud of you, you know. Sophia would be so proud to see how you two seem to be coping. Me, on the other hand... Naomi would be ashamed of me, to be honest. After all my talks about always persevering through hardship, I chickened out and tried to take the coward's way out."

"We're mothers, Deb. We're allowed to be weak every once in a while, when it comes to our children."

"I know it's been hard," Tanner said, his voice surprisingly gentle. "But you can't do this, Deb."

"Do what?"

"You're destroying yourself. You look like a mess! You have obviously been drinking... too much..." Tanner frowned at her, then looked at his wife. He knew well that Debbie never used to drink. "You're coming to stay with us."

"WHAT?" Deborah exclaimed; she was not some damn child! She didn't need a babysitter! "You think you have the right to take me away from my only home? The only place where I'm connected to my daughter?"

"You heard me. And I don't give a damn on whether this offends you. Besides, you don't even sleep at your house anyways!" the Waller patriarch said sternly.

"He *is* right. I'm going to your house to get some of your clothes, and you're staying with us. We'll get a room ready for you," Diana agreed with a strict look coming over her face.

"It doesn't matter where you are," Tanner said. "You will always be connected to Naomi. That house is toxic for you. We're not going to let you keep living like that."

"But..." Debbie looked at her friends in disbelief.

They were treating her like a broken soul that couldn't take care of herself. She was a grown woman. She could think for herself. At the same time, she knew deep down that it was time to face reality. She needed help, just as Tanner had said. She needed someone to hold her when she cried and make sure she stayed healthy. Karl couldn't be that person for her anymore, and maybe he didn't want to be.

"No. You're not arguing. You're not staying in that hellhole one minute longer!"

Debbie had to stay in the hospital for the next few days for observation. The doctors had to determine whether she was still a danger to herself. Debbie was still resistant to the Wallers caring for her, but if she didn't agree to it, she couldn't leave the hospital.

When she was released, Diana rolled her out to the parking lot in a wheelchair. "This isn't necessary," Debbie protested. "I didn't have surgery or anything. I can walk just fine."

"Maybe," Diana said, sounding more chipper than usual, "but you deserve a break. You need to let somebody else take care of you for once."

They got to the Wallers' car where Tanner was waiting for them. "Don't try to argue with her." He chuckled. "It'll only make her want to pamper you more."

"Pamper?" Debbie laughed. "You make it sound like we're going to a spa."

"You'll be in my care," Diana said proudly. "So that's even better. This will be good for the both of us. Maybe we'll start feeling happier in each other's company."

"Why is it any different now?" Debbie asked as Tanner helped her into the car. "We saw each other before when I didn't live with you."

"That's the thing!" Diana beamed. "Now I'll be on call for you twenty-four-seven. Whatever you need, I'll be there for you."

"Can you get me a bottle of Chardonnay?"

Diana looked at her with cold eyes and crossed her arms. "I'm getting rid of all the alcohol in our house. You won't touch a drop."

"Jeez. I'm only kidding!" Debbie said with a half-smile.

The drive to her house was quiet. No one was sure what to say, if there was anything. Debbie stared out the window and sang hymns in her head. They sounded strange at first, but quickly became a comfort.

Debbie and Diana walked upstairs to Debbie's bedroom. Tanner followed them. Debbie breathed deeply, as memories of that night when they found the girls flashed through her mind. Diana rubbed her back and told her to walk slowly. There was no need to push herself.

As Diana packed a bag for Deborah and handed it over to Tanner to take down to the car, the two women sat down in the master bedroom.

"I still wonder how you and Karl do it, stay in this house after all that happened." Diana said as she watched her friend go through the clothes in her wardrobe, looking for something to wear.

At first, it seemed as if she wasn't going to answer, but then, after a while, she came out of the walk-in closet with a simple, but pretty, sunflower dress. "Because, in a way, Karl and I are still hanging on to the hope that all of this has been a very bad dream."

Diana was sad when she heard this. She stood up from the bed and went to hug her friend. "You know you'll have to let go one day, right? But it's okay to take your time too."

Deborah nodded at this, then began to dress up. As she did, she saw Diana go through her jewelry box.

She took out a diamond brooch Karl had bought for their last wedding anniversary and admired it. "Karl bought this for you, didn't he?"

"Yeah," Deborah answered, as she finally got the dress on. "He took Naomi and me to this restaurant for our wedding anniversary. At first, I thought it was odd, him bringing her with us to celebrate what should be an event for just the two of us, but I finally realized she was a big part of our marriage, and I guess it was only proper that she celebrated it with us. Of course, we dropped her over at your place when it was time to do other, more adult things." This last part was said with a small smile at Diana, which she returned. "Naomi picked that out for me. Karl had already gotten me something, but Naomi saw that as we passed a jewelry store and insisted he bought it for me."

"And where is he now, by the way?" Diana finally asked the question she and her husband had been wanting to ask for some time now.

The out-of-nowhere question seemed to throw Deborah back. She didn't expect to be asked about her husband. She blinked fast before answering.

"He is at the lake house," she answered. Panic jolted through her as she pictured Karl relaxing on the water without a care. "Wait, has anyone told him about... this?"

"No. Tanner and I thought about it, but decided that maybe you would want to do it yourself. You're going to tell him about this, right?"

"Yeah, I guess I will," Deborah answered, looking at the floor and clearly dreading that conversation.

"But why would he leave you alone at a time like this?" Diana asked.

"Don't blame me... or him. Honestly, I think we just both needed time apart to come to terms with what happened."

"But that's not the way to go about it, Deb," Diana said. "Trust me; you have to deal with this as one. You must find the spark that reminds you both that you are one single unit."

"Don't tell me how to handle my marriage!" Debbie shouted and pounded her fists against the dresser. Then she slumped onto the bed and apologized for her outburst.

"I'm only trying to help," Diana said softly. "I hope you know that. When children are taken from a couple with so much love in their hearts, that love is so fragile and easily broken. You two have to remain strong and be a united front. You can't let loss tear you apart. I know it's not really my business, but you guys are our closest friends. We want you to be able to work past this. I know you still care about each other, and you shouldn't be afraid to keep loving him. Naomi would want you to be happy. When Karl gets back, I'll give him a stern talking-to. He shouldn't have left you, and for this long."

Debbie let a laugh escape her lips. A tear fell down her cheek and Diana wiped it away. "I guess it's just so hard for him. I know how much I serve as a reminder of Naomi to him, so I can't blame him if he always associates me with her memory."

"That is nobody's fault, I agree. But he should see it as a way to remember all the good and wonderful things about her instead. Please tell me you'll go meet him."

"Yes, of course. I've been thinking about that already," Deborah said, realizing it was time that she and Karl started to heal as a family.

In her opinion, the separation had been a good idea at the time, but maybe Diana was right. They needed each other, now more than ever.

SCARS

CHAPTER **TWELVE**

KARL'S FOOT BARELY COVERED the knife Destiny had kicked his way. Just in time too, because the blonde girl entered the room. Destiny looked at him with an expression of terror on her face, but nearly sobbed with relief when she saw his feet hid the knife.

The blonde girl glared at Karl, but said nothing. That was when he noticed that she had a mobile phone glued to her ear. Her fingers were digging into the phone's edges, and Karl noticed she had long, messily painted nails.

"Get over here!" she screeched into the phone. "Daddy needs your help!"

Karl heard the person on the other side, and this person seemed to be incredibly pissed off, shouting and cursing. The words the man used were words that made Karl blush. The man seemed to know every vulgar synonym for the word "vagina," and he was calling Laura each of those words.

What is wrong with these people, seriously?

Karl knew it wasn't good when the blonde girl's face screwed up into a scowl.

"Listen, you cocksucker. Get here NOW! I don't give a shit how many times you call me a cunt, I want you to get here because Daddy needs you, and he won't ask for you. It's probably because *you* are such a cunt. He knows I am better at helping him than some loser!"

Karl's eyes widened. He couldn't believe the old man condoned this language. Then again, this was the same man that let his children become criminals. Using the correct language didn't seem to be high on the priority list.

She walked into the next room and kept screaming at this person for possibly ten minutes before she returned to the three captives. There, she demanded that the person on the other side made their way to the Williams's house. She gave the exact address, and even added some directions in a baby voice to patronize the listener, before she violently hit the red button on the phone's touchscreen. The girl almost broke a nail as she did so, and Karl wished for it to break. He almost laughed at how petty that wish sounded. He was honestly wishing for a young girl to break her nail? How low had he sunk?

Laura sat down on the couch opposite them and kept an eye on her captives, a pair of garden shears in her hands. Karl had no idea when the ironically named Tiny had returned with the "sharper" shears she had requested. She kept playing with them and pointing the points at each of them in turn with a cruel smile on her face. She also kept saying, "snip-snip-snip," followed by a maniacal laugh when Destiny winced.

She was a true sadist, Karl realized, a sociopath. But he was a surgeon, not a shrink. Nonetheless, he knew that sociopathy was a medical condition. Although, he wondered if she was controlled more by her genes or by her life circumstances. Perhaps both.

"Look what I found!" the girl's boyfriend called from the kitchen, holding several large bottles of dark liquid in his arms. "These people have a cellar! And this is just the beginning!"

He handed a bottle of red wine to his girlfriend and to her father, and another one to Tiny. The four bottles of wine were polished in half an hour, before they went for seconds. Paddy made another two trips down to the cellar in the time they were waiting for the person Laura had screamed at over the phone.

The robbers were now drunk. Karl could tell, as the small-built girl kept laughing uproariously, her voice not the one she had used earlier. It was a voice he heard lately from his wife whenever the whiskey tended to talk too much. People always said brandy had no brakes, but apparently it was whiskey that turned people into sobbing messes of emotions.

It was one of the reasons why he had left. He couldn't stand to see his lovely wife turn into an alcoholic. He had even tried to get her help, but to no avail. Deborah was stubborn, and usually that was a good thing, because she offered a balance to Karl's apathy. But she'd refused to stop drinking.

The robbers started playing a drinking game—every time that Karl looked at them, they each took a swig of wine.

"Like we'll be gone!" Laura cackled loudly. "He... he keeps looking at us, Daddy, like he is praying for us to be gone!"

She took a generous swig of wine, and was disappointed to find that her bottle was empty. She thrusted the empty bottle at her boyfriend and he laughed, opening another one before handing it to her.

His life wasn't the same either; just like Debbie's was now nearly controlled by alcohol, guilt controlled his. He had grown weary of the silence he and his wife had lived in. He was convinced that she blamed him for their daughter's death, and he couldn't exactly blame her for this sentiment either. He should have looked at the security footage more, he should have paid more attention. He should have hired a security company, he shouldn't have left two teenage girls home alone, he should have forced them to lock the doors, he should have called them when he saw that the door was open. Had he seen the door was open? But even if he hadn't, it was no excuse for missing it!

The look of terror on his dead daughter's face was one he would never forget, and when—if—he found the monster that killed her, he couldn't be held responsible for what he would do to the man. Karl was sure that murder would be the cruelest that the killer would meet. Karl had fantasized about castrating Petersen and forcing him to eat his own sack. The monster would probably get a kick out of it too. Murder and rape wasn't enough; self-cannibalism seemed like it would fit right up there with the rest of his crimes. Karl was sure they weren't limited to murder and rape, but he'd never asked the police for more information.

The robbers all went to the kitchen. Karl's eyes flitted to them, but they were all looking at something else. Something Karl couldn't see. At least they weren't drinking to his nervousness this time.

He bent down as far as he could, which wasn't very far, and tried to see how he could pick up the knife. He had a gag in his mouth, so he couldn't kick it up into his mouth—not that he was that agile in the first place. His best bet was to get off his shoe, and then to pick it up with his foot. But what then?

He looked behind him to see how low the chair was, noticing that, if he just sent his legs backwards underneath the chair, he would be able to get the knife near his hands. But how would it work then? He wouldn't be able to get it into his hands, just near them, and he wouldn't be able to pick it up either.

The door opened, and in came a large man. It was a sight that caused revulsion to rise in Karl Munson's entire body, a deep-seeded hatred that he would not forget. He would not be able to.

It was the same man that had plagued his dreams for the last year and a half. This man made him see red and it made his hands tense up and strain painfully against the constraints around his wrists. He had to keep himself from jumping up and assaulting this man, because he knew he would just make matters worse for Fred and Destiny if he did. He took a deep breath and glared at the man. Then again, how would he jump up? He was tied and gagged.

It was a man whose face and silhouette he had memorized, a man he didn't think deserved to live, a man who was no man. It was someone that Karl had seen more than a year ago from his security footage the night his daughter and her friend had been murdered. It was the man whose face he had memorized from the photo the detectives had given him. The man whose crimes now included home invasion and robbery, it seemed.

The man was Mitch Petersen. No, he was not a man; he was a monster. A cruel, useless living being that served no purpose on this Earth.

"Mitch!" Laura screeched, throwing her arms around him.

He grunted in response, patting her half-heartedly on the back. He wasn't very happy at being called to this place, it seemed. Though his shoulders did perk up when he saw the wine.

Behind the monster came a small, young woman. She was also blonde, like Laura, but more strawberry blonde than the ashy blonde that Laura was. Her hair was tied into a high ponytail, and two large silver hoops hung from her ears. She was dressed a faded jean miniskirt that hardly covered her ass and showed that, apparently, she had no underwear on, and a flannel button-up shirt. She also wore knee-high boots.

And around her neck? The leopard necklace that had been stolen from the Munson home the evening their daughter was killed. Karl couldn't believe it. He was so close to the monster, yet he had no way of catching the man and castrate him.

As he stared at the necklace around the newcomer's neck, his vision clouded over, and it was the only creak by his side that served as a reminder that he was currently outnumbered and in no position to pose any real threat. As it was, he knew for sure that, if he could get to Mitch and choke the life out of him before the others got to him, he would gladly take it. But he wanted to take his time when he killed the man who had ruined his whole life, who had taken the sunlight out of his world. He wanted to give him pain like no one had ever felt, and then do it all over again.

As he stared at the necklace around that girl, he couldn't help but think that it looked entirely out of place on that sweaty, grimy neck. He could still remember vividly the day that he had bought it for Deborah. It was just after she had given birth to Naomi, and Deborah had taken a break from work to take care of their daughter.

Naomi had started teething and every night and day she kept her mother up crying. Karl helped as much as he could, but he could see Debbie was having trouble watching her child cry all the time, even though it was normal.

Then one day, the crying finally stopped and the look of relief on her face was so beautiful, he told her to take time to rest that day. He took a very rare day from work to stay home and take care of Naomi. While Deborah and Diana went to their favorite spa, he took Naomi to the park. Of course, he had to promise Deborah he would call her if anything at all should happen to Naomi, no matter how small. In the end, Diana had to drag her to the car and away from her baby.

At the park, Karl had enjoyed every minute with his baby girl. Then, when it was getting towards evening time, he got the sudden urge to buy something for his wife. He'd walked into a jewelry store and asked to see a collection of some of their more expensive earrings. But Naomi saw a necklace on one of the display case and began to point to it, chattering in that baby talk that made her look so cute.

Without wasting time, he asked for that one instead. It wasn't as expensive as he'd wanted to spend, but Karl knew that it was more precious than anything else in that store. As did Deborah when she wore it for Naomi as they put her in the crib for the night. It wasn't the last time that Naomi would help him pick a gift for her mother; but that necklace was the first thing that they shared as a family.

And now, looking at it on the neck of a girl who was the total opposite of his wife for whom it was meant, Karl felt a rage so deep, he knew he would murder someone without a worry on his conscience.

Petersen looked at the three captives, nonplussed, and moved to the kitchen to join his comrades. For now, Karl had no idea who these people were. He just assumed that the elderly man, the one with the cancer sticks glued to his fingers, was this man's father. Tiny must have been his brother then, and the girl with stubs for teeth, Laura, his sister. They were a family of thieves, a family that enjoyed ruining the lives of others.

Paddy went to the cellar again to get more wine, Tiny accompanied him. They came back with a dozen bottles. The bottles were passed around as though they were beer cans, and they drank some more. Soon everyone was laughing happily, as though they were celebrating a wedding or a birthday, rather than ruining the lives of three people that had never done anything to harm them.

The longer Karl stared at the monsters, the more his blood boiled. He was more determined than ever to get out of that chair. He wanted to scream and use himself as bait while Fred and Destiny made their escape.

He had to play this smart, however, and he knew one wrong move could cost them their lives.

CHAPTER **THIRTEEN**

MITCH PETERSEN STAYED IN THE KITCHEN for a long time to ensure that Petersen senior was fine.

"What the hell did you call me for, Laura?" he demanded from his sister. "I don't see Pop having any problems!"

He took a large swig of wine, sloshed some of it down his front, and set the bottle down, hard. He put it down so hard on the island counter that the glass splintered into a dozen pieces. He laughed at this, and Karl hoped that he had sliced his hand open.

"She said *what*?" the raspy voice of the old coal miner demanded. "Laura, you twat, there ain't nuttin' wrong with *me*!"

"You're coughin' somethin' awful, Daddy!" the young blonde woman said, glaring at her brother, "and Mitch is the only one you'll ever listen to!"

Laura was the only one that Karl could see, and she had wrapped her arms around herself in self-defense. Karl thought that, if he allowed himself, he would feel pity for the stubbed-tooth young woman. But she had been the one to terrorize the elderly couple, so his sympathy soon dissipated.

If Karl had any doubt about who the newest person was, he didn't have that doubt anymore. Laura had just confirmed that it was Mitch Petersen, even though he'd had absolutely no doubt about it before. He'd had to make sure. And now he was. The newest arrival was the monster that had ruined his life.

"He's always coughing, stupid!" the new female arrival said, laughing at Laura.

She seemed to be a teenager, or just out of her teens, and Karl wasn't surprised. All of Petersen's victims had been teenagers, and the trend would certainly not come to a halt now. He had chosen as his girlfriend—though Karl suspected she was more of an accessory than anything else—a young girl. This young girl—Joy, he later found out was her name— didn't seem very bright. She did whatever the monster told her to.

The monster, Joy, Laura, and Paddy returned to the captives. Karl only had eyes for Mitch, and the man noticed it.

"What's the matter, faggot?" he asked, pulling Karl's hair, forcing his head back. "Why you keep staring at me like I'm a piece of meat?"

You raped and murdered my daughter and her friend.

"I ain't into faggots, and especially not one like you," he spit out as he slapped Karl harshly across the face.

The surgeon was powerless against the great brute that glowered at him, and he knew it. The only weapon he had was out of reach for his hands, but situated beneath his feet, waiting. He didn't know how to get it, but he would really have liked to shove that knife into this monster's throat.

He knew there would be blood if he shoved it into the jugular and that he would be on the receiving end of it. He would probably taste blood too, if he didn't have a gag in his mouth. For a single moment, Karl wondered if all blood tasted the same... metallic, warm. Then he shook himself mentally and glared at his captor.

"Did that hurt, fuckboy?" Mitch asked as he pulled Karl's head to the back entirely.

Karl's neck strained; he felt as though it would snap in two if he didn't do something about it. He jerked his head away, and the brute in front of him laughed.

"Where did this one come from? I thought it was just the old people that lived here," Mitch asked, turning to his sister.

"He said he's their neighbor." She shrugged. "We couldn't just let him go, so we tied him up."

"You said there weren't any neighbors!" Mitch surged forward and slammed his sister against the wall.

The wooden walls shook and the girl flinched. Her boyfriend's eyes widened as he downed half a bottle of wine, then tossed the bottle aside. It broke as well.

"Get off her!" Paddy screamed, launching himself at Mitch's back.

All that he managed to do in his drunken state was to latch onto Mitch's stiff arm, since Mitch was much larger than he was.

"Get off me." Mitch flung Paddy aside as though he was a piece of meat and turned away.

"Oh, Paddy!" Laura screeched, and promptly attached her lips to his.

Karl was again glad for the gag that prohibited him from throwing up at the thought of kissing that dirty, drug-infested mouth. He was sure that both the cause and cure for syphilis could be found in her mouth, and her stubby teeth probably held some new form of bacteria that could probably cure the common cold.

Though he surely wasn't brave enough to test that idea. He might contract some sort of disease that wasn't yet discovered by science. He allowed himself these dark thoughts, because he felt that he would go insane otherwise.

He could have handled being held captive the stubbed-tooth bitch and her family, but not being held captive by the monster that had now attached his own mouth to the teenage slut's mouth.

His hand was shoved in underneath her short skirt, and there was no question as to what he was doing by the moans that echoed around them. Karl closed his eyes and tried to block the sounds. But his eyes just stopped him from seeing, not from hearing, and that somehow made it all worse...

It was deep into the night when Karl jerked upright. He'd fallen asleep. Or he thought it was deep into the night, there was no clock on the surrounding walls and his arms were tied behind his back, so his wristwatch was also out of his line of sight. So, he just accepted that time had passed, and that it had been hours.

Please let it have been hours. *Please let it have been hours.* He didn't want to be there. He was miserable, and he had to fight tears from rolling down his cheeks. He was angry and saddened at the same time, and the two emotions opened another wound that he had managed to hide, even from himself. The wound that was his daughter. The last few weeks had been nearly blissful as he didn't have to think about it. His life had taken a turn for the better.

But misery enjoyed company, and it wasn't only applicable to people, but to emotions as well. The misery in his heart attracted more misery...

The knife. He looked at his neighbors; both of their heads were lolling on their shoulders while they slept. Karl looked around. Their captors were hidden in the kitchen. They were now either passed out or half-heartedly drinking from another bottle of wine. Someone had taken some food from the freezer and was frying it. The smell of eggs drifted to Karl and his stomach rumbled. At least they weren't being tortured anymore. At least they were left alone. At least... for now.

Karl looked down and moved his feet. The pocketknife still lay beneath his feet, undiscovered. It was so close, and yet so far.

But they couldn't afford to be asleep. What if they were given the opportunity to escape and they were asleep for it? Karl started to tap his feet on the wooden floor, watching the kitchen with a keen eye so he didn't wake the Petersen clan. Fred was the first to wake up, his head jerking sharply.

Then Destiny woke up, though much more gracefully than her husband had. She seemed dazed, and then realization took over. They were still not free. It wasn't a horrible dream. This was their reality, and it was a horrid reality.

Karl cocked his head to the knife and moaned in frustration.

There was a loud bang from the kitchen, and Karl covered the knife with his feet in fear. The pan with eggs had fallen onto the floor, and Mitch yelled at the teenaged girl for being incompetent. He was calling her "useless, stupid, disgusting..." These were the nicer adjectives. Karl tried to block those words out. He didn't feel sorry for Laura, but he did feel sorry for Joy. She was pretty and young. Even if she wasn't all that smart, she could have had a very different life.

Tiny woke up and threw Paddy off him.

"Get off me, ya cock-lover!"

This was the first time Karl had heard the large man speak, and finally understood why his name was Tiny. His voice was considerably less manly than the others'.

"I told you," said Mr. Petersen, laughing at the expression on his daughter's face. "That boy of yours ain't right, darlin'. He's a freakin' cock-lover; jus' look at how he was cuddlin' and smoochin' ol' Tiny over there."

"Shut up, Daddy," Laura shrieked, glaring at her father.

"Ya boy's a faggot, and you gotta accept that! Let 'im love men, if he wants to, darlin'. But don't force the man to lick your damn pussy if he don' like it! I'm just sayin'."

"Pop, I think you'd better shut up, or Laura's gonna turn your oxygen off," Paddy said, his voice freakishly high as he said it.

He was clearly more afraid of Laura than of her father, and Karl vaguely wondered why. But then he knew. Laura was a psychopath amongst the crazies.

"Oh, *now* he speaks! He's a bit smarter, this one, eh Laura?" her father asked, as Tiny shivered.

The large man stood from where he had passed out at the kitchen counter and stalked around the house. Karl heard him open doors and close them, riffling through things, and even dropping objects a few times.

In the kitchen, the fight went on, and Paddy just tried to say that he wasn't gay, with the Petersen patriarch and the youngest Petersen's insults just growing in creativity. New swear words were invented, and Karl made a mental list of them to use if he ever decided to become a criminal.

Dogcunt—said to Laura as her father struggled for words when she accused him of being gay himself.

Pussymouth—said in reference to Paddy who seemed to enjoy cunnilingus.

Cuntshit—Karl didn't even want to know where that one came from, because the whole image made him cringe.

Fatherfucker—instead of "motherfucker," directed at Mr. Petersen to insinuate that he had had that type of relationship with his father and was now homophobic because of it.

Those were the ones that stuck. There were, of course, a lot more, but they weren't as imaginative. Or entertaining. Until their argument was quite rudely interrupted by Tiny laughing exuberantly.

"Hey, Pop! Mitch! Look at what I found!" He was giddy and sounded like a twelve-year-old that had just won his first football game.

The massive man sauntered into the living room from one of the rooms with a gun in hand. Karl's eyes widened. What? He'd found a gun?

This got Mitch's attention, who had been busy been inquisitive with Joy's legs and breasts up until this point.

"Where did you get that?" Mitch demanded from his drunken brother. Tiny wielded the gun as though it was a simple flag rather than a weapon that could destroy lives.

"In one of the closets upstairs," Tiny said.

Mitch shoved him aside before running toward the hall too.

"Which closet, you idiot?" Mitch screamed from a room.

Tiny made his way there, tumbling down more than twice. This man was clumsy. "And ammo!" the high voice said again from the room.

The two brothers spoke in muddled voices, and then there was the thundering sound of feet coming back. Mitch came into view and hurled Fred's chair around with surprising ease.

"What the shit is this?" he demanded, ripping the dirty sock from the old man's mouth.

"It's a gun, young man," Fred said, confused.

Karl realized he was patronizing Mitch Petersen. He also knew *that* wasn't a very wise thing to do.

"I can fucking see that, stupid nigger!" Mitch slapped Fred harshly with a hand that was easily the size of a dustbin lid.

Or so it seemed to the surgeon.

Fred's head was thrust to the side and spittle flew out of his mouth.

"This was hidden in the armoire next to what I assume is your bed. Are there any more guns in this house?"

"No," Fred said immediately.

Mitch narrowed his eyes suspiciously. And this probably meant that the old man would get another slap to the face. Karl's eyes widened, not for the first time that day, because Fred was a lot older than Karl was. He couldn't keep taking this level of abuse.

"Let's try that again," Mitch said softly as his younger sister entered the room.

Karl immediately knew it was a trap. Mitch speaking "gently" was suspicious in itself.

"Do you have any more guns in your house?" He pulled back the tiny amount of hair that Fred had atop his head.

"No." Fred spat accidentally as he said it.

Mitch slapped him hard across the face at this and continued to scream at him. More spit flew, and Fred tried his best not to react. Tiny jumped him, bashing his fists into Fred's skull. Fred disappeared from view, and Destiny screamed, horrified, into her gag. Tiny seemed to enjoy this and renewed his efforts.

When Mitch let up, so did Tiny. He was a deep red in the face, and Karl just knew he would be swollen after this ordeal. If they survived it, that is. That seemed less likely with every moment that passed by.

"Look, asshole; tell me where the other guns are, and I won't kill your little wife here! You tell me where they are, and I won't fuck her throat in front of you until you fucking tell me!" the Petersen monster roared, and what little color there was in Fred's face, vanished.

Mitch turned and opened his buckle, when Fred's broken voice screamed out.

"In the kitchen," he cried out, his voice broken. "Under the kitchen sink."

"Paddy, check under the kitchen the sink!" Mitch yelled loudly to the kitchen, where the order was followed by the opening and closing of cabinets.

"Woah," Paddy said, entering the living room, holding a large gun in hand. "Look, Mitch, it's a 12-gauge semi-automatic shotgun! It was taped to the top of the sink, and it's loaded!"

Mitch took the gun from his sister's boyfriend and whistled, impressed. "This is some firepower, old man!"

"Any more?" Tiny demanded, raising a massive fist to hit Fred's head again.

"That's all!" Fred squeaked, closing his eyes as he expected the blow to fall. "I swear. That's all!"

"Good," Mitch said, and he shoved the dirty sock back into the old man's mouth. "If I find any more, I will kill your pretty little wife first and then you."

Karl protested this by screaming against his own sock, but it didn't help. Mitch met his eyes and laughed loudly.

"You can do nothing, fuckboy. *Nothing,*" he said almost lovingly, and it was clear that he was in his element.

The monster was having fun. It was disgusting.

The guns were taken to the kitchen, where Mitch lay claim on the shotgun and Tiny on the gun he'd found upstairs. Paddy was angry that he didn't get one, and he was even more aggravated when the slutty teenager was entrusted with Mitch's knife.

"But that's your special knife!" Paddy argued, his eyes on the dagger. "Why does she get it?"

"Because she isn't an idiot!" Mitch knocked Paddy against the head, and the blonde teenaged girl stuck her tongue out at him.

Karl would have liked to argue, but Joy seemed to be less dangerous and the better option between the two of them, and Karl preferred her being armed rather than the third man.

Mr. Petersen came into the living room, flipped his captives off, and struggled walking towards the master bedroom. Tiny soon came to help him, and Mr. Petersen kept swearing loudly all the way there. The old man was hacking awfully, attempting to cough his lungs out, it seemed, and he wanted to lie down. He didn't want to be in the presence of *niggers and fuckboys*, so he preferred the long struggle towards the room. Granted, there were probably a total of eight yards, but the man took about ten minutes to reach the destination. His trusty oxygen tank was carried behind him, and Karl wondered how a man could live that way.

An hour later, Destiny's head drooped to her chest. Her head then lolled to the side and Karl could see the whites of her eyes. Fred's eyes widened, and he started to groan into his gag. No one knew what was going on, but Fred was freaking out so much that he freaked out their captors too. Laura was the first one to him, and she ripped the gag out of his mouth. She was whispering about how Fred was the hardest person they had ever come across in their line of work, and he was also the most annoying. Then again, they didn't know that Karl had his own beef with Mitch.

"What?" Laura sneered at him.

"My wife has diabetes..." he said, gasping at the air that filled his mouth. "Her blood sugar is low. She needs to get to a hospital."

"And why we would we do that?" Laura asked.

"Because she will die otherwise," Fred said. "I know you aren't bad people, and you wouldn't want anyone to die."

Fred was wrong. Karl knew about Mitch's history, and was willing to bet that the others were equally as careless about the law as he was.

"He thinks we're good people," said the girl's boyfriend, leaning in the doorway. "After all he's suffered... Ha! Gag him, baby girl."

Paddy grinned at Fred, an awful smile in place.

Laura looked at her boyfriend, questioningly, before hesitantly putting the gag back. At this point, Karl was somewhat surprised that Fred's false teeth hadn't come out, unless he hadn't been wearing them when the Petersen's had attacked.

"Mitch!" Tiny screamed and came running down towards them. "Mitch! Laura!"

Laura was the first to meet her brother, followed by Mitch. Both demanded to know why he was calling them. They were "busy." Mitch was zipping up his jeans while he was talking, so it wasn't exactly a riddle as to what the man had been doing.

"Pop's not feelin' good," Tiny said, worried. "I think we..."

"Oh, my goodness!" Laura interrupted. "You? *Thinking?* Tiny, you should stay away from such dangerous activities. Your brain might explode."

"Shut up!" Tiny screamed. "Pop's not breathing well. We gotta get him to a hospital."

"And why now? Are you growing a conscience, Tiny?"

"No, Pop needs help." Tiny said, but his sister didn't believe him.

"Oh, please! You've been eyeballing this old lady ever since we got her! Now that she passed out, you can have some granny pussy!" Laura cackled, and Tiny turned to his brother, hoping for some understanding there.

"What do you mean Pop ain't breathing?" Mitch asked quietly, but instead of waiting for an answer, he went to see for himself.

He wasn't there long. "Yeah, we gotta get Pops to a hospital."

"You mean Tiny was right?" Laura asked, shock evident on her young face. "Well, fuck me."

"Paddy, go get the car." Mitch tossed a large bunch of keys at the man, who caught it, though he fumbled at first. "Tiny, you and I go get Pop. Laura, Joy, keep an eye on this lot." He indicated to show that "this lot" meant the three tied up in the living room.

Five minutes later, the two brothers came downstairs with their father, whose eyes were severely unfocused.

"Mitch, you gotta stay," the old man said, lifting and pointing a tired finger to Karl, Fred, and Destiny. "You can't let the girls look after them. You and your little girlie stay, and Laura come with."

"Let's just get you to the car, Pops."

The three men struggled to get out of the front door—not all that surprising, considering that Tiny had to leave the door by crouching and turning slightly to the side. Paddy had brought their car right to the front door—in Karl's full view. It was an old car, kind of beat up too, as though it had been driven for ages and never got a service or a repaint. The car hacked almost as much as Mr. Petersen was. No, it wasn't a car, but a truck. If Karl had it right, it was a golden Chevy truck too. It would have looked good if they hadn't ruined it.

Soon the captives outnumbered the captors, but the three of them were still tied up, and Destiny's head was still lolling on her shoulders.

Karl looked at Fred, trying to see if he was still conscious. He wished he could check their pulses to see if they were still alive. The possibility of being left alone with a family of psychopaths brought stark terror to his mind.

Wake up! He tried to scream, but his body was drained. He was hungry, thirsty, and afraid of dying.

Debbie would never know what happened to him. She would live out her life thinking she'd been completely abandoned without a word. Karl couldn't let that happen. He needed to get home to his wife.

CHAPTER **FOURTEEN**

SUNDAY MORNING CAME and the Wallers had convinced Debbie to go to church with them. She stayed outside at first, but she couldn't hear anything that was happening. Finally, she got the nerve to go in. Her steps echoed and she held her purse close to her chest. It was like her own version of a security blanket. She'd been having withdrawals from alcohol, which was usually her safety net. The Wallers were very good about keeping her away from drinking.

Even when they went to another friend's house, or out at a restaurant, Diana would watch her like a hawk. Debbie thought back to last night, when she'd been sitting on the couch, watching TV, and drinking water from a glass usually meant for whiskey. Diana stormed in and grabbed the glass, smelled it, then handed it back.

"Holding this glass comforts me!" Debbie huffed. "It makes me feel like I'm not at the kiddie table. Adults get to drink alcohol, you know."

Diana sat on the couch beside her friend and wrapped her arm around her. "There was a time when drinking wasn't even an option to you. Do you remember those days? You used to say to me, 'if God wanted me to drink, he wouldn't have given me the choice.' Now it's like you need alcohol to survive. It's your strength. I know you think it helps you, but it doesn't. You should come out with us tonight. You haven't left the house since you moved in with us."

Debbie listened intently to her friend while staring into her glass. "Things have changed. People change. I get why people have drinking problems. I get why it's so easy to sin and be part of this exciting rush that you get when you sip a good glass of wine."

"There's a difference between drinking for fun and drinking for sorrow," Diana said. "Have you considered maybe seeing a therapist? Or someone who can help you get over your drinking? Like Alcoholics Anonymous?"

Debbie scoffed. "You would love that, wouldn't you? Crazy Debbie heading to see a therapist because she's too far gone. Or Crazy Debbie going to a group full of losers who have nothing better to do on a Friday night. That'll help you feel better about yourself, won't it? Then you'll know for sure that you're better than me."

Diana stood up and crossed her arms; she towered over Debbie and glared at her. "Why do we keep going in these same circles? One day you're happy that we're helping you, and the next day you're biting my head off for trying to help. I know I'm not better than you. That's a solid fact. Tanner and I have gone through so many rough patches. More than a couple should ever have to go through. If you're going to keep acting like a child, then you might want to consider heading back home. There's no room for this much negativity towards your only friends." She breathed deeply, hoping she hadn't gone too far.

Standing up, Debbie hugged Diana and kissed her cheek. "You were always so good at bringing me back to reality. My stubborn brain just couldn't get anywhere without you. I don't want to go to meetings or a therapist. I've already tried that when we first lost Naomi. I just don't think that that is the right path for me anymore."

"Why not try going to the church with us tomorrow?" Diana asked sheepishly.

She'd been pushing Debbie to go with her for weeks, and Debbie always lashed out. This time, Debbie smiled and hugged Diana again. She pulled a cross necklace out of the pocket of her bathrobe and held it in her palm.

"I was thinking about that, actually. Maybe church will be good for me. Now, if you'll excuse me I'm going to bed."

"Goodnight, Debbie."

"Goodnight, Diana. Please wake me up tomorrow so I can get ready in time to leave."

Debbie knew that turning to religion wouldn't work, but perhaps turning to God was the last thing to try to find her way back to peace. She kneeled beside her bed and held the necklace in both hands.

"It's been a while since we spoke, so I don't really know the proper way to do this anymore. Thank you, God, for saving my life. As much as I want to see Naomi again, I know that someday I will see her again. We have this hope. Please know that I'm thankful that You brought the Wallers back into my life. They invited me to church, but honestly, I'm scared to go. I pushed away everyone at church, and they must think I'm a lunatic. I've heard many rumors going around about me. I don't think anyone believes in me anymore."

Debbie settled into bed and held the necklace to her heart. Then she continued.

"Please send me as much strength as You can. I need it. Facing everyone again will be the second hardest thing that I'll ever have to do, aside from seeing Karl again. I still haven't decided how to handle that. Maybe my day at church will help me. Please take care of him too, wherever he is. In Your Son's name I pray, amen."

With that, she fell asleep at peace.

At church, Debbie stood by the door, listening to everyone sing their hymns. Diana waved at her and urged her to come inside. The song ended, and everyone heard Debbie walking between the pews. She shuffled into a seat near Diana and heard whispers from everyone around her. Surprisingly, she wasn't hurt by that. She wasn't ashamed of the last couple years. She didn't feel the pain that usually overran her entire body. She felt peace in the House of God, and in that moment, everything was clear. She knew what she had to do.

Deborah glanced at the clock on her dash. it was 9 p.m. She had been driving for three hours straight, and she decided that it was time for a pit stop. She was ravenous, despite already having eaten the bag of crisps in the car and having downed a whole bottle of Coke. She didn't even like soda, much less a cola, but she was driving at night and had thought the sugar would be a good idea to keep her awake.

The problem was that the whole bottle had filled her bladder, and she was praying for some place on the road to be open so that she could run to the bathroom.

She'd been staying with the Wallers for weeks, and they had inspired her, and reassured her of her decision to go talk to Karl. Yes, they'd lost their daughter, but they hadn't stopped living. Diana had confided to her that things had been rough for a while, though.

"Tanner and I couldn't talk. We couldn't even look at each other for a while!" Diana had said.

Tanner had been working late, and the two women had decided to go out. They had decided to go to a quaint little restaurant, small and cozy, and one their fellow church members went to. At first, Deborah had been wary about this, but Diana had sworn that no one would pass judgement on her.

"Karl and I are still like that." Deborah had replied, taking a sip of her water.

"Yes, well, you two need to sort it out. Or do you want to lose your husband too?" Diana had said it rather harshly, but Deborah knew her friend was right.

"How did you do it?" Deb had asked, meeting her friend's eyes. "How did you and Tanner move on?"

"We didn't, Debbie. We learned to live with it. It's awful not having Sophie around, and even just saying her name hurts. But Tanner and I had been together for long, and he's my best friend. We just sort of started there. We didn't put any expectations on each other. We just started where we'd started at the beginning. We didn't rely on sex or marriage, but on that friendship we had built years ago." Diana had smiled absently. "We didn't even kiss for a while. We just... got to know each other again outside the roles of mom and dad, and I saw he was still the same guy I fell in love with at college. He is still the same nerdy guy that jogged with me, but always a few steps behind so that he could watch my butt. He was still the action movie lover... and we made time for each other." Diana had said and gave her order to the waiter that had just arrived.

"So... I have to get to know my husband again?" Deborah had asked and gave her order to the waiter too. "How do I do that?"

"Just be with him. Even if it's awkward, or if it's silence, just be with him. I know he misses you just as much as you miss him. Why else would he bother to call every day? You never pick up, after all." Diana had said, and Deborah felt her cheeks grow warm.

She had been guilty of ignoring her own husband, and that wasn't right. She needed to fix it. If she could.

"And pray," a new voice had said.

Deborah looked around, and was surprised to see Mary Gomez, Pastor Mark Gomez's wife, standing behind her. She was clutching her handbag to her chest and was looking at the Munson matriarch with wide eyes. She'd cleared her throat and sat down next to Diana.

"Prayer is important. We worked with Diana and her husband in their grieving, and we would like to help you as well."

"I invited her," Diana had said quickly. "I am sorry, but you need help, Debs."

Deborah had glanced down at her half-empty glass of water, and swallowed thickly. "I know," she'd said in a small voice. "I know I need help, but..." Her eyes had burned, and she'd blinked rapidly to get rid of the tears.

She hadn't cried in over a year, and she hadn't been planning on starting now.

Mary had reached for Deborah's hand. "I know, you don't have to say anything more." Mary had spoken so kindly that Deborah looked up.

Mary was, without a doubt, very beautiful. She had dark curls that she always tied into a high ponytail, and a blemish-free face that would make anyone jealous. Yet, she was the humblest and kindest person that Deborah knew, including the pastor himself.

"Go to him!" Diana had said. "You know where he is. Go to him. Take off from work and go find your husband again."

Of course, their conversation hadn't ended there, but Deborah had already made up her mind at that point. She'd wanted what Diana and Tanner had and what Mark and Mary had; she wanted to be happy again. She wanted her best friend back, and she wasn't going to sit idly by as he just drifted away from her.

She had rushed home, packed and got on the road. She was going to fight for her marriage. And save it.

Debbie made a left turn as a gas station popped into view, nearly sighing with relief. If she really sighed, her bladder might not have held up. She screamed at the petrol jockey to fill her car up before she ran to the bathroom.

Once done, she paid for the gas and debated on whether to buy a large Red Bull or not. She was vehemently against energy drinks, but she was exhausted and needed the energy. It was better than Coke, she finally decided, and told the young man to ring it up for her. She also included a lot of candy and junk food for the rest of the trip.

It was almost midnight when she finally arrived at their summer house. The lights were all on and her heart leapt at the thought that her husband was still awake. She hauled her suitcase out of the car and made her way to the house.

That was when her heart stopped. The front door was open. She knew her husband and knew he would *never* leave a door open. Not after what had happened to Naomi. He had grown paranoid about closing—and locking—doors. He had yelled her continuously to close their front door, and he got up at least thrice each night to ensure that all the doors were fully locked.

Deborah forced herself to breathe. Maybe Karl had let go of his paranoia toward doors because he was in a small town where nothing ever happened. Maybe he had learned to ignore his paranoia. Maybe. Maybe it was something else.

She went inside, the wheels of her luggage scraping against the tiles.

"Karl?" she called.

When she got no answer, she repeated his name. Still, there was nothing. On the kitchen counter stood plastic bags that had been half-emptied, with milk and bread still in them. Next to them lay her husband's car keys and his mobile phone.

Now she allowed herself to panic. The open door, and her husband didn't have his phone with him? He had sworn to her before he'd left that he would always have his phone on him if she ever needed him, no matter the time of day or night. He would drop what he was doing and go home.

But...

Wait, Deborah. Don't get excited, don't get upset. Maybe he went jogging. AT MIDNIGHT? Maybe he's sleeping. Go check.

She made her way to the bedroom, but found no husband. He wasn't in the spare bedroom either, or in Naomi's room.

How long had he been missing?

Wait. She dug out her phone and checked her call log; he hadn't called her that night. He called every night. There were no texts from him either, and that was very unsettling. Maybe he was next door?

She didn't want to wake Fred and Destiny, but at the same time, she was desperate to find Karl. She paced in the kitchen and stared at her phone. Who could she possibly call? Everything was closed, and in this town, most people went to bed before the sun went down. She thought that he might have driven down to see her, but his car was there and again his phone never left his side.

A sinking feeling filled her stomach. She had no choice. She had to check the neighbors' house.

SCARS

CHAPTER **FIFTEEN**

DESTINY WILLIAMS' HEAD had been lolling for a while now, and suddenly her head fell back. The whites of her eyes weren't visible anymore, and Karl knew she had lost consciousness entirely. It wasn't a good sign, and he was sure she would die before this night was over. His heartbeat rapidly in his chest as fear rose in his chest.

Karl started to scream in panic, and so did Fred. They screamed as much as they could with the gags in their mouths, and Karl forced the sound coming from his throat to be louder. Nothing came of it, so he screamed even louder, causing his throat to become raw and angry at him.

Thundering steps ran towards them. It was Mitch and his teenaged girlfriend. He did always like them young. And the girl seemed to be at his disposal, happy to serve her monster of master.

Mitch looked at the three of them in turn, then his head snapped his head between Karl and Fred. He smirked as he saw the unconscious woman. Mitch decided that it was time to torture Karl, it seemed, because he forced the gag out of the doctor's mouth. Karl's tongue was dry; the sock they had stuffed in his mouth had taken all moisture. He swallowed, willing saliva to fill his mouth before he could speak. He was thirsty.

"What the hell is all this noise about?" Mitch asked, his face close to Karl's.

Karl had so many things that he wanted to say to this man, but now was not the time.

Mitch sat the bottle of wine he'd just drunk clean down near Karl, and waited for Karl to speak. He did so impatiently, even going as far as to start tapping his boot.

"She's diabetic and she passed out. She needs to get to a hospital, or something," Karl croaked.

His voice sounded strange to him, but he guessed it was due to lack of use. His tongue was dry. For the first time in his life, his tongue wasn't moist, and that was dangerous. He was becoming dehydrated, or rather he was becoming severely uncomfortable. He knew that he could go for three days without water, but his body wasn't playing along with that little theory. He was in the beginning stages of dehydration, and he didn't want to die. Not before getting the bastard back for killing his daughter.

"And why exactly should I care?" he demanded from Karl.

The teenager gently touched his arm to get his attention. He looked around to face his girlfriend. "WHAT?"

She winced as though he had lifted his hand to her. Something told Karl that Mitch often *did* lift his hand to hit his girlfriend, and that was why she was so submissive. She only stood up against him when Mr. Petersen came into the discussion, telling Karl that Joy was more afraid of the Petersen patriarch than she was of Mitch. What type of family were they? What monster did Mitch stem from?

"Maybe... maybe we should help. Maybe we can... I dunno, give her something sweet to drink... or a bit of water?"

"No! Would Pop do that? He would just let the old bitch die!" Mitch answered, glaring at the passed out old woman. "I can't believe you're taking their side. You're supposed to love me!"

"I do, Mitch. Baby, you know that I do. But would your dad be happy if his people are dead before he actually wants to do it?" Joy asked.

Karl didn't know what to think, but he didn't dare interject. The girl might accomplish something, while he would just make things worse. The girl seemed to have the unique ability to placate Mitch, because his breathing calmed.

"Pop wouldn't care, as long as they're dead," Mitch shot back, and Joy lifted a light eyebrow.

"That isn't what happened last time, remember? There was a kid, and he was throwing up something bad. I told ya'll to take him to a doctor. But no! And then the kid got dehydrated and died right there. And do you remember what Pop did to Tiny?" the girl demanded, her eyes flashing to Karl's for a brief moment. "He beat up Tiny so bad that he couldn't sit for a week, baby. Do you want him to be angry at you like that too?"

"Fine. Help the old bitch, but I'm not staying. I gotta piss," Mitch declared, gagging Karl again before walking away towards the kitchen, completely apathetic.

Joy sighed heavily, her ponytail falling over her head as she did so. She closed her eyes for a moment to collect herself, then disappeared to the kitchen to get a knife. The young blonde girl slashed through the zip ties around Destiny's hands and helped the old woman to lie on the floor. She was laid down behind the chairs, where there was space, and now Karl couldn't see her head, just her legs.

Fred kept staring at all of this, incredulous.

Destiny seemed to be limp, and even groaned slightly, as Joy arranged her limbs to be in a more comfortable position. Joy also took the gag out of the older woman's mouth gently and smiled a syrupy smile at Destiny, as if though Destiny wasn't being held captive and tortured in her own home at the moment, but at a comfortable hotel.

"Don't worry, ma'am. I know what to do. My little brother is diabetic. See?" she asked Destiny, who only nodded feebly. "So, you just lie here. Okay, mama? Imma go get you some water now, okay?"

The young girl disappeared to the kitchen with the knife and came back with two glasses, one with water and the other one with what Karl assumed was orange juice. There was no chance to even try and pick up the pocketknife that lay on the ground, and Karl was getting annoyed. Were they never going to get out of this hellhole?

Joy lifted the elderly woman's head and helped her drink the water. The young girl put the juice on a small coffee table behind her. Destiny cleared her throat when she was done, drinking about half the glass of water, and put on her best sympathy-attracting expression. Karl could see this in the television's reflection, but didn't draw attention to himself.

"Young lady, might I trouble you for something to eat?" Destiny said softly, her eyes large and teary. "If I don't eat, I'll pass out. Dear, I might even die."

She looked at Joy with large eyes and her voice cracked as though she was terrified. Joy seemed to be having an internal struggle before she nodded and flounced to the kitchen. More noise from the kitchen followed.

Karl saw a hand slowly reaching underneath his chair, an old, wrinkled hand, and he moved his foot off the knife. Destiny's hand closed around it and she was busy with his ties next. Destiny managed to cut his ties, and then put the knife back where she had found it. She got up and sauntered between the chairs as the young girl came back, her arms outstretched, as though she was a zombie. She moaned for effect and the young girl ran to her side, alert.

Joy gave Karl and Fred a once-over, to make sure that they were still tied up, before giving all her attention to the elderly lady. Karl kept his arms at his back and kept hold of the black zip tie, sure that it would attract attention.

"I'm allergic to cheese!" Destiny cried out, and fell to her knees, sobbing. "I'm... I'm allergic... I don't want cheese..."

Joy kneeled next to her, and her back was turned to Karl. Karl and Fred met each other's eyes, both relieved that Destiny wasn't really dying. It had all been an act. And she was damn good at it too.

"That's okay, Mama," Joy said. "There's some peanut butter on this sandwich. Is that okay?" Joy seemed to be truly sorry, but Karl was beyond caring at that point.

He picked up the wine bottle that Mitch had left near him earlier, lifted it as high as he could, and hit the blonde girl over the head. Glass shattered, but luckily the Williamses had a carpet and the noise was mostly absorbed. The girl hadn't been cut, luckily. Or rather unluckily, because she would be better off dead. Karl then started at his own thoughts.

The petite blonde fell to the carpet with a dull thud, unconscious. Destiny scooped up the knife again and cut her husband loose. She forced the half-empty glass of water into his hand.

"It's been hours, my love. You have to drink," she whispered to him urgently. "You'll dehydrate if you don't, Fred. I already had water."

Fred gulped the water down. Karl wasn't offended that they didn't think to offer him any water, because he had already taken the glass of orange juice that Joy had bought earlier and gulped it down.

"Quiet," Karl whispered to his friends, putting a finger to his mouth.

The elderly couple immediately fell silent, clutching at each other. Joy was passed out on the floor, and they had no idea where Mitch was.

"I'm going to go looking for him. Stay here," he instructed before disappearing to the kitchen.

Karl picked up a large knife that the robbers had used earlier when they were making steaks and went to the deck. He fully expected to find the monster there, but he was nowhere to be seen. Karl was suddenly glad that he wore sneakers, because they were by far the best shoes to use when sneaking. The outdoor lights were off, and it must have been past midnight at this point.

The surgeon crept around the corner while clinging to the wall, the knife ready to attack. He tuned his ears to listen if he heard any footsteps, or maybe even the familiar sound of someone peeing on the ground. Nothing.

He walked around the house, looking at the entire deck. He didn't find the looming shadow of Mitch Petersen, much to his dismay. He walked around again, as quietly as he possibly could. He found nothing. He found no one.

Did... did Mitch Petersen leave? Karl could hope, but he didn't want to put his money on it. Petersen was apathetic enough to just leave his girlfriend with a dying woman, but he was also a psychopath who seemingly wanted his father's approval. He wouldn't just leave without ensuring that he would get it. Would he?

Would he?

There was a bloodcurdling scream from inside, and Karl's heart jumped into his throat.

The scream wasn't from either of his neighbors, and it wasn't one that bore good news.

Should he go back to his summer house and call the police? But he couldn't leave his neighbors on their own. Then again, the girl was passed out and the large man was gone. He was nowhere to be seen. He wasn't around the house, and he wasn't in the house.

At least, not as far as Karl knew. Instead, due to the screams, and since the monster would hear them eventually, Karl rushed back towards the house.

SCARS

CHAPTER **SIXTEEN**

FRED LOOKED AT HIS WIFE. Yes, she was a very good actress, but not that good. She was obviously very sick, and very weak. He took his wife's hands in his.

"Go to our bedroom and lock the door. You should be safe there." He kissed her hands and pulled on her hand and led her to the master-bedroom at the end of the hall.

It went slowly. He helped her each step of the way; she was weak for more than her just being a diabetic. Her foot was mangled, as was his, but he was functioning on adrenaline alone.

Both senior citizens were also exhausted. He heard his own breath coming and going, and he was suddenly glad that he had quit smoking decades ago, otherwise he would be as sick as the old man that had been taken to the hospital earlier.

His entire house was a mess; drawers were pulled out, clothes and random items lying everywhere. In their bedroom, everything was even worse. Their safe had been found too, and broken into. Destiny's jewelry was all gone, but Fred's coin collection was still in there. Pity too, for the thieves that is, because his coin collection was worth a lot.

Destiny's clothes were scattered across the entire room, some of it torn up. It was worse than just thievery, it was destruction. Destruction that was fueled by a deep unhappiness, Fred thought. Everyone seemed to force their laughter or their happiness. Laura did so to make her father happy. Fred had seen her looking at her father, even while she was snipping off their toes. She had a desperate need to be accepted by him.

The father was a bit of an interesting case to look at. A redneck, evidently addicted to cigarettes, and seemed to think that he could justify his behavior and his children's upbringing by blaming his wife for dying.

"Be safe." Destiny whispered to him, her eyes wide, brimming with tears. "And know that I love you."

"I love you too." He kissed her on the cheek quickly.

Fred took his wife to their room and closed the door behind him. He tried hard not to see the heartbroken look his wife gave him. She was now silently crying, two wet stains could be seen glinting even in the darkness of the night, as if telling him to be careful. As if... she was saying goodbye. She seemed to know something that he didn't. He heard the lock click behind him, and he heard the dresser scrape across the floor as Destiny pushed it to the front of the door. Good. She was smart. Their captors would find it hard to enter the room then. Maybe Destiny could escape. Though he realized that this was wishful thinking at its best.

Fred turned away and made his way to the china cabinet that stood in the hallway, limping down the stairs one at a time, cringing each time the muscles in his foot contracted. The cabinet was mahogany, ornate and pretty, and he opened the glass doors. In the cabinet was a bunch of things that were rather unnecessary: Destiny's porcelain dolls and porcelain plates with several patterns on them. But underneath the second shelf was Fred's reason for allowing this silly cabinet: a six-inch Colt Python revolver. His last secret weapon that he had managed to hide from the thieves.

He shakily dislodged the revolver, causing the mass of porcelain to shake slightly, and checked it. It wasn't loaded, unfortunately. He made sure to close the cabinet again. He knew there was ammo in the spare bedroom and made his way to it. Or he tried to, because as he turned, Joy stood in front of him.

"You think you're so fucking smart, don't you?" Joy asked, taking a step closer.

She had an angry bruise on her forehead from where she fallen.

"You think I am just some frail little creature?"

Fred gulped. *This girl must have the world's thickest skull!*

She suddenly seemed utterly terrifying. Gone was her airy, self-involved aura, replaced by a darkness that scared him.

What was this woman capable of?

Joy knew that people always assumed she was simply either a dumb whore or a quiet, fragile little mouse, depending on the situation. For the most part, she did not care what people thought about her, anyway, as long as it did not affect her relationship with Mitch. Her whole life was centered around Mitch and pleasing him. It did not matter what it was that he was asking for or what he needed at the moment, Joy was ready to give it to him at any cost. Some people might have termed their relationship sick or vulgar.

She had heard the whispers of how the love she was rumored to have for Mitch was sick. But it was more than that to her; it was simply a case of the devil you knew. Mitch would allow her to do anything that she wanted to do, as long as it didn't bother him at all. She also liked to think that in a way he loved her as she did him.

The first time they had met, Joy was on the floor at the mercy of Drexler, her pimp, who was beating her for not bringing back enough money to meet her nightly quota. It wasn't the first time that this had happened, and Joy already knew to curl into herself and protect her kidneys and face.

But the beating that day was especially fierce as her pimp already had two of his girls run out on him. Sometimes Joy wondered why she also did not run away, but she knew how much more dangerous it was out there for a young streetwalker without the protection a pimp. As it was, she knew she was probably going to have to go to the hospital after this. Again.

Then she had heard a yell and a scream, and looked up to see her pimp flung against the wall. She looked to the side at her savior and saw a large terrifying looking man who peered down at her while still on the ground. He seemed to consider her for a moment before looking up at Drexler. Her pimp was slowly standing up from the floor.

"And who the fuck are you?" Drexler asked, already reaching for the gun that Joy knew he always kept in his waistband.

If the man was scared he did not show it; he just looked down at her again, and then back at Drexler. "Why are you beating her?"

"I don't see how that is any of your business." Drexler spat as he got really close to Joy and the new man and started brandishing the gun.

For emphasis, he kicked Joy again, and then one more time.

"She's my bitch. But, like I asked, how is it any of your business?"

"I am bored, and I kinda want to fuck her." This time the stranger's tone turned very menacing. Even Joy got chills. "I'm the only one allowed to beat any bitch I'm fucking."

"You really are ready to die, ain't you, motherfucker?" Drexler was screaming at the tall man by now.

But the man only seemed to smile at this. Then, with a speed that seemed almost impossible for someone of his size, he slapped the pistol out of Drexler's hand and the three watched it sail a few feet away. He then wrapped his hand around the pimp's neck and lifted him easily in the air, until his legs were dangling below him.

He drew his hand back and released a blow that had Drexler screaming out silently as his fist plowed into his midsection. He dropped the now thrashing man to the floor, and stepped aside, as Drexler curled into a ball wheezing as he fought to get breath back into his lungs.

The man took out a knife, with the letters "MP" engraved on one side and a penis on the other side, and stabbed Drexler on his thigh without saying a word. Drexler let out a loud scream. He then took it out and cleaned with Drexler's shirt before putting it back in his jean's back pocket. And, without one glance at Joy, who was still lying on the floor, mouth opened in shock, the stranger walked out of the alley.

Joy quickly got up, stopping to deliver a swift kick to Drexler right in between his legs, she made her way out of the alley, hurrying to catch up with the man who had just saved her life. He walked for a while without saying anything to her, then looked back at her.

"How old are you?"

"Twenty-five." She lied immediately, not wanting him to think she was a baby.

But it was clear that he did not believe her. She had been with him ever since, happy to oblige him whenever he wanted to fuck, and in all that time she had known how good and kind he could be when he was happy. But, when he was upset that was when the real beast, the monster, woke up.

So, she always made sure not to upset him. Not because of the fact that he got violent when he was upset, but rather because he was not happy when he was upset. And Joy would never allow anyone upset her Mitch.

Not even an old man who thought he could play on her intelligence and saw her as weak.

Joy laughed and stepped closer to Fred. Her memories of Mitch's heroics fueled her rage. She was willing to do anything for him.

"Your wife's next..." Joy whispered.

Before Fred could respond, she held up a hand, an engraved knife, and plunged it into the side of his neck. Fred first let the revolver drop to the floor, then he fell to his knees.

He had not thought the girl was capable of this. She seemed to be the only one with a single ounce of kindness in her. Now he saw that she was brutal. She was still a puppet of her boyfriend, but she was a killing machine, nonetheless. She had no sympathy. She was a sociopath. She was... she was...

Fred Williams closed his eyes as dark red blood stained the carpet. Dead. The last thing he heard was a high-pitched screaming coming from the girl.

CHAPTER **SEVENTEEN**

ITCH PETERSEN WAS MANY THINGS. He was a lover of life (and of taking life if the television could be believed), he was a lover of wine (really, any alcohol would do), and he was a lover of his family (though not messing around with his family, and especially not with his old man, who was a terrifying man if you believed all the stories he told his children. Yes, Mitch did believe them, because he'd seen his father commit some of the acts). And he was also a lover of sex. Just ask Joy and every other girl he fucked.

He was also a car enthusiast, and the fact that he owned a beat-up truck was something that hurt his pride immensely. He wasn't some poor sod that could go around in a truck, it was very noticeable, and it had gotten him caught the first time. It was why he'd stolen a little Ford Fiesta with peeling paint from an unsuspecting college student, after he slit her little throat and came on her young body.

He'd left her there at the university parking lot. He wondered what had happened to her... Nah, he really didn't care.

This was why, when he had seen the garage keys hanging in the kitchen as he was on his way outside to take a piss, he took it. These people were all rich. They thought they were too good for normal society and therefore isolated themselves. They thought that they were above everyone—above the Petersen clan and many others like them—that they just chose to leave them to fend for themselves.

It wasn't a bad life, if he had to be honest. Every month or so, they broke into a house of someone who looked rich after Paddy and Laura stalked the people for a very long time. Usually just two people: a couple, two teenagers who were home alone, a mother and her child. Mitch liked it when it was the mother and daughter, and the child was anywhere from fourteen to eighteen. He would rape the daughter in front of her mother, and watch the mother beg him to stop, beg him to take her instead, to torture her instead. She wished. He never did fuck the mothers, though, because they were too old and too loose.

But Paddy and Laura hadn't done their homework, because now there was a third person tied up in the house. The neighbor, they said. But from which side? These people didn't have *neighbors*.

These stupid rich people spent money on dumb things like dolls and fucking plates! And they didn't even use these plates; they were just propped up in an ugly cabinet for people to look at. Why plates? What was so special about something that you just ate your food in? It was a waste of money. It was a waste of space. *Fucking rich people...*

And he had seen the safe. They had a collection of money—of *money*. How stupid was that? They hoarded money as though it would feed them once the apocalypse came. Stupid people. All rich people were stupid. But... the jewels. Gold and silver with diamonds and rubies.

Joy had liked *that*. She had slipped a diamond bracelet onto her wrist the minute she saw it and gave Mitch a long, tongue-filled kiss in thanks. Joy absolutely loved jewelry, and Mitch was only too happy to oblige his girlfriend. She would pay him back later. *Probably with her ass*, Mitch thought to himself.

It was because of all the expensive things in their house that he thought to go and see what car they had. And he wasn't disappointed, though rich people hardly ever disappointed when it came to cars and jewels. This had to be the old man's pride and joy, but soon it would be Mitch's. He was 40 yards away from the house, having left his girlfriend alone with their three captives.

He had no worries about Joy letting them go, because she was an idiot, but she wasn't that much of an idiot. Joy was a little fierce killing machine—or she could imitate Laura to the best of her abilities. He'd seen it happen before, and he had been severely impressed. It was one more reason to keep her around, if not just for the fact that she was a tight little sexy fuck. She would help the old bitch, and then tie her up again. If she wanted too to fuck either of the men, she could; he had no worries about that. She was a horny little one too.

Fucking nympho!

That was why he loved her, really. If he didn't see it happening, he was happy. If he did see it, however, there would be no guarantee that either of them would make it out alive.

Inside the garage stood a car that elicited a whistle from Mitch. The red and black 1970 Plymouth Hemi 'Cuda was beautiful. He knew his cars. Oh, this was a car that he liked very much. This was a car that he wanted, but it was one that he didn't want to share with his family. Joy was the only one he would allow to ride in it.

This... this was his baby, he decided. No one else's. Not even his father would be allowed to touch it. He was afraid of the old man, but that fear was slowly dissipating, because the old man was obviously dying. Pop would leave the family business to Mitch. Laura was too young and Tiny didn't have the brains to do what they were doing.

He unlocked the car, got in and started the engine. He had to check that the vehicle actually worked, because otherwise he'd be stuck with a stolen piece of scrap that would just stand around their already crowded yard.

The car roared to life, and Mitch closed his eyes, listening to the powerful roar. Yes, this... this was his car. He didn't realize a car could get him hard until now, and he almost laughed at his own boner. He had to get back so Joy could help him... alleviate his problem. That ass was waiting for him and it wasn't going to fuck itself, after all.

Soon enough...

He made sure the car was in neutral and stepped on the gas. Another, a more powerful roar, filled the garage. It sounded like angels were singing to him, as though they were *serenading* him. This must be what heaven felt and sounded like. He left the car running and got out. He opened the front of the car and whistled again. V8 engine—powerful, *powerful* stuff.

SCARS

CHAPTER **EIGHTEEN**

KARL FROZE AS SOON AS HE ENTERED the Williams house. The scene wasn't a good one, but then again, when he'd left, there had been someone lying unconscious on the floor, surrounded by broken glass, and his neighbors had been clutching each other in fear.

Now, the girl was gone; the only evidence of her presence was the fact that the carpet was indented. Yet she was gone, even the knife she'd held onto was gone. Where was she? The entire living room stank of blood, urine, and wine. Karl vaguely wondered if the piss-smell had been there all this time, or if it had happened while he was gone. Did someone wet themselves? He disregarded this and went in search of his friends.

The doctor turned to the hallway and froze again. Joy was standing over something, her head tilted towards a person on the ground. Her hands were red, as was her ponytail. A knife was raised in her hand, also dripping with deep red liquid, as though she'd just pulled it out, with a pool of what was unmistakably blood pooling at her feet. She stood in it, her boots splashed with dark spots of blood. Karl thought of her as bathing in the blood of older, wiser ones to gain immortality.

She moved, and Karl saw Fred.

Fred. Fred was... Fred was dead? How... how could he be dead? Where was Destiny? Where the hell was Destiny?

Panic started to rise in the surgeon. Where was the old woman? Was she dead too? Was she lying on the kitchen floor? Was she possibly alive? Karl hoped, but he didn't want to find his hopes crushed by her death.

The girl turned around slowly and seemed surprised to see him. Her mouth hung open and the hand around the knife was limp. Then she launched herself forward—all five feet and two inches and one-hundred-and-ten pounds of her—and tackled him, a homicidal scream accompanying her attack. Karl couldn't hear anything, just his own heart beating. He just saw her teeth flash and the glint of a knife.

But she was silly if she thought she could overpower Karl. For one, he was larger than she was. She slammed into his frame, the knife held tightly in her hand, and he swept her up and tossed her onto the floor. There was a sickening crunch followed by an echoing clatter. She had landed hard on the tiled hallway, and his knife had gone spinning out of his hand. He was without his weapon, without any type of defense.

He knelt down beside her, not caring that she still had a bloody knife in her hand.

"Did you kill him?" he asked quietly, pointing at Fred's dead body.

He knew she did, but he had to make sure before he did anything more. He didn't want to attack an innocent person, though she was caught, quite literally, red-handed. But he needed to hear it from her own mouth.

The girl gurgled and laughed. Karl sprang to his feet and kicked her limp body. He didn't know or even care where he kicked, he just kicked everywhere he could reach, but he kicked with fury that he had never felt before. He didn't care about what the morals or ethics regarding hitting women at that point, because this girl, whom he had given the benefit of the doubt, was no human. She was a monster. Like Mitch. But Karl didn't know why he was expecting something different from a girl who had spent her time cohabitating with a rapist.

He kicked her—in the gut, in the face—and she just kept laughing. Blood poured out of her nose and from her mouth from where he'd dislodged a few teeth. But she just gurgled some more, laughing wetly, spitting the blood out of her mouth onto the tiled floor.

When she'd stopped laughing, Karl stepped on her right hand. She had managed to keep her knife in her hand, as though it would save her life. It didn't. And he put more weight on her hand since she didn't let it go. He kept putting weight on it until her hand went limp, he heard even more cracks as the tiny bones in her hand broke, and the knife fell to the floor. Karl kicked the knife out of the way and turned. Maybe... maybe Fred *wasn't* dead. Maybe Fred was just unconscious. Karl was hopeful, but he knew from the blood and from Fred's body not moving that he was dead.

He knelt down beside his friend of about five years and reached out a shaky hand. He forced his breath to still and his heart rate to go down, otherwise he wouldn't be able to concentrate on taking Fred's pulse. When he could hear again, he put his index finger and his middle finger on the pulse point in Fred's neck.

Nothing. Not even a faint heartbeat to betray life, to betray that he had not died and there was still a glimmer of hope to cling to.

But no.

Fred Williams *was* dead.

And Karl allowed himself a brief moment to grieve. The moment was cut short by another homicidal cry from Joy, who had slashed the knife he'd been carrying earlier into his shoulder, and pulling it out again with immense strength. He cried out in pain, staggering backwards and into her and slipping on her spit and blood. She ducked down, and he tripped, falling on his newly wounded shoulder. He cried out again, and the teenaged girl stood over him, the knife in hand. She looked menacing and, with her swollen face and blood dripping from her nose and mouth, she looked like a macabre angel.

"You can't win," she said, smiling a bloody smile at him.

Karl sprang to his feet, ignoring the pain in his shoulder, and launched himself at her. She stood her ground, but he was stronger than she was. With a lot of moaning and groaning, he pushed her through the kitchen, bumping into the counter island and into an open drawer. She cried out in pain as the drawer hooked her exposed hip, but she kept forcing her own strength against him. She wasn't planning on giving up. Nor was Karl, as a matter of fact; as he struggled against her, his bleeding shoulder protesting heavily against him for putting more strain on it.

Karl twirled them around in their dangerous dance and pushed her out of the house onto the deck. She lost her footing for a minute and slid away from him, but she ran at him again, waving the knife in the air. She was pushed a couple of yards away from him, but she surged forward to attack him again. She brandished her weapon at him and caught him with it in the arm. A loud groan escaped his mouth, but he allowed the knife to dig into his arm, because it meant he could overpower her, and he could think and fight through the pain. He walked backwards towards the railing of the deck, unsure as to what he was doing, but he was just getting her out of his way—and out of his nightmare. Her eyes widened when she hit the wooden railing, and she glanced at the knife digging into his arm. She pulled at it, but it wouldn't give way.

Her eyes widened even more when the railing gave out beneath her from their combined mass, and she screamed when Karl let go of her without realizing that the railing had given way beneath her. He stumbled backwards, and didn't hear the scream until it was too late. He didn't hear the sickening *crack* until it was gone, or the splash of water that followed.

He blinked, confused. Where was the slutty teenaged girl? That was when he saw the broken railing. That was when fear struck his heart. He went closer to the railing, his heart beating erratically in his chest once more. He inched closer, slowly, agonizingly. Karl was terrified of what he would to see.

His heart stopped when he saw over the edge. The girl lay at the bottom, where the water was calmly lapping at her feet. Her head had met the lake beach rocks, and it was split open. Even in the darkness, he could see her blood staining the otherwise clear water of the lake. She was dead. She had met a violent end, not unlike that of Fred. And though Karl was sorry for the violent end the girl met, he wasn't sorry that she *had* met her end. She had killed Fred, she hadn't tried to help them, not really. She was trying to help Mitch when she gave Destiny that food and drinks. Not them. She was just as guilty as the rest of the Petersen clan.

He turned to the side and emptied his stomach's contents onto the wooden deck. Had he done that? Had he killed her? He must have, there was no other explanation for what had happened.

"Fuckboy!" a familiar voice yelled, and Karl whirled around.

Running towards him was the massive brute, Mitch, pointing a shotgun at him, sprinting from the Williams' garage.

SCARS

CHAPTER **NINETEEN**

ITCH HEARD HIS GIRLFRIEND'S TERRIFIED SCREAMS and turned off the car. He cocked his head slightly, and first he thought he had imagined it. It was entirely possible, because his hearing wasn't what it should be. He liked to think that the screams of all the girls he fucked made him a little deaf. Not screams—their moans of begrudging pleasure as he pounded their pussies, wet or dry, until lubrication came. Either their bodies started to enjoy it, even if their minds didn't, even if tears poured down their cheeks and they screamed, or they started to bleed.

He liked the latter. He liked to see the blood stain the sheets beneath them. The smell, the colors, the groans, and their tight pussies clutching around his cock as he came and he squeezed their dying breaths from their small, young, tight bodies...

He shook his head, pulling himself out of his thoughts. He hadn't had a fuck like that in months; he had to make a plan.

Maybe he had heard incorrectly, and the car had made the weird sound. The car, while it was very impressive, was old, and it was possible that it had simply screeched.

There it was again. No, he hadn't heard incorrectly.

It was not the car.

It was the dulcet tones of his girlfriend. But it wasn't the vocal tones he was used to. She liked to be very loud during sex. Paddy hated it. But he adored her moans of pleasure.

However, this certainly was not pleasure; it couldn't be. It was utter terror. These were the sounds that the teenaged girls normally made if he wasn't quick enough to cover their mouths.

He put his wine bottle down and grabbed the shotgun the old man had stupidly told them he had, and ran out of the garage. The fuckboy was standing on the deck, where a massive chunk of the railing had given way only moments earlier.

Mitch stilled for a single moment in time. Joy had fallen through that railing, and he knew... He just *knew* from the thud and the sickening, nauseating crunch that she was dead.

His heart stopped. Then... rage.

The fuckboy staggered back and hunched over, throwing up. A bulky wetness hit the wooden deck, and Mitch could see the yellow chunks from the man's stomach.

Disgusting.

Mitch Petersen could see past the deck, since the garage was higher than the deck on a hillside, and at the bottom, on the rocks, lay a pair of butt cheeks that he knew very well. It was the ass he liked to fuck.

Her denim mini-skirt was flipped over her bare ass. Mitch looked further toward her head. Her head was shattered. Blood stained the water. And this red wasn't something that he liked seeing. It wasn't something he usually saw. He usually saw a brighter, more vibrant red. The red spread through the water and surrounded Joy's head.

Rage.

He had one emotion running through his large body, his blood pumping through his veins, angrily, pushing him into action. One emotion that he rarely ever felt, even with his idiot of a brother and slut of a sister.

"Fuckboy!" A primal scream escaped his mouth and he surged forward, the shotgun raised. The fuckboy saw him, his eyes widened, and he ran away, limping. Mitch ran to the deck, gun in his hand, but he ignored the fuckboy for now. The man disappeared into the kitchen, presumably. Mitch stopped at the railing, lurching dangerously. A meaty hand shot out and he stopped himself from falling over the broken deck too.

He had... hoped. He had hoped against hope—hoped against what his eyes had told him—that Joy was still alive. He had hoped that her eyes, the ones that stared up at him, would have a slight shine in them, and Joy's mischievous smile that told him that she was in on whatever the fuck they were doing, and that she was having fun.

But, no. Her eyes were empty, her mouth was open. The final feeling that the girl, who had just started college, had felt was terror and shock. Terror at falling to her death, and shock at the finality of it all.

Mitch let out another pained yell at the sight. He then whirled around, furious, and ran into the house, his footsteps thundering beneath him. Alcohol fueled his rage and he couldn't stop running, couldn't stop screaming. He was in unimaginable pain. This was something that Mitch had never felt before, it was pain that was something else entirely from the physical pain he felt whenever he and Tiny fought.

Inside the kitchen, he saw nothing. He heard nothing in the house but the soft tick-tock of the clock against the wall and the drip-drip of a broken wine bottle's wine dripping onto the floor. He picked up a half-drained bottle of wine and knocked it back. This wasn't the sweet stuff he'd drunk in the garage. It was thick and bitter, which explained why it was only half-drained. But he drank it all, forcing it down his throat. Bitter, like he was.

"Come on, bitch!" he screamed, yelling for the old woman.

She wasn't tied up anymore. The chairs were abandoned. He stomped down the hall and paused when he saw a dark shadow. He felt around blindly against the wall for a light switch. He finally found one and light flooded the hallway.

At his feet lay the old black man. Very obviously dead, and very obviously not from a heart attack. He didn't know who the man was, just an old man who had been caught up in his father's madness. In the Petersen Clan's insanity. The old man had stopped bleeding at his feet, the blood now completely dried up. The man's shirt was stained dark red, and his clothes were torn.

He started to laugh. It was an empty sound, one that echoed through the hallway. The large man laughed and laughed, his eyes fixated on the old man's body. Their victims often ended up dead, though never would they normally have been found. Not for a while, at least, because they were careful. Mitch immediately knew who had done it, and he didn't know if he wanted to laugh or cry. He would have screamed at her because of her stupidity, but now he missed it.

He lifted the gun and aimed down the hallway. There was nothing, but he pulled the trigger. Loud bangs echoed through the hallway, and the bullets hit the doors, the floor, the wall... Everywhere. The steel bullets clanged around, and he let up from the trigger. It hit the lightbulb and the lights flickered out. Darkness fell, and this time the silence was missing.

There were sounds coming out of his mouth. Screams. He was cussing like a pirate.

He didn't know what they were. They sounded like... like he was crying. It sounded like he was sobbing. He was surprised, because Mitch Petersen had never cried since he was a baby. Mitch Petersen hadn't felt anything in a very long time. He wasn't talking about physical pain—no, that he felt daily. However, anything else, emotionally speaking... no. Nothing. Until now.

CHAPTER **TWENTY**

LAURA CURSED LOUDLY, the stream of words was something that she was not proud of. Her father shot her a mean look, but she just ignored it. She was on Paddy's lap in their beat-up old truck as they were taking Daddy to the hospital. Tiny was driving like a maniac. Not that it really surprised her, because Tiny had the brains of half a noodle. Tiny never got his license, but their Pop taught them all how to drive since a young age.

He'd done it on an old dirt road near their rundown house back in the mountains. Their house was a little wooden cabin with three rooms. Daddy had one room. the biggest room in the house, with a fridge and a TV in it. The TV and fridge were things that they had gotten from other people's houses they had broken into. These were the houses of rich people that hardly spent time in their houses, using them only as vacation homes.

The whole clan—except for Mitch, who was always off one some stupid mission or another—had stayed in the house for a long while. The family had finally shown up after two months to find the Petersen's squatting in their home. Daddy had knocked the man out with a shovel, and Tiny had tied the woman up before she could say anything.

They had started with scarves and torn linen back then. They usually just used whatever they found lying around—rope, linen, scarves, zip ties, etc. Laura had then also tortured her first victim, and she had thrown up just after she'd done it. Later, much later, she'd gotten used to it.

She had to. Because she didn't have anyone else in her life. Her mama had died when she was just a little kid, and her daddy had to bring her up. He did an okay job; he was just trying to provide for her and her brothers. She was spoiled, but her brothers were spoiled even more.

The blonde woman would never admit it, but she would do absolutely anything to get her father's attention, even murder.

Luckily, she never did. She was a thief, she was a sadistic little bitch, and she often relished in the screams of the people she tortured, but only because of the look her father gave her. It was a look of pride—a sick look of pride that she took an interest in her father's hobbies. Later, when her father had trouble moving and when liquid started to fill his lungs, when the years of working in a mine and smoking like a damn chimney took its toll on him, it became her responsibility to torture their victims.

She didn't want to. She hated it. But she could never show it. She could never show how much she hated what they did, how they made a living... How they plundered, drank, and stole to get by. Daddy could never have afforded a way for them to get an education further than the ninth grade—and she secretly resented him for that.

A fifteen-year-old Laura had been forced to take up the mantle of torturer. It made her daddy happy, it made her happy to make him happy. She didn't like to do it, but she did it because of him. She did it because she had no one else to look after her.

Mommy had died when she was not even a decade on the Earth. She barely remembered her mother—tall, blonde, pretty, and loving. Laura didn't know much else, except that her mother had made her feel warm and loved. It was a feeling that Laura had not felt in years.

She had wanted to get away from him, but she had nowhere else to go.

The other rooms in the house were hers and Tiny's. Mitch didn't live with them. He lived in a shitty trailer with that slut. God only knew what that fucker did in his free time, though Laura had a bit of an idea. She had read about a serial killer and a serial rapist that invaded homes, fucked teenagers, and killed them. And she had the idea that it was him. It finally made sense why he kept that little slut around. She was an idiot!

He had just turned up one day with her in tow, and no one had any idea why he kept her around. Everyone knew that Mitch wasn't the relationship type. Besides it was hard to imagine any woman would want to ever be in a relationship with someone as vile as him. At least until Joy. The girl seemed to truly adore her brother. She never understood why or how. But she was the only one that he actually showed any iota of care for.

When Mama was still alive, things had not used to be as bad as this. Of course, Daddy had always been crazy with a shady life, but Mama provided an insulation from all of that. Laura hadn't even known she had a father until the funeral for her mother, where she saw an old man smoking continuously and swigging from a bottle. It was after the burial that she was told the man was her father and she would now be staying with him. Numb out of her mind and feeling adrift, she had been desperate for any support she could get.

But it hadn't been long before he showed her that if it was warmth and love that she was looking for, she should not expect anything from him. Thrust into a world of men, with the dumb Tiny, the cruel and vicious Mitch, and her new, clearly unloving father figure, Laura had to learn how to cope. She could still remember snide remarks from her classmates when they found out who her family was. For a girl who grew up with the confidence of the love of her mama and the trust that nothing bad could happen to her, it had been hard for Laura to deal with the cruel rumors of people who were supposed to be her friends. At home, things had not been much better either, as Daddy had believed in an every-man-for-himself philosophy. Laura even had to fight for food at home; not that there had ever been enough to eat.

Then, one day, she'd come back home from school crying, and Tiny was the first to see her. Of all the men in the house, he had been the only one who seemed to be kind to her. He'd asked her why she was crying, and she'd told him that some girls in school had called her names and talked badly about her family. Frothing with rage, Tiny had grabbed a baseball bat and was about to go down to the playground and teach the girls a lesson. Then, her father had come in and demanded to know what was happening.

After Laura had finished narrating what had happened in the same way that she had to Tiny, she had waited for her father to get angry on her behalf just as her brother had. However, this had not been the case. Instead of empathy or compassion from her own father, he burst out into laughter, pointing at her and laughing until tears ran down his eyes. Then, suddenly, he'd stopped and looked at her.

"So, you tellin' me that a bunch of pussies made fun of you at school and you come home bawling. You're no daughter o' mine! Your mom spoilt you rotten, girl." He spat on the floor and then walked out.

That was how Laura knew that any sign of weakness was not acceptable in this family. The next time she had been teased, she'd waited until Abbie, the ringleader of the girls, was walking alone, taking a shortcut home. Then she had sneaked up on her and hit her on the back of her neck with a stick. Abbie had fallen to the ground and, for a moment, Laura had thought she was dead. But then she'd seen her still breathing faintly, and quickly ran away.

When she'd told the story at home that night, she had been praised and applauded, and for the first time, Daddy had been really proud of her. She became his baby girl that day. That night, she got to serve herself food first. And even Mitch, her older brother who seemed to ignore her most of the time, smiled at her. Finally, she had become a part of the Peterson clan. And even though she'd felt sick to her stomach at what she did to get there, Laura had just been happy to finally feel love of some kind.

At school the next day, all that everyone could talk about was Abbie, who was still at the hospital. Apparently, the blow had knocked her out, but there would be no lasting damage. Still, Laura had found that she had to lose more and more of herself to gain just a little bit of love from her father. But earn his love she had, by becoming the ruthless, heartless, and sadistic monster that he wanted her to be. She became a true Peterson in actions and deed. Maybe not in heart, because for everyone she tortured, every drop of blood she spilled, she felt herself lose a part of herself. So much so that she needed to escape the guilt that always seemed to plague her.

She had tried a lot of things, tried doing good when she could, far away from the eyes of her family. But that didn't work. She had even tried running away from home once, but had come back after only two days, when she'd realized she could not live, or at least survive, without her family. For the two days that she had been away, no one had looked for her or even noticed that she was even gone. And when she had come back, her father had just handed her a crowbar and told her they were breaking into the neighbor's house that night.

Laura had finally tried drugs. First, she'd tried weed—smoked it, made them into brownies and ate it. Then, she'd tried coke, but it was too expensive. And then she'd stuck to meth. She had to get her hit, because it was how she managed to cope. Life sucked.

Laura pulled her thoughts away from her past.

Daddy sat between her and Paddy, and Tiny. He was coughing awfully, hacking up slime every now and then that he smeared across the dashboard. Laura had to keep herself from throwing up. This wasn't something weird, she'd seen her daddy throw up slime a ton of times. But he was next to her, and she heard how hard it was for him to breathe. He was wheezing, and he kept his oxygen mask over his mouth, though it didn't help much.

She smelled them all. She smelled the sour-sweat smell of her brother's sweat, mixed with the smell of wine, and it nauseated her. The young girl felt sick. And it wasn't just the smell of sweat, alcohol, and cigarette smoke that churned her stomach.

It was the memory of the old man's screams. It was the memory of the blood spurting from the old man's foot as she snapped off his toes, happily counting the seconds and cuts it had left. The man's muffled screams and tear-filled eyes as his eyes begged her to stop. And then again, he'd begged her to stop when she'd moved to the old woman, trying to tell her to torture *him*. She didn't know why, or how, this man could love someone so much.

Tiny turned the car sharply and Laura clutched at the door handle to make sure that she didn't fly out the window. Paddy closed his arms around her waist, and her father grabbed her other arm. She was momentarily touched at the idea that they were trying to save her, but there was no time to dwell on it as they turned into the hospital's parking lot.

They bustled out of the car. First Laura, then Paddy. From the other side, Tiny climbed out, rushed around and helped Daddy from the car. Tiny was strong enough to lift their father and carry him into the hospital, but the old man cursed at him.

"Let me walk, you, stupid boy!" Daddy screamed at him, and Tiny stared dumbly.

"What am I s'posed to do, Pop?" he asked, standing and hunching his shoulders.

Laura looked at him, thinking it was absolutely hilarious that Tiny tried to make himself smaller, because it was impossible.

"Just help him," Laura snapped at him, and she looked at Paddy, who jumped into action.

Paddy took one of the old man's arms and Tiny the other, while Laura carried his oxygen tank.

When they got closer to the hospital doors, she noticed something that felt weird. Sure, they were a bunch of weirdos. They were four people walking up to a hospital—an old man with a long, dirty beard who was close to losing consciousness, a mask glued to his face; a massive man with hands the size of dustbins lids, be it small dustbins, with very little hair on his head, and a very stupid expression on his face; a tall, lean guy with bloodshot eyes and a wispy beard; and a blonde crack whore carrying an oxygen tank.

But the gazes they were getting were highly suspicious. There were people talking into phones and glancing at them shiftily, and then they quickly looked away.

"Petersen..." Laura heard her last name as they were about to enter the hospital. She dropped the oxygen tank.

Paddy looked around at her, eyebrows raised, but she had backed away from the three of them.

"Laura?" Paddy asked, and she just shook her head slowly.

He walked closer to her, leaving her father dangling off Tiny's arm.

"No," she said, taking another step backwards.

She didn't want this. Paddy was confused, and he kept coming closer to her. Her brother had turned around to look at what was happening too; her father's eyes were closed and his inability to breathe became evident.

Behind them, Laura saw the glint of extended arms with a handgun. An officer at the hospital must've recognized them!

"Halt!" a voice yelled, and Laura pushed her boyfriend away from her, into the line of fire, and she ran.

"Freeze!" the voice screamed, but Laura didn't stop.

She ran, her blonde hair whipping in her eyes, blinding her at times. She had to get away. Her footsteps thundered beneath her and she only came to a halt when she had found their car. She hid behind it, glancing over the front of the car at what had happened.

Her father was on the floor, his oxygen tank away from him, the mask ripped from his face. Tiny was running too,

Paddy was running too. They both ran towards the car, but they were both larger than she was, slower.

Tiny turned around, cursing. He slammed his fists into a wall, tears streaking down his cheeks. Laura wanted to go to her brother, to help him. To hug him. She was one of the few people that could soothe his pain. Were they caught? It all happened so quick. Of course, their faces had been all over the news. They were the notorious Petersen Clan—home invaders, thieves, murderers. Sociopaths. Psychopaths.

Laura saw how Tiny tried to take his gun out from his pocket. Shots rang out. His entire body shook as multiple bullets hit his massive body. Tiny sank to the floor, and it all ended. Tiny stopped moving, his massive body now submerged in a pool of blood.

"Tiny!" she screamed, not really knowing what to do or where to go.

Paddy was lucky. He was also shot, but in the leg. Laura saw him collapsing on the lobby floor, unable to run any further. Another armed uniformed man had caught up to them and was restraining Paddy, as the first one who shot was radioing someone.

Laura exited the doors quickly and ran. She continued to ran away from them, no longer looking back. If only she had the vehicle keys! But she ran, not knowing where to go.

Even though she hadn't been hit, she pain was excruciating. She know what to feel or to think. She didn't know if to laugh or to cry. Her heart needed to stop; it needed to be cut out and... She just had to stop feeling this confusion and pain. She wanted the voices in her head to stop screaming. She couldn't breathe.

I can't be alone! I can't be the only one left.

So, she ran some more. Away from the commotion. Away from the sirens. Away from the hospital. Away from her reality.

CHAPTER **TWENTY-ONE**

THE POLICE HAD A LONG LIST of things that Mitch had done — armed robbery, murder, rape. Photos of him were plastered all over the news. People had come forward with their stories about their daughters, even younger than Naomi. Parents who were broken-hearted about teenage girls being strangled while they were being raped.

The first girl on record was Hannah Hill, a cute girl with long ponytails, big brown eyes, and an innocent smile. She had been fourteen years old when she had been hunted, like an animal, through her own house. Her older brother, eighteen, had been busy in his bedroom with earphones in his ears, playing video games, where the sounds of zombies and shotguns drowned out his sister's cries.

He'd found her body half an hour later. Her clothes had been torn, the mattress beneath her a pool of blood.

Girl two had been Sherry Daniels. Fifteen, brunette, bright blue eyes, a little pudgy. She had been home alone; her parents had quickly run to the grocery store. They hadn't even been gone for twenty minutes, and when they'd returned, their baby girl was dead too. Her eyes wide open, her mouth also opened in her choke...

Her parents had found her body on the couch. Her throat was bruised. She had been cut all over. Blood covered the creamy couch. Mr. Daniels had committed suicide that evening. Mrs. Daniels was in rehab.

Girl number three had been Joanne Gomez. Seventeen. Black hair, brown eyes, short, petite, gymnast. Rosina Lang had been girl number four. Redhead. They had been the first girls that he had attacked together. He had attacked the redhead first, leaving her body on the stairs. A blunt hit to the head had done it. Then Joanne, who he had brutally sodomized right before slitting her throat.

Then there had been Brittany Miller, girl number five. She was a runaway who he had found at a park.

These were all girls who came from good families, most of them from wealthy parts of the country. Most of them who lived in safe neighborhoods. Or so it was believed. Yet this monster found his way into their homes or found them wandering alone outside.

And murdered them.

Hannah, Sherry, Joanne, Rosina, Brittany... All innocent girls. Their innocence stolen from them; young girls who had been forced to grow up too fast, only for their lives to be taken from then while suffering.

Mitch really had no particular style... as long as they were young. He had read or heard somewhere how pedophilic tendencies were a sign of a serious underlying psychologic pathology. During his last stint in prison, Mitch had to spend time with a therapist who liked to throw a lot of big words around. Mitch knew that it was all a con, all an attempt to psycho-manage him. But this wouldn't swing him in the least bit. It all made sense to him. Some men liked big boobs and others liked skinny women. Mitch... well, he liked them young. That was his thing. He liked them unripe, before they saw how cruel the world could be and have their innocence stolen from them. He enjoyed being the one who stole that innocence.

And so far, there had been no survivors.

⁂

Karl limped into the house, hearing the agonized scream coming from Mitch. The sound was strangled and pained, which surprised Karl. As he staggered into the house, tired, Karl fell next to Fred's body. The old man still had the knife sticking out of his chest, and Karl ripped it out of his body.

On the other side of Fred lay a revolver, and Karl swiped that too before he got up and sauntered down the hall, his leg protesting painfully beneath his weight. He heard the man screaming outside, his rage making him pause for the briefest moment that allowed Karl to escape.

Down the hall he went, the gun in one hand, the blood-stained knife in the other. He walked up the stairs, clinging desperately to the railing. He made his way to where he knew the master bedroom was, and tried to open the door, but it refused to budge. Locked.

Karl's heart jumped into his throat as he heard the giant enter the kitchen behind him. Karl tore himself away from the locked door to the bathroom, where the Williamses had an old-fashioned bath-shower combination, and Karl hid behind the dark curtain. Terror overloaded his every sense.

CHAPTER **TWENTY-TWO**

MITCH STARTED TO WALK down the hall. He walked up the stairs, breathing heavily. He chose to look in the furthest rooms first, because those were the rooms that he would have hidden in if he was trying to hide. He had played this game many times with Tiny and Laura, though he always lost, because what type of big brother would he be if he allowed his idiot siblings to know just how fucking stupid they really were.

Laura was a freaking meth-head, her boyfriend was a jobless bum and just kind of rode their wave of good fortune. Good fortune that Pop, Mitch, and Tiny accessed by breaking into houses and stealing things. They could always sell jewels, and that was why they targeted rich folks. Of course, they didn't sell the stolen jewels close to the places that they had invaded—now *that* would be something Tiny would have done. Named Tiny for the size of brain, he was.

They sold everything two towns over and made sure that Paddy did it.

Laura used to do it, but when people saw her stubby teeth, they called the cops, or the hospital, to help the *poor young girl.* Paddy looked sort of normal, albeit ugly and with a funky mullet. He always said it was for his girlfriend's medicine. The only meds that his slut of a sister took, was the crap turning her into a fucking rotten corpse.

The room at the end of the hallway was empty. It was a small room, only had room for a double bed with purple covers and a little dresser. There was even a pretty little decoration on the bed, and Mitch couldn't help but think how much Joy would have liked it. Ah, well, that cunt was dead, and soon her killer would be dead and gone too. He didn't even bother to look under the bed, because the covers didn't quite cover it entirely and the bed way was too low for even a cat to hide under.

Purple. The color of royalty. These people really did think of themselves as better than everyone else, didn't they? They were real snobs.

Now, where the bloody hell was that limping fuckboy?

He screamed inside his head.

He didn't want to say it aloud because he was afraid that the bastard might hear, entirely forgetting that he was breathing heavily, his footsteps were as loud as thunder, and he had already sent a dozen shots through the hallway.

That fuckboy had glared at him with so much hatred that Mitch could have sworn he felt it as though it was radiation. He honestly had no idea who this idiot was, but he knew he had to get rid of him. If he let the man live, the man could identify them all. His father, his brother, his sister... him. Even that idiot his sister was fucking. Fuckboy knew them all, and that was not good.

Next, he found a bathroom, where he switched on the light. When he saw the tub, he laughed.

Old-fashioned niggers, huh?

He left the bathroom as he had found it, because he saw no one in there. All that was left was the closed door, the one where his brother had found the gun earlier. The biggest bedroom in the whole house, and the only place that fuckboy would truly deem worthy enough to hide in. Rich folks were so utterly predictable, because they just fled to the places of comfort.

The girls he fucked always ran for their bedrooms. He knew that by now. Each girl he'd fucked, was one he had stalked first. A month, maybe two months before his attack, he would start watching them. Joy would nag and nag that she missed him and whatever the fuck else, so he even took her along with him. She was the one who had said the girls went to their rooms, because that is a girl's so-called "safe space." Mitch made sure that there was no such as a "safe space" for the little cunts. He didn't know why the girls didn't run out the front door. He couldn't exactly follow them outside and fuck their tight pussies on their driveways, could he? Those idiotic cunts chose their wealth, their comfort, above their safety.

It was their own fault that they ended up where they did.

The monster threw his body against the door, trying to open it, ignoring his thoughts. It didn't budge, and he did it again. Again, it didn't budge.

He cursed loudly before pointing the shotgun at the lock. He fired, and the door's lock shattered, making a hole in the wooden door as well. He threw his entire weight against the door again, and this time it moved. Only a little, though, because there was something barring the door. He repeated his act, throwing his whole body against the door, and whatever was in front of the door finally gave way.

He strode in as though he owned the place—only to find that no one was in the room. At least, no one that he could see. But these people had to be here somewhere. Maybe the closet? He trudged over to the closet and shot a round of bullets into it. There was no screaming, so no one was in the closet. He turned. These people had a large TV in their bedroom, and he made note of that. He could use a new TV. It was at least 60 inches, and it would fit perfectly on his bedroom wall.

This bed was high enough for someone to hide under. Maybe either the fuckboy or the old bitch was hiding there,

Mitch thought. He stooped down to look, but found only shoeboxes and dust. He made a mental note to come look in those shoe boxes later. Old people kept all kinds of things in shoe boxes—cash, guns, booze, condoms, vibrators, flesh lights, credit cards... You name it, they saved it. Mitch usually gave Tiny the flesh lights, seeing as no girl in their right mind would want to fuck the ugly son of a bitch that was his brother.

Mitch stilled, looking for a clue as to where his prey was. The windows were closed and all of them had burglar proofing on them, the white bars now kept the burglar inside, and with the thief, the victim. There was no way that the fuckboy or the old bitch could have climbed out. He laughed at the idea of the woman climbing out a window. She would break a neck and then he wouldn't have to kill her. He laughed loudly at the idea, and his heart leapt at the thought.

Now, where would the fun in that be?

There was a small loveseat in the room and piled on it was a ton of clothes. Perhaps... perhaps under the pile of clothes? The old woman certainly was small enough, and fuckboy could curl his body into a ball to hide under it. Mitch knew that he would not have had a chance to do this. He hadn't had enough time. But maybe the old bitch was crying her lungs and eyes out underneath these clothes.

He cocked the gun and shot at the heap of clothes. Once, twice, thrice, before deciding that there was nothing and no one there. There were no screams that filled the air, no movement that betrayed a sign of life, no blood that stained the clothes or couch to show a sign of death, no sound of bullets hitting anything but cotton and stuffing. It was a sound that Mitch was familiar with.

Wait. What was that? He heard... he heard *crying*. Soft crying, mind you; and it came from... it came from the closet? The one that he'd just shot the hell out of? How in hell was that even possible?

He stormed to the closet and wrenched the doors open. Only to find that it wasn't a closet, but a hidden bathroom.

Fucking rich people!

He growled in rage and was surprised by the porcelain toilet lid being brought down on his head. He lost focus. His head hurt like shit, and he was sure that there was blood coming out of his ears. He sank to the ground, his massive body unable to keep him upright when his head spun. The gun clattered onto the floor, away from him, and all he saw were blurry shapes. He saw a pair of bare feet trying to escape, so he threw out a meaty hand and the woman fell, her knees connecting hard with the tiles.

Mitch reached for the gun, forcing himself up, and his heart stopped when an icily cold voice spoke behind him.

"Freeze."

CHAPTER **TWENTY-THREE**

TO KARL'S IMMENSE SURPRISE, the monster stilled from where he had been scrambling on the floor. Around him lay the remains of the porcelain toilet bowl's lid. The doctor shot a look at his elderly neighbor, and despite being exhausted and terrified, she seemed fine. Her whole body shook in terror, she breathed heavily, and her face was stained with tears. She looked relieved at Karl's presence, and she looked as though she wanted to hug him, but she stayed rooted where she was, except she lowered her hands.

"Get up. Hands in the air," Karl ordered, keeping the revolver aimed on Mitch Peterson.

He stood slowly and put his massive hands in the air. He glanced around for something to defend himself with, since he had lost his shotgun. It lay a few feet or so away from his boot-clad feet, near to where Destiny Williams stood. Destiny stared at the shotgun, her agitation evident.

"Destiny, you okay?" Karl asked, his brow furrowing in concern.

The woman looked at him reproachfully, her entire body heaving with her attempts to breathe, but she nodded.

She was not okay, Karl knew, nor would she be. Not if she found out about her husband's body at the end of the stairs. Not if she knew about the body of the young girl polluting the water just outside her home. Not if she knew her life had just been thrown on its head. Not if she knew what Karl knew.

Karl still had Deborah, and he would go back to her if he made it out of this alive. He would go on his knees and beg her to give him a chance. Because if there was one thing he now knew, it was his love for that woman. And he had acted like a complete idiot for the past year. Their daughter hadn't been the glue that had held them together, Karl knew, and her death wasn't going to be what tore them apart either. Not if he had anything to say about it.

Karl saw it too late. He was so busy keeping an eye on the Petersen monster, he didn't see his elderly neighbor throw her old body towards the shotgun in a desperate attempt to end their nightmare. Karl, however, did see Mitch throw himself towards the gun. He didn't fire his revolver.

Mitch and Destiny wrestled over the shotgun, and the gun was pointing at Destiny's chest. Karl Munson was too slow to react. The next thing he knew, the shotgun went off.

Destiny's body fell backwards and she hit the floor with a dull thud. At the other side, Mitch had hit the ground too, though Karl didn't care enough to make sure if their captor was all right, he just made sure that he was out cold. He stomped on Mitch's face, breaking his nose, for good measure. When Mitch had seized the shotgun, he'd pulled the trigger immediately.

The birdshot had hit Petersen in his face. It must have been what had caused him to go unconscious. Blood flowed from his broken nose and bullet wounds into his eyes. The deep crimson liquid would blind him if he came back from dreamland.

Karl moved to Destiny, whose chest was leaking copious amounts of blood, and took her hand. She was still alive, but Karl knew she wasn't going to make it. Too much trauma, too much blood loss, too little strength in the frail old woman's body.

"Destiny..." he said, and her brown eyes found his green ones.

His throat felt thick with emotion, and everything, or anything, he would have said to her was gone. She squeezed his hand, tears flowing down her wrinkled cheeks, and she closed her eyes. The moment her eyes closed, she gave up. Her life was over. A long, fulfilling life was now over.

At least she didn't have to see Fred's dead body. At least she didn't have to see what was coming next. At least...

Karl folded Destiny's arms across her chest gently before turning to Petersen. The feeling Karl felt was one of unmistakable hatred and anger. A wish to get revenge for Naomi and Sophie, and Sherry, Joanne, Hannah… and all the other girls—nameless girls who were not reported missing because they were not loved.

The surgeon allowed himself a moment to grieve for the loss of his neighbors. The loss of Destiny and Fred would hurt a lot, and it would crash into him later, where he would collapse in a puddle of tears. But that moment was not now.

Mitch Petersen was lying on the ground at his mercy. And this was a moment that he, Doctor Karl Munson, could not pass up. The monster liked to ravish innocent girls and take their lives? The monster liked to tie people up and rob them?

It was time for payback.

But he was terrified of the man waking up before he could do anything. He rummaged in Fred and Destiny's drawers and found some sleeping pills, which he forced down Petersen's throat. Mitch's throat refused, but Karl sat on the man's chest and pushed the blue and white capsule down his throat, then poured a bottle of wine that stood on the chest of drawers down too to make sure it went down.

Through all of this, the monster didn't wake up. It was a blessing, because there was no way in hell, on Earth, or in heaven—okay, possibly in heaven—where Karl could overpower Mitch. Mitch was twice his size, and the size of his muscles spoke volumes about his physical prowess. Karl wouldn't be surprised if Mitch frequented a gym to get these muscles. He also wouldn't be surprised if Mitch took a bunch of steroid shots to help build them.

Karl dragged the huge man down the hallway, not caring if the man hit his head and it caused permanent brain damage. He hoped it would. It took him ten minutes, but it was only because Mitch's belt kept catching on the door hinge. After a few minutes of struggling, Karl gave in and took of the man's belt, tossing it aside.

Once in the living room, Karl set to using a knife to cut Mitch's clothes off. After the shirt, it was the pants, and then the briefs. Karl didn't look at the man's private parts, afraid that what he might see would give him nightmares.

Oh, but how he wanted to cut that thing off!

For months after Naomi and Sophie's murders, Karl had had nightmares. He'd dreamt his daughter was calling him, begging him for help, but he was too busy socializing to help her. He had dreamt that he was the monster who stole his daughter's innocence and life. He had dreamt that he was Mitch Petersen, skulking outside the Munson home, watching the two teenage girls, and what played in Karl's mind was the security footage of the two girls swimming outside.

Karl had dreamt he was the monster perched outside the Munson house in a tree, watching the married couple fight and their marriage fall apart, and he dreamt that this monster laughed at their misery. He had dreamt he was Mitch Petersen, and that he was now raping Deborah, while forcing Karl to watch, unable to change anything or stop it. Then the dream would end with two meaty hands wrapping around Karl's neck as the monster teased him about the murders, and how there was nothing he could do about it.

The zip ties were still on the kitchen counter. Karl took the whole packet with him to the living room, where he forced the naked man to sit on one of the chairs. It wasn't an easy feat; the man was heavy and Karl still had a bad ankle. Finally, Mitch Petersen stayed in a sitting position, and Karl went to work. He tied Mitch's hands together, but he wasn't an idiot.

Mitch was freakishly strong, and he could easily break the single pair of zip ties. So, Karl put two more around his wrists. He tightened them as far as he could, not caring if he cut of the man's circulation to his hands. Those hands—the murder weapons—should be the first to go.

He then put the zip ties around Mitch's arms and around the back of the chair. Five zip ties around each arm, tightening them as far as he could. He did the same with the legs. He noticed long kitchen rags with an image of a rooster on the counter. He grabbed them all, and with them, he tied the monster's ankles to the chair legs. Tight. This way, he wouldn't be able to move around.

He finally shoved a dirty pair of socks into the man's mouth.

When he was finished, he stood back and watched his handiwork. He was satisfied. He had caught the monster.

Now what?

What would he do now? He now had the upper hand. He had the monster tied up and at his mercy, he was alone and whatever he did to the man... well, no one would know. Destiny and Fred were dead, as was the young girl that had killed Fred. It was just him and the monster who had stolen his daughter's life. Him and a man who deserved to get what he had given so many young girls.

Mitch Petersen deserved to have his penis sawed off with a blunt knife, his hands cut off with a blunt axe, to die a slow painful death, while a poisonous plant was shoved up his butthole, deep, to torment him from within. Or maybe a burning needle could be inserted into his penis? Karl had read something like that somewhere.

But if he did what his mind told him to do, what would *he* be? He would be no better than the monstrous man before him.

Then the question would arise: who was the monster and who was the man?

SCARS

CHAPTER **TWENTY-FOUR**

DEBORAH WAS APPREHENSIVE. The lake house door was open—something Karl had been very paranoid about ever since Naomi died—and everything was left as though he had made a very quick exit. Something was wrong. But what?

Was he hiding from her? She'd considered it, but after looking everywhere, even in the closet, she'd concluded that something had happened to him. She picked up the nearest thing just so that she had something to hold. It was a book. She clutched it close to her chest and closed her eyes.

What if something bad happened to him? Not Karl. Please, not Karl. I don't think I can survive without him. I don't... I can't go through it alone.

Deborah heard some commotion coming from the Williamses', but she decided it was none of her business. More than anything, she just didn't have the energy to deal with someone else's problems. Besides, she didn't want to make something out of nothing, and in all honesty, she had her own issues to deal with here.

Exhausted, she closed the door behind her. She locked it for good measure, and packed the groceries away. Finally, she settled down in front of the television. She would wait here for her husband.

Upon turning on the TV, a horrific news story awaited her.

"Authorities were notified of the Petersen's Clan's presence this morning by an anonymous caller. The Petersen Clan had been on the run for more than eight years. During these years, the family has committed multiple crimes, including home invasion, murder, and theft. The scene that follows contains graphic material and younger viewers should look away," a newscaster said, and the scene changed from a generic news broadcasting view to a camera outside a hospital.

Deborah held the remote control with both her hands as she watched the news.

"The Petersen Clan had been apprehended earlier today. Four of the family members had been on their way into the hospital, presumably due to the father Mr. Jerry Petersen's ailing health." A picture of an old man with a lot of wrinkles filled the screen.

"The occurrence turned into a bloodbath when one of the family members tried to escape. Miss Laura Petersen, 22, managed to escape police custody. Her father died of oxygen shortage soon after. One of the family members, Rommel 'Tiny' Petersen, was shot on sight as he tried to escape and fight back, and Paddy McCormick, another member of the clan, surrendered." Now there was footage of a man with a short, stringy beard and the ugliest mullet being led away in handcuffs. He struggled to walk and the officers were essentially carrying him.

"Miss Petersen is on the loose, and the public should consider her armed and dangerous."

At this point, Deborah turned the volume up.

"Furthermore, besides Laura Petersen, two more members of the Petersen clan are at large. Miss Joy Brooks—" A photo of a pretty blonde girl was shown on the screen. "—and Mitch Petersen."

Revulsion fueled Deborah as she saw the man who had ruined her life.

"Mitch Petersen is also wanted in a series of rape and murder cases, and any information on him will be appreciated. The toll-free number at the bottom of the screen can be called with any information relating to the Petersen Clan members who are still at large."

Deborah reached for her mobile phone to save the toll-free number, just in case. She had barely saved the number when her phone vibrated, nearly making her jump out of her skin. She recognized the number as the Williamses' landline.

"Hello?"

Why would her neighbors be calling her? Unless something had happened to Karl? Had... had Karl succumbed to the urges she had succumbed to? She'd had someone to bring her back to life, to help her get on her feet, and to feel better. Did her husband?

"Debbie?" Karl said, and Deborah was filled with relief.

He was alive, he was next-door, he was okay! He'd probably just forgotten to close the door. He was okay... Wasn't he? He had to be! He wasn't dead! That was all that mattered, and she felt a stray tear escape her eye as relief flooded her again.

"Deb, please," he sounded like he was on the verge of crying. "I... I need you." He sounded more than just like a crying man, but like a captured man.

Worry overtook the relief she'd felt just a few moments prior. "What is it?"

"Deb, I got him," he said. "I got the monster. I have Mitch Petersen."

"What do you mean you got him?" she asked, clutching the phone.

"I have him! He is tied up in front of me. Literally." His voice sounded shaky. "Please, get up here!"

"What? I don't understand." she asked. "And why are you calling me from the Williams'?"

She had no idea what was wrong with him, but she knew that he needed her help. And that was why she was here, wasn't she?

"We are at Fred and Destiny's house."

Deborah remained silent, not letting him know that she was next door.

Karl continued. "We... good God... Deborah, they attacked us! The Petersen's attacked us. Or... no, they attacked Fred and Destiny, and I just sort of stumbled on it. And the others left, and left us with Mitch and some other young girl. And... I have him, Deb."

He went on to tell her that they had been made to watch the people kiss in front of them, fight, use drugs, drink, burgle... And when he started to tell her about the torture of the Williams', Deborah had to ask him to stop.

As Karl kept talking, she was looking through the window towards the neighbors'. Unfortunately, but she couldn't see much. She didn't know if any of it was true. She had no way of knowing. It could be true. But it could also be false. Karl might have had a nervous breakdown and imagined it all. He might have done something awful too. What if he had been the one to attack their neighbors? Was that what all the commotion was about?

"I am on my way," she said and hung up.

SCARS

CHAPTER **TWENTY-FIVE**

KARL SET THE LANDLINE DOWN, ending the call with his wife. She wouldn't be here for a few hours. Or so he thought. He looked at the man before him, still very unconscious, his head lolling to the side.

The doctor made his way to the kitchen, opened the Williamses' fridge, and grabbed the coldest thing that he could find, a carton of vanilla flavored soymilk. He drank deeply, relishing the amazing feeling of the milk soothing his aching and drying throat. Karl decided that this beverage was his new favorite thing to drink and was disappointed when he found out that he had downed the entire purple carton. He put the empty carton on the table, and something caught his eye.

A wallet. A brown leather, probably faux-leather, wallet, with thick wads of cash sticking out of it. The money wasn't what called Karl's attention, however, it was the fact that this wallet... it just called to him. He picked it up and flipped it open. Mitch Petersen's ID smiled up at him, and Karl cursed at the smug smile that the man wore in the photo. It was an expired driver's license from West Virginia.

He didn't know what made him do it. Curiosity, probably, but started to flip through the wallet. He put the cash on the table, and thought that the wallet was still too thick. He investigated some more, and finally pulled out the ID card. With it came a dozen or so pictures. School pictures that the monster could have easily found online.

Karl went through all of them. Sherry, Hannah, Joanne... Sophie. And, finally, the beautiful girl that was his daughter. That was Naomi. She was smiling serenely at the photograph, her eyes showing happiness.

Karl collapsed into the closest chair. And he lost it. He sobbed like he had never sobbed before, anguished sobs echoing through the house. Tears he hadn't shed when Naomi first died, pain he hadn't expressed, now came to the fore. And with it, came the grief of his friends, Fred and Destiny, who had treated him like a son.

All the variations of questions starting with the word *why* ran through his head. Why them? Why did their daughter have to suffer? Why had he chosen their house? Why had they chosen *this* house? Why had God allowed this to happen? Why did God punish *them*? What had they done that had been so utterly terrible that God felt it necessary to take their child from them?

"Yo, fuckboy!" the voice called from the living room.

Karl sobered. *So, the monster awakens.* Karl walked to Mitch and stood in the doorway, leaning his right shoulder against the frame. The surgeon glared at the other man, hatred evident. Karl Munson didn't know how frightening he looked. His face was swollen, his lip was bloody, he was covered in dirt and grime, and blue bruised had started to appear all over his neck and arms.

"What?" Karl barked at Mitch, but before Mitch could answer, Karl was on top of him.

His clenched fist met the larger man's jaw.

"You monster!" And Karl was sobbing again, both of his fists now raining down, hitting Mitch in the face.

Blood came out, but Karl didn't stop. His own fists had started to bleed, but there was no stopping. Nothing but hatred and pain filled the room. Karl experienced the deepest hatred he had ever felt for this man who had destroyed his life, who had taken his baby girl from him, and who was the reason why his marriage was in shambles. He saw that Mitch was swollen beneath his punches, but he didn't stop. He didn't even stop when he heard a crack in his own hand.

He stopped when he heard Deborah's voice.

"Karl?" she called, worry evident in her voice.

That was fast... Too fast!

How did she get here in just a couple of minutes?

"I'm in the living room," he called back confused, and he heard her light footsteps running to him.

She saw him first. She was shocked at his appearance, bloodied and bruised, but she didn't ponder on it for too long. But her attention was quickly drawn to the naked man tied to a wooden chair.

"You monster!" Deborah screeched launching at him with a hammer in hand.

Karl slapped his hands over his ears at the sound his wife made.

She launched herself at the monster, but she couldn't do more than spit on him before Karl's arms closed around her waist and taking the hammer from her hand with the other.

"Who are you people?" Mitch managed to grunt.

"He doesn't know who we are, Deb," Karl said, suddenly calm. He kept ahold of his wife, more for his own sanity than for hers. "How did you get here so quickly?"

"I had just gotten next door when you called."

Karl smiled, and hugged his wife one more time, dropping the hammer on the floor.

After a few moments, he then turned to his hostage. "You know, Petersen, let me tell you a story," he started, and he felt his wife start to shudder as she cried. "There was this girl, Naomi. She was beautiful, you know? Sixteen years old, and she was this champion swimmer. She could hold her breath for a minute and a half, and she loved to swim. Even outside of the championships, she loved to swim. She loved to play volleyball. And she was good at it too." He had to bite back the sobs. He felt warm tears mix with the blood and grime on his face, but there was nothing he could do about that. "Naomi was really smart. She had straight As, and she liked it when her dad helped her to study. She thought her dad was the smartest man in the world! And she was a blessing sent to him. She was his and her mother's little miracle. She was so caring, and she loved to help others. A selfless soul. Loving and lovable. Her father was just very happy about her."

Karl looked at his wife and took a pause. "And so was her mother," he continued. "That girl, Naomi, was a treasure to the mother and father. A blessing. A gift. You see, the couple had not been able to conceive a child for *years*. They had to look at professional insemination, and then, their girl was born."

SCARS

CHAPTER **TWENTY-SIX**

MITCH WATCHED THE COUPLE before him, confused. He could barely see them, but he knew that it was the fuckboy that stood in front of him. Why the hell was he telling him this? He didn't care. He didn't give a shit about any of this! Why should he? It wasn't his story. It had nothing to do with him!

He could understand why fuckboy had beaten the shit out of him, drugged him, and tied him to a chair. He knew that he wanted to get even. Shoot, they would've done the same, if not worse. But why in the world was this on the table?

"And then, when the girl was getting close to her seventeenth year," the man in front of him went on, "someone broke into our house. He had stalked our house for months, apparently. He knew our schedule. He knew that we would be at a party and that our daughter would be home alone. Only, she wasn't alone; she was with a friend."

Mitch had noticed the changed in pronouns. "The", "She", "her"—they had all changed to "Our". He looked at the couple again.

"That monster took my daughter—our daughter—from us. And you know what?" Fuckboy paused. "That *monster* was you."

Wait.

The rich folks in Pasadena. The one where he got Joy her favorite necklace—the golden one with some sort of cat on it. The freaking disgusting rich people who had too much and showed it off? Who thought that money could save their sorry souls and fix everything?

Now... now they had caught him. Mitch felt his heart rate go up to a mile a second, because he had never been caught before. He had never been stopped. He had done it all. No one ever caught him. He had raped about twenty girls in his life, murdered more than half of them. And now he was caught. His dick was hanging out for them to see, and he suddenly feared for his life. He was afraid for his dick. He had lost his girlfriend already; he couldn't lose his cock too!

He must have known, must have predicted, that at one point in his life, he would have been caught. He'd liked to think that he was invincible, that he was untouchable, that he was a god! But now, Mitch was faced with his own mortality, his little life in the hands of two people who felt he had wronged them.

For him it was just a good fuck. The young ones had such little tight pussies, and they got even tighter when he strangled them. Joy's pussy hadn't even been that tight anymore.

"Your father is dead," the woman said.

He liked her voice. She sounded like she'd been crying. He liked that. But he didn't like the message her voice gave him.

"They apprehended your family at the hospital. Your sister fled like a coward and left your father to die."

His eyes went wide. He knew his sister was a pussy, but he didn't think that she would just abandon them!

"Your brother is dead too," the woman went on. "Rommel 'Tiny' Petersen? They shot him as he tried to run away. Isn't it funny that his name was Tiny? He wasn't a small man in the least."

"He didn't have a lot of brains," Fuckboy supplied and, while Mitch knew it was true, he screamed into his gag.

"They got this guy called Paddy," the woman went on. "Paddy McCormick. He told them everything."

"Wait, what?" Fuckboy said. "How do you know all this?"

"It was on the news," the wife said. "But they said that Mitch was still missing. And his girlfriend."

"The girlfriend is dead," Fuckboy said almost coldly. "We fought, she fell. She died."

"And no cops have shown up here?" she asked, and Mitch saw a devious glint in her eyes.

Fuckboy shook his head.

"Oh... well, isn't this fun?" She looked at Mitch, gently disentangled herself from her husband's grip, and strode over to him. "Well, well, well. Looks like Mitch is having trouble with his luck." She looked at his cock and laughed. "I get why nobody wanted to *do* you with that thing. It looks like a diseased cucumber."

"I think more like a rotten pickle," her husband supplied, now standing next to her.

Then Fuckboy looked him in the eye. "I could do it, you know." He held up Mitch's own engraved knife and held it next to his penis. "This knife is sharp, and your thing would be cut off in a minute. No. In a second. But there's no fun in that."

Mitch gulped. There was absolutely *nothing* he could do. He couldn't scream, he couldn't fight back. He had tried, but the zip ties were wound too tightly around his body. His legs were wide open, his balls open for them both to see, and his butt was easily accessible. It was a nightmare! They were probably serious. How the hell was he supposed to get out of this?

Would this be how he went? He had never imagined himself being on the other side of torture.

"We could cut his penis off," the wife said, "and feed it to him."

No!

The couple looked at each other and grinned maliciously.

"Or we could shove a wine bottle up his ass."

No!

"Do you think he'll be able to handle it?"

"Or we could just slit his throat," said the man quietly, pensive. "Send him to hell where he belongs."

He looked at Mitch with a hard stare and Mitch gulped again. He didn't want to die. HE DIDN'T WANT TO DIE! He was sorry!

No, he wasn't.

Not really.

Mitch didn't know what it was like to feel sorry. He didn't know anything but lust and anger. Lust for tight young bodies that refused him, and anger at the world. He didn't know why he was so angry all the time, but he had learned to live with it.

"But we aren't monsters... Are we?" The man was having second thoughts.

It was fun to imagine torturing the man who took away their pride and joy. What would Naomi have wanted? Would she want them to take their revenge before calling the police? Would they even bother calling the police? The whole family was basically dead. It would be easy for the police to find the teenaged girl and send her away for life. They could pretend it was self-defense, that they had no other choice but to hack him to bits.

The couple looked at each other and smiled kindly. For a moment, their connection was reborn. They were lost in their own world.

"No. We wouldn't be able to live with ourselves if we did all of that," the woman said, as they both backed off. "We aren't this, Karl. This... is not who we are."

"But..." He struggled over his words before looking at Mitch again. "What he did to Naomi..."

"Is unforgivable," the wife said and reached out to take the man—Karl's—hand. "But... honey, this is not who we are. We are not monsters. *We* do not kill."

"Just this once? No one will know."

"*We* will know. *God* will know." There was a moment of silence before the woman continued. "Think about our daughter." Her voice was now so soft and tender that even Mitch would have melted. "Is this what Naomi would have wanted?"

"It is what *I* want!" Fuckboy shouted as he launched himself at Mitch again.

Mitch felt the fists hit his already hurting nose and jaw. He didn't think he could handle it anymore. He would soon pass out from the pain.

"I want him to suffer too," the wife said behind her husband, her voice very calm. "But this? It's not okay. Karl, this isn't helping. It isn't healthy. Don't you think the others deserve justice too?"

"This *is* justice!" Karl screamed, and Deborah pulled him off Mitch.

She shot Mitch a death glare, but turned to her husband, holding onto his arms. She clung to him tightly, because her fingers started to turn white.

"This is revenge. And this... this isn't you. Don't let this monster change you."

"Who is the monster and who is the man?" Karl mumbled, collapsing into his wife's arms.

She held him. She cradled his head to her bosom and made little *shhh* noises to placate him. He wept harder, sobbing his heart out, and she just held him.

Mitch was dumbstruck. Joy had never held him like that. She had never, she'd just bent over and put her ass in the air for him to fuck. She hadn't lain next to him or made him feel better. Never. Ever. She'd never asked why he was so angry or how he felt.

Mitch felt something else. He wanted what these two people in front of him had. He was angry that he didn't have it.

"What *would* Naomi do?" Karl asked his wife, lifting his head, after what felt like an eternity for Mitch.

An eternity where new *things* wrestled in his chest. Jealousy. Fear…

The woman held out an arm, and Mitch saw an old, worn-out black bracelet on it. The ones he saw the kids make at survival camps and church camps. The white letters *WWJD* on it.

Great. These people were Jesus freaks. Well, for once, Jesus freaks might be a good thing for him. Mitch didn't believe in anything; he just knew what his body wanted and he went to get it. He'd met a bunch of Jesus freaks in his life, and he didn't like them. They were always telling people to have hope, to believe that God had a plan for them and whatever else. They were dumb, blind sheep.

"We're not bad people," Karl said, looking at Mitch. "We are not… you."

"Naomi would have…" The wife swallowed, as though the thought and the words physically pained her. "Naomi would have forgiven him."

The man smiled, though it didn't dry his eyes. "Yes, she would."

"And so shall I." The wife said while taking her hands off her husband's arms and striding over to Mitch.

He looked at her as best he could, but the closer she came, the blurrier she got.

"I forgive you, Mitch Petersen."

He felt something. He didn't know what, but he felt *something*. It was light in his chest. It was an alien feeling to him.

"I forgive you," Karl said, surprising Mitch, because suddenly Karl was at his right side. "I forgive you. And—" But whatever he wanted to say was cut off, and he turned and ran to the kitchen.

Mitch, for some reason, felt elated. He felt stronger, he felt like he'd just smoked some of that high-quality weed Joy always gave him.

The wife didn't look angry anymore. She looked as though she felt pity, as if she was sorry for him. Mitch didn't understand why she felt sorry for him, or why they forgave him, or why they were so obsessed with what their daughter would do.

When Karl was in the kitchen, Debbie looked at Mitch and smiled. "We've waited a long time for this moment. To face the man who ruined our lives and took away everything that was good. Not a lot of parents get to face the monsters that destroyed them. We are blessed to be standing in the room with you. We have all the power now. For a moment, God is giving us the power to make a choice. We could either kill you, and know that you'll never hurt another woman again, or we could turn you over to the authorities."

Mitch rolled her eyes. He couldn't believe the bullshit she was spewing.

Debbie went to the kitchen to be with Karl; he had just gotten off the phone.

"How did you get here so fast?" Karl asked.

"I was already here," she said, a tear rolling down her cheek. "When you were away, I did a lot of soul searching. I reconnected with the Wallers and they helped me realize that this marriage is worth fighting for. We deserve a good life, Karl. I want our life back. I love you. We need to be together."

"I love you too," he said and pulled her in for a kiss.

"I'm so sorry that I didn't get here sooner. Maybe then none of this would have happened…"

Karl placed his finger over her lips. "Don't do that. Don't blame yourself. The only person to blame is the monster in the living room. You hear me? Him and his family are awful people who do awful things to good people who are more successful than them. None of this is your fault, okay? We're together now, and that's all that matters. The past is behind us."

"Okay." Debbie smiled. "But before we move forward, there's something I have to tell you. We really do need to talk."

"Let's not focus on that right now. We should wait for the police. I got hold of Detectives Park and Ramirez. They'll be here as soon as they can. The local sheriff is on his way too.

He should be here soon. They told me we must stay put and keep an eye on him. Do you think we can handle that?"

Debbie nodded, and they both returned to the living room.

Karl touched Mitch's shoulder. "I called the police. They're on their way."

Deborah touched his other shoulder. "We'll pray for you."

What would praying help?

These people were crazy.

※

As Mitch remained captured by the Munson's, Laura was trapped by something too. Her own guilt. She ran as fast as she could away from her family. She stopped by the side of the lake, no people or animals in sight. Laura was completely alone. She sat on a rock, trying to catch her breath and to stop shaking. She buried her face in her hands and cried.

"What did I do to deserve this life, Mamma? Why did you have to leave me?" She thought back to all the pain and suffering she was responsible for.

She remembered how desperate she was to have a loving father when she'd first joined the family. She did everything for him and at what cost? Laura was now alone, with no family and no boyfriend. Even if they were alive, they surely wouldn't forgive her and take her back. She had nothing. She had to live in the wilderness for the rest of her life.

"I don't know how to take care of myself," she whined to the wind. "I can't do this alone, Mamma. Why won't you come back? Can't you come home?"

She listened to the owls' hoots and the soft crash of the rippling water hitting the shore.

"Who am I kidding? I don't deserve a good life. I was destined to live a life of crime and heartache. I want to come see you, Mamma. Would that be okay? Do you think you would like that?"

Laura stripped down to her underwear and walked towards the water. She dipped her toe in and shivered from the cold.

"I'll come find you. We'll be together forever."

Laura walked through the shallow water and walked until she couldn't keep her head above water anymore. She let out a deep breath and sunk beneath the small waves. She let herself go and drifted to the bottom of the lake.

CHAPTER **TWENTY-SEVEN**

K ARL FELT LIGHTER THAN HE HAD FELT IN AGES. In over a year and a half, to be precise. Ever since his daughter had been taken from him. He felt as though a weight had been lifted from his shoulders, and he knew it was because he'd let go of the anger and hatred he'd held in his heart for so long.

He'd gone to the kitchen to call the police, and Deborah had given her cell phone to him. It was a toll-free number.

"This way, we'll get quicker results." She shrugged, and he took her phone. "It's a hotline for him. It was under the news report where they said his family was killed."

"This is the Petersen hotline. How may I help you?" a male voice said, obviously bored.

He was probably someone in his early twenties who didn't think the call would amount to anything.

Well... Karl thought sardonically. *Surprise!*

"I have Mitch Petersen. I have him tied up in a house."

He heard what appeared to be the man on the other end falling off his chair and scrambling back up to get the receiver. "Can you repeat that?"

"I have Mitch Petersen. My wife saw this number just beneath a news report earlier," he said in a monotone voice. "Listen, please just hurry."

"Are you serious?" the young man on the line asked. "Describe him to me."

Karl heard the young man calling someone, probably his supervisor, to hear their conversation. As Detectives Park and Ramirez had told him before, they had most likely had several calls that had led nowhere.

"Tall, muscled, dirty blonde. Um... I don't know...?" He didn't know what else to say, but he described him as best he could. "Look, he was here with a girl and she's dead now. So, send the authorities and an ambulance to this address, and hurry."

He heard the detectives' voices in the background asking if it was Karl. Karl shouted that it was him and he rejoiced when the detectives said they would come out there personally. He gave the man the address and his name and then hung up. Karl finally put the revolver down; he had been carrying it without realizing it. Curiously, he opened it.

There was no ammunition in it. He would have shot blanks. And that was good, he thought. He wasn't a killer, and he didn't want to be a killer. He was just a man. That was all.

It wasn't long after he hung up that the local police showed up at the Williams house. The sheriff, only made known by the presence of his shiny badge, took one look at Karl and raised his gun. Karl wondered how bad he looked if his appearance caused so much alarm in the other man. An ambulance's sirens reached Karl's ears, and several more police cars stopped outside the Williams residence.

"I am unarmed," Karl said, putting his hands defensively in the air. "My name is Karl Munson. I called the hotline. Petersen is inside, sir."

The sheriff lowered his gun and offered Karl his hand. "Sheriff Stone."

Karl shook it, and then realized his hand was sore. He looked at it closer when he withdrew it and saw that it was blue and badly swollen. It was broken.

He sighed and motioned for the sheriff to follow him inside the house.

"Good Lord!" said the sheriff. "What happened here?" He had seen the chaos in the kitchen.

"The Petersen's were having a party," Karl said easily. "Except for the purple empty carton of soymilk. That was me."

"You mean the whole family was here?" Stone asked, shock evident on his face.

Two deputies followed him and looked around the estate.

"We got a call from a woman earlier, saying the Petersen's were on their way to the hospital here. She was cut off before she could tell us more, though. We sent some troops to the hospital, just in case. These folks are dangerous, you know." He shrugged. "But a couple of the security guards spot them before we got there anyway."

Destiny, Karl knew. She had called the authorities to stop them Petersen's. Clever lady.

"Yeah, they were. The old man kept talking about how proud he was of leading his children into a life of crime. The big one was sort of an idiot, and the girl... Well, she just disgusted me."

"Wait..." The sheriff put a hand on his arm. "Start at the beginning."

"I will," Karl said simply. "But first, you have to get him out of here."

They had arrived in the living room, where Mitch was sitting, still tied up. The sheriff motioned for the deputies to arrest him, and they snipped the zip-ties off first before they slapped a pair of glinting stainless steel handcuffs on his wrists. One deputy read him his rights as they led him outside. They had conveniently forgotten to take out the gag.

"My wife will be back shortly. She just went to get me some clean clothes," Karl explained, although he realized, too late, that the sheriff would never have known about his wife's presence if he had kept his mouth shut. "There are three dead bodies here," Karl went on. "I think you better get those out of here too."

"Three?" Sheriff Stone repeated, shocked.

"Yeah. His girlfriend tried to attack me, but she went over the deck into the lake. Smashed her head open." Karl looked white as he said this, the nausea obvious at the memory. "One is in the master bedroom, and the other one is in the hallway. Fred and Destiny Williams."

"How come you're here?" Stone asked, a notepad in his hands, scribbling away furiously.

"I live over there," the surgeon said, pointing to his house. Its lights were visible across the clearing. "I thought I heard something and came over. Found my neighbors bound and gagged, with their toes and fingers being cut off."

"Oh," was all the sheriff could say.

"I should mention..." Karl said, just as Deb returned. "Mitch Petersen raped and murdered my daughter over a year ago." He took the clothes from his wife with one hand and thanked her. "I—"

"I would have killed him," Sheriff Stone said bluntly, interrupting him. "This son of a bitch doesn't deserve to live. I would have killed him and cut of his dick off for good measure before I killed him. You folks are better than I am, that's for sure. I would have even covered for you guys, ya know? I would've understood. If you'd killed him before we got here, I would've given you a high five. He's an animal, and… well, I'm not that strong. But I need ya'll to come down to the station to make a statement."

"Oh, no," Deborah said. "First, my husband is going to be checked out by a medic, and *then* we'll tell you everything."

CHAPTER **TWENTY-EIGHT**

AFTER EVERYTHING WENT WELL at the hospital and with the police officers, Debbie and Karl were allowed to go back to their lake house. They slept on the living room couch until late the next morning. Debbie was the first to wake up. Karl had his arms around her, and they were both enveloped in a blanket. She tried to stand up without waking him, but he started yawning and stretched out his arms.

"Good morning," Debbie said cheerfully, and for the first time in a long time, she actually meant to say good.

"Hello, my love," he replied and kissed her cheek. "I can't believe how fast we fell asleep.

"I can! You had the most exhausting and terrifying night of your life." Debbie hugged him and stood up to go to the bathroom.

"Wait," Karl said and pulled her back down. "Don't leave just yet. We should talk. You said you had something to talk to me about, and it seemed very important."

"Let's not worry about that, dear," Debbie said, and laughed nervously.

She took care of her needs and came back to his side on the couch. She knew exactly what she wanted to say to him, but suddenly she found herself at a loss for words. She was afraid, scared that he might judge her for her actions.

"You can't fool me, Deb," Karl chuckled. "It's not like we recently got married. I know something's up."

Debbie turned to him and grabbed his hands. Tears formed in her eyes and the smirk on Karl's face turned into a frown. "I did something. Something bad."

"It couldn't be any worse than what we thought about doing to Mitch." Karl tried to laugh, but no smile broke out on Debbie's face like he'd wanted. "Okay, you're scaring me now."

"When you were gone..." she began. "I was very low. More than low. Lower than rock bottom. I was alone. Depressed. Lonely. I pushed every single person out of my life, and the one person I needed had abandoned me."

"I didn't abandon you..."

"Please, let me finish, babe." Debbie plucked a tissue from the box on the coffee table and blew her nose.

Karl went to get her a glass of water. When he returned, tears poured down her face. She cried harder than when she was mourning Naomi. This time, he didn't want to run away from her tears. She was expressing exactly what he'd felt the night before. He put the water on the table and rushed to hug her. He rocked her back and forth and spoke to her in a soothing tone. "It's okay, Debbie. Just talk to me when you're ready. Don't push yourself."

Debbie rested her head on his chest and stared into nothingness. If she had to look right at him when she spoke she feared she would break down again. "One night, I just wanted the pain to go away. I wanted to pause my life and forget about everything that happened. I needed to sleep. I don't remember the last time that I slept well. I had no other option. I was drunk and stupid, and I don't know what came over me. I'm so sorry, Karl! I'm sorry!"

She broke down crying again and Karl held her closer.

"It's okay, you're safe here. Whatever you did, you can tell me." He had his suspicions about what she had to say, but he didn't want to jump to any conclusions.

"I was in our room, thinking about Naomi. I tried to pray, but I'm not totally sure what I said. I took pills. As many as I could to go to sleep. I didn't want to hurt myself. That wasn't the intention. I'm so sorry, Karl."

Karl started crying too. His hands shook, and he couldn't control his whimpering. "I'm sorry, Debbie. I should have been there for you. I should have known what you were going through. Please forgive me. We agreed to separate. I thought time apart would be good for us."

Debbie covered Karl's mouth. "Don't do that. No more excuses and nor more blame. The past is over, and I'm okay. Diana and Tanner let me stay with them for a while. They helped me realize that we needed to save this marriage. I found my faith again, and I feel like a whole new woman."

"You're the same woman that I've always known and loved. Nothing has changed between us. Not really. We're a little stronger than before now. But our love never died." Karl kissed her forehead and hugged her. "I'm sorry I wasn't there for you, but things will be different now. I'm never letting you out of my sight!"

"What about when I go to work?"

"I'll set up surveillance cameras throughout the office. I'll put my own personal cameras all over town, so I can track every step. I'll watch you from my phone and I'll set up alerts for when you might be in danger."

"That's a little overboard." Debbie chuckled and kissed Karl.

"You're worth it, baby."

The two of them laughed and then jumped when someone knocked on their door.

"Could that be the officers again?" Debbie asked.

"I don't know, but I doubt it," he replied in clear confusion, and got up to get the door. "They said they'd leave us be for a few days."

Karl smiled when he opened the door and saw Detectives Park and Ramirez.

"Hello, Dr. Munson," Detective Ramirez said with a smile. "We hope we're not interrupting. We just wanted to come and check on you and see how you're doing."

"We planned to come by last night, but we had to stop by the Wallers first. Then it got late," Park explained. "We told them what we knew of what happened up here and assured them that Mitch Petersen would be behind bars for good. Mrs. Waller was so happy that she made us cupcakes. In the middle of the night! What a lady."

"Yes, she is quite the woman," Karl said and invited them inside. "Debbie, the detectives are here."

Debbie put on a bathrobe and rushed into the kitchen to greet their guests. She made coffee and the four of them sat around the kitchen table. Karl made everyone pancakes for breakfast. Karl didn't realize how hungry he was and had to make more portions than usual. They ate and chatted, celebrating the arrest of Mitch Petersen, the monster.

"So..." Debbie said, and wrapped her hands around her warm mug. "Do we get to become honorary detectives or something for catching Mitch? Well, Karl caught him, but I helped in a small way."

"We'll be forever grateful to you and your husband. You've been through so much, and we're glad it's over now," Park said.

Ramirez nodded in agreement. "You didn't deserve the life you got. Life dealt you quite the hand, and we're so thrilled you managed to stay together. We see so many couples split up over lost children. It just breaks my heart."

"It wasn't easy in the least," Karl said, "but we're stronger now after all that hardship."

"If you two ever need anything, like counselor references or even just a friend to talk to, don't be afraid to reach out to us." Ramirez handed a business card with her personal cellphone number on it to Karl. "I meant it. Day or night, we're here to help you move past this."

"I'm pretty sure I already have your numbers, but I'll keep it just in case," Karl said and put it in his wallet. "I was planning on taking Deb out on the boat today. And seeing as you're out here, would you care to join us?"

"No, thank you," Park said. "I've got to get home to see my wife and kids."

"I just got engaged, so I have a lot going on as well," Ramirez added.

"It's amazing how much can happen in a couple years. Congratulations!" Debbie said. "Life keeps moving and everyone has new adventures around every corner."

"I'm confident that your life will get better," Park said as he put on his coat. "It may not seem like it now, but it'll get easier. You'll never forget Naomi, but you'll be able to figure out how to live without her and honor her memory. I'm not very religious, but I respect those who live their life by a certain faith. I hope you two are still holding onto that, because it can be comforting to think that you may be able to see her again in another life."

"We will see her again, I know for sure," Debbie said, and walked the detectives to the door. "When we do, we'll be sure to tell her about the great people who helped catch the man who killed her."

"Thank you, Mrs. Munson," Ramirez said. "Blessings to you, and thank you so much for breakfast."

"It was our pleasure."

Karl and Debbie stood at the door, feeling the cool morning breeze on their skin.

"I hope they get home safe," Karl said. "We don't need any more tragedy in our lives."

"I didn't think you wanted to go sailing today," Debbie said when they went back into the house. "I thought we were doing that at the end of the week?"

"Why wait? It's a beautiful day!"

It was in the will of Destiny and Fred Williams that they were to be cremated and thrown into the lake together. Usually these things took days, but the police officers wanted to put their bodies to rest as soon as they could. They gave half of the ashes to the Williams's children, and kept the other half for the water. It was comforting to know they would always be watching over the Munson's, no matter where they went.

After the Munson's went sailing, they spent another week at the lake house before going home. The Williams house was still a crime scene, but most of it had been cleaned up by then. Karl wanted to go over there before they left, but thought it'd be too difficult.

The Munson's slowly packed their things into Karl's car. Debbie decided to leave hers up at the lake house in case they ever came back. She thought about buying the Williams property when it went on the market but didn't want to live with so many memories of the past. She was surrounded by the past and needed to find a way to move forward.

They stopped for a late lunch at a diner just outside the city. Debbie and Karl sat across from each other in their booth. They couldn't stop looking at each other or holding hands. The waitress thought they were newlyweds, so they went along with it. They pretended they were coming back from their honeymoon in Mexico. The entire wait staff loved them.

"Hey, Karl?" Debbie asked near the end of their meal. "Do you think we could stop somewhere else before we get home?"

"We can do whatever you want, love. The only thing I want right now is to pamper and love you until you can't take it anymore." Karl kissed the back of her hand and she blushed.

"Well, I don't know about you, but I haven't been to Naomi's grave since the funeral. I was thinking we could buy her some flowers on the way there too. I know that she loved daisies, but roses seem to be a more powerful way to express love. Plus, it'll be like on *The Bachelor* when they give out roses. We loved that show, remember?" Debbie stopped talking when she saw the solemn look on Karl's face. "I'm sorry. It was a stupid idea."

"No, no!" Karl smiled and stood up to shuffle into Debbie's side of the booth. "I was just trying to remember the last time that I went to her grave. I don't think I've gone since the funeral either. This will be a great way to end our trip. Honestly, I miss home. I need to get back into my own bed, and maybe start working again."

"Yeah, you freeloader!" Debbie teased. "Get a job, bum."

The couple started kissing like when they were younger. The waitress whistled at them and they stopped, embarrassed.

"Let's pick that up when we get home," Karl whispered and helped Debbie put on her coat.

When they arrived at the graveyard, they sat in the car in the parking lot.

"I thought this would be a lot easier. She's our daughter," Debbie confessed. "We should be excited, shouldn't we?"

"I've been away from home for so long, it feels strange to be back," Karl said. "It's like I'm walking into an old childhood home. It feels like I've been away for ages and it's different, but familiar, you know?"

"I know what you mean," Debbie said. "For the longest time, I felt like I was having an out of body experience, just watching my own life like a movie. When God spoke to me, it was like he also gave me back my soul. I was reborn. I was whole again."

"I think I need to go back to church. Maybe we should do that first? It might be an easier step."

Debbie got out of the car and walked over to Karl's side. She pulled him out and locked the car.

"If we don't do this now, I don't think we ever will. Not anytime soon, anyway. Are you with me?" She held out her hand for him to take. "You and me, baby. We have to stick together, right?"

Karl nodded and slapped his hand onto hers. He held it firmly and dragged her up the walkway. "We're coming Naomi! The parents are coming!"

Debbie laughed, and that was music to his ears. "Naomi is rolling around in her grave trying to slap you for all your horrible dad jokes."

"What other kind of jokes would I make?"

Karl and Debbie strolled through the graveyard until they reached Naomi's headstone. They stopped dead in their tracks a foot away from it.

"There it is," Debbie whispered. "That's what's left of our little girl. She's sleeping now."

She crept forward and placed the bouquet of roses near the grave. She knelt beside them and looked back at Karl.

"Could I please have a minute alone with her?"

Karl nodded and stepped back to lean against the tree. While Debbie talked to her daughter, telling her all about Mitch's capture and everything she's missed on TV, Karl did something he hadn't done in a while.

"Thank you, God," he whispered. "Thank You for protecting my wife when she needed me and I wasn't there. I'm so sorry for giving up on You, but at the time I thought You'd given up on me. I now know this wasn't the case. Thank You for not giving up on me. I'm going to go back to church and be the giver I used to be. You've blessed me in so many other ways that I want to be a blessing to others. Please help us get home safely and live a boring life for a while. In Jesus's name, amen."

Debbie walked towards Karl and hugged him. "Do you need a minute with her too?"

"Yes, that would be great. Could I meet you back at the car?"

"Of course," Debbie said and kissed his left cheek.

Karl stepped forward and wiped the tears from his eyes. "Hey, baby. Daddy, here. I miss you. Can you believe it? Can you believe we finally caught the man who did this to us? I wanted to kill him when I saw him. I wanted to rip him limb from limb until all my energy was drained. But, as much as I wanted to hurt him, and make him feel the same pain you did, I didn't want to stoop to his level. If your mother hadn't shown up, I probably would have been that monster. You've always looked up to me, and I couldn't be the one to let you down."

Karl sat down next to the stone and brushed away some dry leaves from it as he continued. "Honestly, I think I can help him. I think that with enough hope and prayer, Mitch can become a better man. I don't know if that's something you want to hear, but everyone deserves a second chance. No matter how much suffering someone's caused, there's always an equal amount they suffered to make them that way. Your mother and I have forgiven him. He's paying for his crimes in a just and fair way, I promise you that. He won't hurt another soul for as long as he lives. But I truly believe that I can help him change. Maybe I can help him become the man that he's supposed to be. I'm not just doing it for you, but all the women that he's hurt."

Karl shifted his weight and took a deep breath before continuing with a broken voice.

"Baby, he took away your future, and in return I'm going to change his. It sounds strange when I say it aloud, but it's the right thing to do. Who am I to play God and decide what happens to others? I'll try to come visit you again, but I don't know how easy it will be. I hope the pain dulls, but there will always be a hole in my heart. Goodbye, baby girl. No one will ever be able to replace you. You're the light of my life, and I promise I will take care of your mother. I too, will become a better man. And I hope... no, I know, that someday soon, I will see you again on that glorious day. That won't happen for a while, but I sure can't wait for the day when I can see your smiling face again. I love you."

Karl got up, shoved his hands into his coat pockets, and turned away.

They drove back to their house and had a lazy evening.

The next day, they decided to start cleaning. They scrubbed every inch of the house until it was spotless. They threw out garbage, wine bottles, and anything else they didn't need. Then they went through Naomi's things. Most of her clothes they kept, because they held precious memories, but they found enough to put together a donation package for the church. They weren't trying to forget about Naomi, but they knew they had to move forward and start a fresh life.

When they finished cleaning, it was past dinnertime. Both their stomachs grumbled. Before they could even begin to discuss what to eat, someone started banging on their door. They rushed to see who it was.

"Karl!" Diana screamed and rushed into the house with Tanner trailing behind.

Diana hugged Debbie. "I heard all about what happened. I'm so glad that you're both okay."

Diana hugged Karl so Tanner could hug Debbie. Diana stepped back and gently punched Karl on the shoulder.

"Why did you leave us? It scared us to death." She hugged him again and laughed. "We missed you so much!"

"I'm not sure what to say here, Diana." Karl laughed and went to shake Tanner's hand. "Are you happy or angry?"

"Well, I promised Debbie I'd slap you when I saw you again, but I could never stay mad at you!"

Karl looked at Debbie with his eyebrows raised. "You asked her to do that?"

"No!" Debbie squealed and playfully shoved Diana. "She's just being an overprotective friend. We'd love for you guys to stay and chat, but we have to figure out what to do for dinner. I just realized there is next to no food in this house."

"No problem," Tanner said. "We were just in the middle of making dinner ourselves when we decided to come over here. Care to join us? Diana's making her famous casserole."

"You sure know how to convince me!" Debbie said and grabbed her house keys. "Let's head on out, Karl."

When they got to the Wallers' house, much of Debbie's things were still strewn about. She looked around, embarrassed, and started cleaning up.

"Don't do that," Diana said and ushered everyone into the kitchen. "Take some time to relax and enjoy the sweet aroma of my cooking."

The Munson's and Tanner sat at the kitchen table while Diana cooked. She was the best cook out of all of them and frankly the only one who actually enjoyed it. The two couples spent the evening talking and laughing, free of alcohol, for Debbie's sake. Free of pain. Free from their haunting past.

It felt like old times. Almost as though nothing had changed in the time they'd been apart.

SCARS

CHAPTER **TWENTY-NINE**

A YEAR HAD GONE SINCE Mitch Petersen had been arrested. There had been a short trial—very short—due to the overwhelming evidence and witnesses. He had wanted to defend himself too. His semen matched those found at the crime scene. He pleaded guilty on ten counts of sexual assault, on twelve counts of murder, and four of attempted murder. His wallet was given as evidence to the authorities, and the video footage of him entering and exiting the various places was more than enough to convict him for several lifetimes without the possibility of parole.

His life was over.

Karl decided to pay Mitch a visit; he had a couple of things to say to him. At some point he had asked his pastor to visit Mitch in prison to pray with him and perhaps give him Bible studies, and the pastor had tried to do so, mostly as a favor to the Munson's. But it was to no avail. Mitch was not interested and even laughed at the suggestion. In fact, he was offended.

Honestly, though, the pastor had just been happy that Karl was talking to him again and fervently attending church again.

"You certainly seem different now," the pastor had commented, "but yes, I will do this. I'm glad you decided to take the higher road, Karl. You would have been in a much darker place had you taken his life."

"I know. But together, Deb and I will get through this, Mark. And with the help of God..." Karl smiled absently, and the pastor put a comforting hand on his shoulder.

"Yes, Karl. Trust God in everything." The pastor smiled warmly. And Karl smiled too.

And now, he was sitting in a visitation room where he would soon see the man who had killed his daughter, and so many others. Karl had done one of the hardest things he had ever had to do; he had forgiven Mitch.

He had also tried his best to move on with his life. It didn't do anything for him to dwell on the past and the things that he couldn't change. No, his focus, was now on the things he *could* change.

The guards led Mitch Petersen into the visitation room. And he looked perplexed when he saw Karl. Karl felt uncomfortable, but he shook it off. Mitch's face was entirely covered in scars. From the birdshot to the face. From the beating that Karl had given him. Karl saw the scars on his own face as well reflected on the glass dividing them.

Very similar scars; yet two very different men.

Karl had made a living removing scars and fixing mostly cosmetic imperfections on other people to make them feel better about themselves. However, he had decided to keep his, as a reminder of what could have been. As a reminder of Naomi. As a reminder of forgiveness. Mitch's forgiveness, as well as his own. Jesus carried his own scars. Why wouldn't he? And seeing Mitch's scars also served a reminder of what a monster could be, thanks to childhood trauma.

The guards stood back a few feet to give the two men the illusion of privacy.

"What are you doing here?" Mitch asked on the hanging phone.

"Hi, Mitch. I came because I have two things that I want to share with you," Karl said, "First of all, your sister is fine."

Mitch looked up at Karl confused. "My sister? What the fuck are you talking about?"

"I figured you might've worried about her. When I found out that she was okay, I thought I'd let you know."

"I don't give a shit about my sister? And neither should *you*, of all people."

"Somehow, I think that deep down you actually do care, Mitch. And you know what, maybe I'll ask her to visit you some time, but only if she wants to," Karl said sternly.

Mitch remained cold. "So what happened to her?"

"Laura tried to drown herself in the lake, but a police officer who had been part of the search party to find her saw her from a distance. He managed to rescue her and resuscitate her just in time, as other arrived at the scene. She put up a fight, but in the end, she made it, as she was taken to the hospital."

Mitch nodded in understanding. "We really fucked her up, didn't we?" He didn't look at Karl as he said it, as if he knew the answer to his question.

"You did. But... I think she'll be okay." Karl did not expect Mitch to reply in such a way.

"Anyway, what's the second thing you wanted to say, Fuckboy. You said there were two things you came to say to me, so let me have it."

"Well–" Karl was about to say something, but Mitch interrupted.

"Let me guess, that you won? That you beat me? That you're glad I'll be dead soon and I can rot in hell?" Mitch chucked. "Well, come on, let's get this done with."

Karl saw him in silence. He knew well that psychopaths and sociopaths can't change. And any small seed of hope for that was gone. Mitch maybe could pretend to find God and to be transformed, but it would most likely be another con job. That's what people like him did. That's the way their brain worked. There would be no crocodile tears for this monster, and justice would indeed be served. But he still was willing to go with this.

"I... I forgive you, Mitch," Karl finally said it.

SCARS

CHAPTER **THIRTY**

THE MUNSONS HAD DECIDED TO VISIT MARY, Pastor Mark's wife, when they returned home. They'd reconciled, though it hadn't been easy. Karl had to learn that God was not punishing them.

"You know, when you were missing..." Deb told him one night. "When I was in that house, and you were gone, I prayed for you. I prayed that you were okay, because I couldn't be alone."

"You've never told me this," Karl said, his tone filled with love.

"I know. Because what happened next... Well, honey, it was rather extraordinary," she said and excitement glowed through her eyes and smile. "Karl... God spoke to me."

"*What?*"

"It's as if he was telling me you would be okay. Like he was telling me to trust Him. And I'm so glad that I did!"

She had then thrown her arms around him in a hug, and he had pulled her closer to him. Yes, they were both middle-aged and their bodies had known better days, but they were *there*. They were *together*. It felt so much better.

Mary had agreed to meet them, to pray for them, and to pray with them. Karl had shed all his anger and fear, and he'd welcomed God. He had been so surprised when Mary had prayed for them, and that she was just there for him.

After a while, the couple returned to their normal lives. Well, as normal as it could get for a surgeon and an orthodontist. As best as it could, for a couple who had lost a daughter and gone through hell and back. It wasn't easy. God knows, it wasn't easy, because they were two very different people to who they had been when their daughter had died, yet they were inexplicably the same.

The house, however, was an issue. It house was too big for just two people to live in. And Deborah wanted to sell it.

"Come on. Why are we staying in this place?" Deborah asked him. "We're not happy in this place, Karl. It holds so many bad memories."

It was dinnertime and they were seated around the table. A table also too large for only two people to share.

"It doesn't," Karl countered her. "This is the place in which our daughter died, yes. But it's also the place where she *lived*, Deb. It's where we watched movies with her, where she practiced her swimming, where she sang, where she danced, where she played, where she grew up…" He swallowed and blinked rapidly, looking up at his wife. "I don't want to move, because I feel like we'll be leaving her behind."

Deborah's face softened. She hadn't thought about it before. "But it's too big, Karl. It's dangerous."

He didn't reply to this, but he did think of a solution. The next day he was off work, Deborah wasn't, and he went to the mall. The mall had an immense pet shop, and it doubled as the Society for the Prevention of Cruelty to Animals. On one side there were cages filled with all sorts of dogs, puppies, adult dogs, small dogs, and big dogs. On the other there were a few other animals as well. A few puppies barked happily when they saw him, each inviting him to pick them.

He found her that day. His puppy, his little girl. She had been sitting in the middle of the cage, not trying to get his attention, but she was looking at him curiously. She was tiny, about the size of a full-grown rat. He didn't even know it was a she until he picked her up.

A miniature red poodle. She was beautiful. She was perfect. Karl had almost already decided that she was his. She nibbled on his finger as he put her back down. He continued to look around.

Then he saw him. Karl saw the dog before the dog saw him. A beast of a dog with sleek brown fur. A Pitbull. He looked angry, but the moment he saw Karl, his face broke out in a friendly, if ugly, smile. He had been hurt. His face was scarred. They had their stories. Stories, most likely, of domestic abuse.

He couldn't exactly lift the Pitbull out of its cage, but he did call the attendant.

"Sir, this dog is a package deal," the attendant said, pointing to the light-haired bitch that was in the cage too. "But this is usually for breeders."

"I want them," he said and looked at the female. She howled at him. He put a hand against the cage for both dogs to smell him. They were just puppies with large floppy ears and excited yowls. They would be perfect.

That day he spent a lot of money on the dogs. The breeding pair was expensive, but he didn't care. He wanted to give them a loving home, not a home where they were expected to produce offspring every six months or so. He had to get food bowls, beds, collars, name-tags, although he had no idea what they were going to call the dogs just yet, leashes, shampoo, toys, pee pads... The list seemed endless, but he was *happy*.

When his wife got home that day, she was surprised by the excited barks of two puppies.

"Karl!" She laughed, picking up the male Pitbull. "What did you do?"

"I made the house a little bit smaller," he said from where he was seated.

Deborah gave him a fleeting kiss and fell next to him on the sofa, where the smaller Pitbull jumped up to lie next to her.

"They are ours. You can name them."

She looked at the two large pups. The female rested her head sideways on top of Deborah's lap, and the male one licked her ears.

"I can't believe you got us dogs!"

"Are you complaining?" He raised an eyebrow, and she shook her head quickly.

"No! It's just... it's surprising, that's all."

Karl pressed a kiss to her cheek. "I hope it's a good surprise."

Deborah pulled both the Pitbulls closer to her. She thought it was funny that her husband had gotten dogs. He had never been the pet type. But she loved her two pups. And she was happy that he had.

She named them Scarface and Princess. Scarface would protect their home and Princess wouldn't let anyone mess with her. They would be her babies.

There they were... the Munson's. Two adults and two dogs. All of them full of scars. Each with their own story. But each of the scars had healed. Forgiveness had made space for love in their lives.

It would be okay.

SCARS

CHAPTER **THIRTY-ONE**

LAURA PETERSEN LOOKED AT HERSELF in the mirror. She had managed to escape the hospital after she'd been pulled from the water, but she had been on the run for so long. She hadn't had any money and had been sleeping on the streets. There was a time when she couldn't afford her meth anymore, and she hadn't wanted to sell her body either.

She found an alley and kicked the addiction there. The withdrawals had gone on for days. Her body had shivered, and she couldn't sleep. She had been awake for three days when she could finally rest. Her heart had been pounding loudly, quickly, in her ears, and she could hear nothing else but her own heartbeat. People had tried to talk to her. She could see their mouths moving, but she couldn't hear them. She'd screamed at them. She'd wanted to be left alone. She hadn't needed help, or money, and she didn't want to fuck.

Not anymore. She couldn't eat, even if she wanted to. She couldn't because she had no money.

Withdrawal was a bitch, she decided, but it was necessary evil. She didn't need drugs anymore. She didn't need to feel numb for everything that her father had expected her to do. She didn't feel the need to please anyone, and that led to her kicking the habit. Yes, her body wanted it. Her body was in physical pain, her mind was playing tricks on her.

And a week later, she woke up, feeling extremely tired, but she felt... *better*. She felt as though she could eat something. The problem was that she didn't have any money. She hated having to do it, but she decided to dine and dash. It would be easier to dine and dash at a local café than it would be to shoplift something from a store.

Laura sidled into a breakfast joint, made herself comfortable, and asked the waitress for a cup of coffee. She perused the menu for the cheapest item on it. She didn't want to cause the diner too much of a loss.

Laura made the mistake of looking up when her coffee arrived and ordering a greasy bacon and egg burger. She made the mistake of making eye-contact with a woman who was sitting on the next bench. She made the mistake of smiling and revealing her blackened, stubby teeth. The woman came over and sat across from her.

"Hi," the woman said, and Laura answered in a hoarse voice.

"Hi." She didn't know what else to say.

Should she let the woman stay? Should she let the woman just... watch her eat?

"Do you have money to pay for this?" the woman asked softly, and Laura shook her head. That was presumptuous. "I'll get it. Order what you want."

Was that too condescending?

Laura stared at the woman. "What are you doing?"

"I am helping you." the middle-aged woman said. "You look like you've been through a lot."

"My father and brother just died," Laura admitted.

It was the truth, and it stung her as she stated it. And while she didn't like her father, she really loved her brother. She loved Tiny. She'd seen the news about his death, and... she'd been torn. She saw that Paddy had been arrested, and that he was serving time in prison for a list of crimes that Laura had to be in for too.

"My boyfriend is in prison, and so is my other brother. My best friend is dead."

Paddy, Mitch, Joy. All of them were gone. All of them had left her alone. And she was still standing.

"I kicked my meth habit recently. At least I think I did. I am... I'm just so... I am *tired.* I'm *alone.* I don't have anyone, ma'am, and I know I messed up a lot. But... I just want... I want someone to... to..." And Laura, for the first time in a long time, cried. "I need someone to care. I want my mommy, I want my big brothers, I want..."

Her life had been torn asunder. Everything she had known and had trusted was gone. Vanished.

"My name is Deborah." The woman said and moved to sit next to Laura.

The lady picked up a napkin and wiped Laura's tears from her face.

"And... well, I don't know why I'm doing this, but I'm glad that I am. Would you want to come home with me? Have a nice bath, eat a home-cooked meal...?"

"I couldn't ask you to do that," Laura said, sniffling.

"You didn't, dear. I *want* to do it."

Laura looked at the older woman, at Deborah, and fresh tears seeped out of her eyes. Brown hair, wrinkles around her eyes and mouth. This woman knew how to laugh. She was happy. Joyful. The woman was kind. She had a sense of peace like the world could not give. It was a joy that did not depend on circumstances.

She reminded Laura of her mother. The woman made her feel warm inside, made her feel like she could be so much more. And Laura leaned towards the woman, throwing her arms around her, and sobbed.

An hour later they arrived at a large house in Pasadena. It was two stories high, and Laura just hoped that she wouldn't be an inconvenience for the woman's children. She was a bum, a meth-head, and a criminal. She didn't deserve any love.

"I think you should tell me your name, dear," Deborah said. "Otherwise I don't know how to call you when dinner is ready."

"L..." She started, but she didn't want her name. She didn't want to be associated with her family, even if she did miss them. "I'm Ariel."

Ariel seemed like a pretty name and was a pretty version of Laura going backwards. "Ariel McCormick." In honor of Paddy.

"I'm Deborah Munson. Nice to meet you. Now, come inside!"

Inside, Laura... no, Ariel... was thrown backwards against a wall as a large dog with scars on his face put its front paws on her torso.

"Scarface!" Deborah chastised the dog, and he got off her. Ariel looked at the dog, her eyes wide. "Oh, don't mind him. He's just a happy pup, and he likes you."

Another dog appeared before the two women, and it howled at them. It had lighter golden skin, and it was... well, it was eyeing Ariel in a way that scared her. Then it bounded towards her, its tongue lolling, and Deborah was screaming for it to stop. But it had thrown Ariel against the wall and was now licking her face. Ariel started to laugh, a sound she hadn't heard coming from her own mouth in a very long time.

"Princess!" Deborah chastised the dog, but Ariel put her arms around the dog in a hug. This type of love was something that she wouldn't mind having.

Deborah led Ariel up the stairs to a bedroom that must have been Deborah's daughter's. It was decorated in all the colors of the rainbow, and Deborah opened the closet for her.

"You're tiny. Do you think you'll fit into these?" Deborah asked, pulling out a pair of jeans. "They're a size four."

"Me too," Ariel said, wondering why the woman was offering Ariel her daughter's clothes.

"Great. Then you can take *all* of this."

"Ma'am..." Ariel said, looking at the woman with raised eyebrows. "You can't just give your daughter's things away! She won't be happy!"

Deborah smiled at her. "Trust me, it's not a problem. She loved to share."

"Past tense?" Ariel asked carefully.

"My daughter died. I never cleaned her closets out, I don't know why. But now I'm grateful that I didn't."

"Oh!" Ariel said, dumbstruck. "I am so sorry, ma'am. But... wouldn't you rather..."

"No," Deborah said kindly, putting a hand on Ariel's elbow. "You take it. It's yours now. It will serve a better purpose this way."

Deborah disappeared out the door, giving Ariel some privacy. She peeled her clothes off and put them in the dustbin. Her clothes were bloody, dirty, and grimy. She had worn a long coat over her clothes, one that she'd found in a dumpster and smelled like smoke and rat pee. She hated the smell, but it covered her up. She stank bad.

Princess stayed with her. The large dog just watched her, and when she made her way to the shower, the dog just lay down in the bathroom, as if waiting for her.

Now she could get rid of it. She didn't know where she would go when Deborah was done with her; but for now, she would use the opportunity to clean herself up.

It was later, a lot later, when Ariel got out of shower, her body smelling like lavender and strawberries. And she put on some of the clothes from the closet. She then made her way downstairs, finding Deborah in the kitchen. Princess was following her, panting behind her.

"Ariel!" Deborah said pleasantly. "Don't you look pretty!"

"Thanks, ma'am," she said shyly, and sat opposite Deborah at the counter island. She did feel pretty. She hadn't felt that way in a very long time. "Ma'am, if I may ask... *Why* are you being so nice to me?"

"Well, it looked like you needed it." The brunette woman shrugged. "And I certainly have more than enough." She gestured around the house. "So why not? Even if you do end up robbing me."

Ariel laughed. "Ma'am, you've been so kind to me. I don't know how to thank you. Stealing from you is not an option. Trust me."

"Okay, well... Then tell me about yourself."

And Ariel did. She told Deborah everything—her mother dying at an early age, her father being a prick and favoring her brothers more, about how she did anything to please him, but it was never enough. And then about how she met her boyfriend, who introduced her to meth. She left out names, because she was quite sure her family was infamous enough for her to be recognized. She told her about how she'd been forced to quit school at fifteen and wished she could finish her education.

She didn't want to be known as Laura Petersen anymore. She used pronouns and tried to be vague, which she realized that Deborah was aware of, but she had said nothing.

"You're welcome to stay here," Deborah said. "We have more than enough space, and Princess likes you."

"I don't want to be a burden..."

"Oh, no, honey!" Deborah said. "You won't be."

The front door opened, and a voice called. "Babe, I'm home!"

"In the kitchen!" Deborah called back. "That's my husband, Karl."

Ariel's heart started to beat loudly again. What if... well, what if he decided that he didn't want her there?

When she saw who he was, she nearly fainted. It was the man that they'd held captive in their last home invasion. *Fuckboy*, as Mitch had called him.

"Oh, hello," he said, equally stunned to see her. "Uh, Debbie?"

"This is Ariel McCormick," Deborah said, pressing a kiss to her husband's lips. "I invited her to stay with us for a while."

"Oh," was all he said.

Ariel closed her eyes, waiting for the bomb to drop. He would call the police, he would throw her out, he would demand his daughter's clothes back...

"Well, welcome to our home."

Ariel's heart sped even more.

Dinner was ready at that point, and Ariel and Karl were just staring at each other. He smiled at her, surprising her, and sat down next to her at the counter island. Deborah dished heaps of food onto both their plates, mashed potatoes, steak, grilled veggies, all food that Ariel hadn't eaten in a very long time. At one point, Deborah's phone rang in the other room and she excused herself.

Ariel turned to Karl. "Why didn't you say anything?"

He shrugged. "Why would I? I've forgiven you for what you've done, and I'm not angry. I'm a bit shocked, but not angry. I mean, what are the chances?!"

"And you aren't afraid that I'll steal from you... or worse?"

"Honestly, yes I do. But I hope you won't," Karl said, "Look, these are just earthly things. And if you decide to do anything stupid, you will most likely lose. Let's be honest. On the other hand, however, you do have a lot to gain, don't you think?"

Ariel remained quiet.

Karl continued, "Besides, I like the idea of having another young woman around, even if it is just to help my wife out with her job."

"Her job?"

"Our friend Mary and Debbie are starting a halfway house." Said Karl. "You know? Where homeless teenagers, drug addicts, abuse victims... where they all can go and be in a loving environment."

"A halfway house?" Ariel repeated. "You mean... a place where someone like me would end up?"

"Yeah, actually. So, you can stay, and I won't say a word to Deb if you don't want me to." Karl smiled again before putting a piece of his food in his mouth.

Ariel couldn't stop herself from throwing her arms around him. He laughed, and she loved the sound of his deep, throaty laughter. She felt warm, she felt... loved. She hadn't felt that in a long time.

"It wasn't easy, you know," Karl said. "My daughter died, and then your family..." He trailed off, but she nodded in understanding. "Well, it wasn't easy for her either. But if she chose you to live here... I trust her."

That was it. No threat. No warning of acting out. Nothing. Grace. Mercy.

But what about justice?

"We had help to get us where we are," Karl said. "A pastor, our friends the Wallers, our spiritual community, and the pups." He frowned, then called louder. "Scarface!"

Steps could be heard as the other dog ran to them. Karl smiled, relieved, when he saw his pup. It was a big pup, but it was his baby, nonetheless.

"We had the church who supported us. And we definitely didn't get to where we are now alone. And... I don't expect you to just turn it all around without help either. Plus, now we can get your teeth fixed! That's what my wife has done for a living."

She was Ariel McCormick. She had a home. And her smile would be fixed, literally and figuratively.

SCARS

CHAPTER **THIRTY-TWO**

GRACE STARED INTO THE FREEWAY without any visible emotion. One could see the nervousness in her eyes. She was scared. She had waited for this day, and now that it was finally here, she was tense. What was she going to say? What was *he* going to say to her? An infinite number of possible scenarios crossed through her mind as she drove to the station.

She was going to see her daughter's killer. The monster in the flesh.

And now she knew his name. Mitch Petersen. She had been right all along; this evil man had been the perpetrator of multiple cases, all similar to the incident with her beloved Brittany.

Grace had been at home doing her usual cleaning rituals when she'd heard the peeping sound. At first, she hadn't bothered to check it. She'd thought an insect or a bird was making the noise, so she'd continued with her chores. But when she'd heard the chirping noise again, she'd realized it was her phone. It had been a while since someone had called her phone.

"Hello...?" she'd answered the unidentified caller, not sure of what to expect.

Was it Tony? No, it couldn't be Tony. Perhaps one of her deserted friends. A telemarketer, perhaps. Who could it be?

"Good evening, Mrs. Miller. This is Detective Ortega," the caller identified himself.

She hadn't expected his call; he had never called her back, not once. She had always been the one making the calls in this relationship with the law. Something must have had happened for him to be calling her. But what could it be? Had they decided to drop her daughter's case already and finally had the guts to let her know? She had grown rigid. Agitated.

"How can I help you, Detective?" She'd inquired, expecting the worst.

"Ma'am, can you come to the station tomorrow? There's something I would like you to see."

"What is it? You never invited me before. Have you decided to drop the case? Please, just tell me once and for all."

"No, ma'am, not at all. On the contrary! We have a big break in the case. We've captured your daughter's killer..."

Grace Miller hadn't been able to believe what she'd heard. Maybe she hadn't heard right. Had he just said her daughter's killer had been captured? "Detective, are you telling me that you have found the killer?"

"Yes, Mrs. Miller. That's exactly what I'm saying."

"I am on my way right now."

"No, we're still working some kinks out. It won't be possible today, but tomorrow would be ideal, if you can."

Just like that, it was over. Wasn't it? As much as she had wanted them to catch her daughter's killer, she had never thought the day would come. Grace had begun to sob, a full-on emotional outburst. The mixture of happiness and sadness was truly a peculiar sentiment.

Grace parked her blue sedan in the parking lot, remembering all the days when she had come to the station. Each time, she had come here asking the same questions over and over. *Have you solved it? When are you going to find the monster who did this to my baby girl?* But never had she expected a positive reply, only a negative one. But now, here she was, case solved, monster behind bars. She couldn't believe it. She'd better not have been dreaming this.

Detective Ortega stood up immediately upon seeing Mrs. Miller walking in, but this time, he didn't run away to hide from her. No, he rushed toward her. That was new. It was weird! Even Ortega's muscles were screaming for him to go the other way, but he had a big smile on his face. He got close to her and they exchanged pleasantries.

"Would you like some coffee?" Detective Ortega asked the woman.

"I am not here for coffee. Please, just stop all the formalities and take me to him."

The detective nodded, as he led her to a room with a one-way window. She sat down as detective Ortega made a call. Then he too sat next to her in the dark room.

"Are you okay?" he enquired again.

"I'm fine," she answered, trying desperately to hide any emotion.

After a short while, the other room's door opened, and an officer brought in a tall man. Young. Fully chained up from head to toes. The officer sat him down and chained him to the desk, then left the room.

Grace didn't know how she was going to react. Would she remain calm? Would she be angry? But upon seeing him, she felt hatred. So much hatred for him that her blood boiled. All she could think about was about her daughter's laughter, her soft hair, her silliness. All things which she would never see or experience again. She wanted to smash the glass, take one of the shard, and stab it straight into his neck. Even though visibly calm, in her mind, Grace Miller had already killed Mitch Petersen, the monster, a thousand times.

Detective Ortega was telling her about him, but the only thing that she heard was his name, Mitch. That was all she needed, a name to blame. She stared at him, eyeing him from top to bottom. Inspecting him. Dissecting him. He didn't look like she'd imagined. She'd expected a wolf, but all she saw was a sheep. A large, strong sheep. But a lamb, nonetheless.

"When are they going to prosecute him?" She cut the silence.

"I don't know. But you'll be informed."

Grace was ready to go now. She had seen the monster with her own eyes. She thanked the detective and left the premises. She got into her car, expecting to feel free, but she wasn't. She still felt down. The weight in her heart was still there. Catching the killer hadn't lifted her spirits. It didn't make her better. In fact, it only made her feel worse.

After her daughter's death, she'd had only one drive, to find her daughter's killer. But now they found him, she was lost. She didn't know what to do. She had no motivation, no cause for living. No purpose. No identity. She was still in her deep dark abyss. She'd believed there would be light on the other end, but apparently there was no light. Only darkness.

She started her car and drove out of the parking lot, not knowing where life was going to take her next.

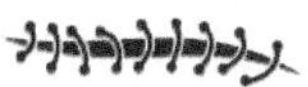

Grace sat in the diner and ordered coffee as she waited for them. She couldn't believe she was reaching out, finally asking for help. She was tired of facing her demons alone. She needed to find a way out of this darkness, or she would certainly go crazy. She'd tried calling Tony, but he hadn't picked up. It had been a while since she had seen him, and as much as she missed him, he had moved on.

The door of the diner opened. She turned around to see who it was, but it wasn't them, just a father and his daughter cracking up about some dad joke. Wherever she turned to, all she saw was happiness and kindness. She saw smiling faces all around, but when she looked at her life, there was only sadness. She was tired of it all, and only wanted her old life back.

The door opened again, and an attractive, middle-aged couple entered, looking around as if searching for someone. They looked at her side, but she didn't know them, so she looked away. Then, a third person came in right behind them. She recognized *him*, Pastor Mark Gomez, with a big smile on his face.

Mark saw her and waved at her. The three of them walked towards her after some hand motions from the pastor. Grace could swear that they were walking in slow motion as they drew close. Maybe it was nervousness playing tricks on her mind. It was too late to back out now anyway.

Grace stood up to greet the visitors. Pastor Mark introduced them.

"Hello, Grace! It's good to see you again. This is Dr. Karl Munson." Karl stretched out his hand and Grace shook it. "And this is Dr. Deborah Munson, husband and wife."

"Debbie is fine. How are you doing?" Debbie enquired.

Grace didn't respond, she simply hugged her.

After the short introduction, they all sat down. Pastor Mark sat beside Grace, as the couple sat opposite them. There was an awkward silence, as no one seemed to know where to start.

Gomez broke the obstinate silence, trying hard to start the conversation. "Do you guys want something to eat? I see you have some coffee already, Grace. I think I'll get the same."

Before anyone could answer, Grace jumped in. "How did you do it? How are you not affected by it? I see you and I can still see the traces of the pain, but you're both radiant with hope. You're shining, smiling at life," Grace asked the couple across from her.

"That is the easy part, Grace. We didn't do anything. It was the Lord that did it all. It's by His grace," Debbie responded with a smile, grabbing Grace's hands on top of the table.

Grace, looking perplexed at them, queried them further, "So, you're saying that miraculously, God came down from Heaven and took all your pain away, just like that?"

"Something like that, although perhaps not exactly like that," Karl added.

"Grace, are you familiar with any Bible promises?" Pastor Mark asked. "John chapter three, verse—"

"That's just poetry, some random words someone wrote a long time ago. They're not real," Grace defended defiantly.

"They're not just words, Grace. As you said, you can see us radiating with hope. Do you think we have the power to do that on our own?" Karl asked. "'For God so loved the world that He sent His Son that whosoever believeth in Him...'"

"'...shall not perish but have everlasting life,'" Grace finished. "But it can't be that easy! I can't believe that, if I just believe in someone, I will not perish. It can't be real."

"No one said it's easy," Debbie responded as she held her husband's hand. "We almost lost everything. We were so low, I thought we would never see the light again. I was angry! And not just angry at him but at the world. Angry at God! Why would He do such a thing to me after I served Him wholeheartedly."

"Well, that's exactly where I'm at right now. I'm just tired of everything."

"But one day, while crying, I felt him. I felt his presence. And I realized I was fighting my battles alone instead trusting Him," Debbie finished.

"We decided to give it all up to Him. Forgiving Mitch was cathartic for us. It was a burden that we let go of," Karl said.

"I don't understand what you're saying. Are you trying to say that I should forgive that asshole? That I should not make him suffer, even though he caused me a lot of pain?" Grace fired back, eyes watery.

"That's right, Grace. Look at yourself! He's not the one suffering, it's you. You're the one going through the pain. You need to let go. Forgiving him doesn't mean forgetting what he did to your daughter," Pastor Gomez said.

Forgiveness. That was impossible. What were they saying? They couldn't possibly be serious! It had to be a joke. How could they expect her to look Mitch Petersen in his eyes and just forgive him after hunting him down for so long? It didn't make sense at all.

"Thank you for the time." Grace stood up to leave.

Pastor Mark tried to halt her, but Debbie stopped him. Debbie followed Grace and caught up to her before she got into her car.

"I just have one more thing to say to you. Why are you allowing him to win? Why are you allowing him to have this much control over you? This is *your* time to be victorious. It is *your* time to shine and heal. Please, just think about that."

With that, Debbie left Grace and went back inside to join her husband and the pastor.

Grace, paralyzed with anxiety, managed to enter her car and sank into her car seat. The seat started to feel unstable, as if it was undergoing transmutation. It felt like liquid. She felt as if she was drowning, deeper and deeper into the abyss. The panic began to sink in. But she was ready to accept her fate. She deserved it, she thought. And she sank into the abyss...

Abruptly, she woke up from her slumber. She had one more thing to do.

Grace was finally face-to-face with the person who had killed her daughter. He stared at her, not knowing who she was or why she was there. People said that those closest to you caused you the most pain, but not in her case. This was him, the source of all her sorrows. The monster. The one who raped and killed her daughter. The one who caused her divorce. The one who caused her depression and made her life a living hell. And only a glass pane separated her from him.

She picked up the phone on her end.

"Hello, Mitch. My name is Grace Miller and my daughter's name was Brittany Miller. She was named after her grandmother and she was a very smart girl. Very social and liked by her friends. She could be a little naughty at times, but my Brittany was a good girl at heart. She never made A's at school, but she had decent grades. She wanted to be a fashion designer when she was older, and she loved to draw." Tears flowed from Grace's eyes.

Mitch didn't say a word. He just listened to the woman on the other side of the glass.

After a moment of silence, she continued. "I know you didn't know her, but she was my girl. She was my little paradise, my everything. But *you* took her away from me." At this, the monster shed a tear in silence. Grace had not expected that. "But I'm not here to tell you about what you took away from me. I'm here to let you go. I'm here to take back my life. To heal."

"Sorry?" Mitch Petersen finally said in his deep voice. That was all he said.

Grace Miller was in awe. Taken aback. She'd thought she would just spew out her grief and he would just stand there like a wall and take it all. But that was not the case. Never had she imagined the monster would apologize for his monstrosity and horror. Never had she conceived the possibility of him talking back to her and asking for forgiveness. Was she imagining this? Was he apologizing, or was this something else? It was more of a question. Was he teasing her?

It didn't matter.

For the first time ever, Grace thought of Mitch Petersen, her daughter's killer, as a human being. She didn't see a monster anymore. Yes, he was still a rapist, a killer, and may other bad things. But he was a human being, a hurt man with lots of demons.

She managed to speak through her tears. "I forgive you. Goodbye, Mr. Petersen." Trembling, and before Mitch could say anything else, Grace hung up the phone, stood up, and walked away.

That was it. She had done it. She had faced her demons and showed them she was far greater than them. She would greatly miss her daughter, forever. But she could now move on in life and finally heal her emotional scars.

Mark waited for her on the foyer. Without a word, they walked back to the parking lot. The pastor opened the door and helped her enter on the passenger side of his car. Moments later, while on the road, he finally spoke.

"How are you feeling, Grace?" he asked while focusing straight ahead.

"I feel... different. I feel... I don't know... lighter, for some reason," she responded. "As if a heavy yoke has been lifted from me. Does that make any sense?"

"Yes, it does. I understand clearly what you mean. Welcome back, Grace Miller. Welcome back to life."

They walked back to the car for the hours-drive. They'd come all this way for these few minutes, and it was worth it.

She smiled in her own seat.

The car continued down the highway, back to civilization. A new world waited for Grace. There was only one way for Grace Miller to go, and that was up. Grace 2.0, a new creation, had been born.

SCARS

CHAPTER **THIRTY-THREE**

LIFE HAD DISHED OUT A LOT to the Munsons. Their daughter being taken from them was still a very sore spot for them, and they now thought they knew why it had happened.

Naomi had already been a good girl. She had been kind, and while she hadn't deserved her fate, Karl thought of silver linings. Her life had inspired so many new things.

The halfway house, for one, which was always filled with people who needed love. Ariel, who had finished her education and now helped Debbie with the halfway house, who was helping drug addicts through their addiction, who had a degree in Social Work, and now officially worked for the Munson's. She still lived in Naomi's old room and she had become a big part of Karl's life.

Ariel had needed so much from them, far more than simply their financial support. She had needed a mother and a father, even at the age of twenty-two. And that was what

Karl and Deb became. They took her in and thought of the girl as their own daughter. She had never stolen from them, except for the stray cookie or two that she sneaked to her bedroom at night. Though that wasn't stealing, since they'd told her to help herself.

And Mitch Petersen? He was in prison.

He was no longer in the area, as he had been moved to ADX Florence, a super-max federal prison in Colorado. He would be there for the rest of his life, serving eight consecutive life terms without the possibility of parole. Karl was satisfied that there was justice in the world for more than simply his own daughter. All the people whose daughters and sisters had died because of Mitch had gotten justice. They were thankful that he was off the streets. However, Karl also believed in and was certainly thankful for mercy.

Mental Health professionals assured Karl that Mitch Petersen was messed up due to watching his father assault his mother continuously as a child. Due to the constant beatings he took from his drunken father as a kid. These adverse childhood experiences taught him two emotions: hatred and lust. This trauma created the monster he was now. And Karl actually felt bad for him.

Both men were scarred for life, both in their bodies and their souls.

Mitch had scars on his hands and on his face; one across his left eye and another one on his nose. Hopefully, those scars served as a constant reminder of everything he'd done in the past. Karl, on the other hand, had scars on his hands and face as well. He had one scar on his lip, and another one near his temple. The scars reminded him of the fragility of life, and how things could change forever in an instant. They reminded him of Jesus, and how He had suffered for his sake. They reminded him of his daughter, whom he couldn't wait to see again in the next life.

Karl Munson removed scars for a living. But Karl Munson was a scarred man himself. And he was finally okay with that.

THE END

ABOUT THE AUTHOR

Obed Olivarría was born in Mexicali, Mexico and spent his youth as a fully bicultural transnational citizen. He has a passion for writing both fiction and nonfiction, public speaking, composing, arranging, and performing music, as well as traveling around the world. He loves the thrill of adrenaline-pumping activities, but also the quiet reflection he gets from writing and creating.

His love for books started at an early age, as his parents were eager readers and owned thousands of books. His passion for writing was born after winning a city-wide short story competition while in high school in Arizona. The publication of this in a local journal inspired him to continue creating worlds and characters in print.

Obed has worked as a youth and young adult pastor, as a graphic designer, as a session musician, as a ministry consultant, as university dean, as school administrator, and school psychologist. Having worked at every level of the education system, from pre-k to university, has given him an expedition to the human psyche. He has a dynamic love of life and ministry, and he is a deep thinker, and an honest intellectual to the Christian gospel.

Obed lives in sunny Orange County, California with his charming wife and two energetic children. Obed hopes to continue writing inspiring books that entertain, but also challenge the status quo. Personally, he would like to visit every country in the world, drawing inspiration from these travels for another great story.